Lucretia P. (Lucretia Peabody) Hale

Seven Stormy Sundays

Lucretia P. (Lucretia Peabody) Hale

Seven Stormy Sundays

ISBN/EAN: 9783744746533

Printed in Europe, USA, Canada, Australia, Japan

Cover: Foto ©Andreas Hilbeck / pixelio.de

More available books at **www.hansebooks.com**

SEVEN

STORMY SUNDAYS.

"The sun shall be no more thy light by day; neither for brightness shall the moon give light unto thee; but the Lord shall be thine everlasting light, and thy God, thy glory." — ISAIAH lx. 19.

THIRD EDITION.

BOSTON:
AMERICAN UNITARIAN ASSOCIATION;
WALKER, FULLER, AND COMPANY.
NEW YORK: JAMES MILLER.
1866.

NOTE.

I HAVE to thank two of my friends for the use of two sermons which I have heard them preach, and which would not be otherwise published. I must express my acknowledgments, too, for two sermons by Rev. W. B. O. Peabody, never before printed. I believe the sermons of Tholuck and Bretschneider have not been translated before.

CONTENTS.

A STORMY SUNDAY.

THE RHODODENDRONS.

"Praise God, for wondering eyes his world of love to see!
Praise God, for thought which wanders always free!
Praise God, for faith, which bends a willing knee,
Draws me to him, the while he smiles on me."

A STORMY SUNDAY.

THE RHODODENDRONS.

" What went ye out into the wilderness to see? A reed shaken with the wind? But what went ye out for to see? A prophet? Yea, I say unto you, and more than a prophet."

WHAT went ye out to see
O'er the rude sandy lea,
Where stately Jordan flows by many a palm,
Or where Gennesaret's wave
Delights the flowers to lave
That o'er her western slope breathe airs of balm?

All through the summer night
Those blossoms red and bright
Spread their soft breasts, unheeding, to the breeze,
Like hermits watching still
Around the sacred hill,
Where erst our Saviour watched upon his knees.

The Paschal moon above
Seems like a saint to rove,
Left shining in the world with Christ alone;

A STORMY SUNDAY.

Below, the lake's still face
Sleeps sweetly in the embrace
Of mountains terraced high with mossy stone.

Here may we sit and dream
Over the heavenly theme,
Till to our soul the former days return;
Till on the grassy bed,
Where thousands once he fed,
The world's incarnate Maker we discern.

O cross no more the main,
Wandering so wild and vain,
To count the reeds that tremble in the wind,
On listless dalliance bound,
Like children gazing round,
Who on God's works no seal of Godhead find.

Bask not in courtly bower,
Or sun-bright hall of power;
Pass Babel quick, and seek the Holy Land:
From robes of Tyrian dye
Turn with undazzled eye
To Bethlehem's glade or Carmel's haunted strand.

Or choose thee out a cell
In Kedron's storied dell,
Beside the springs of Love, that never die;
Among the olives kneel,
The chill night-blast to feel,
And watch the moon that saw thy Master's agony.

Then rise at dawn of day,
And wind thy thoughtful way,
Where rested once the temple's stately shade,
With due feet tracing round
The city's northern bound,
To th' other holy garden, where the Lord was laid.

Who thus alternate see
His death and victory,
Rising and falling as on angel wings,
They, while they seem to roam,
Draw daily nearer home, —
Their heart untravelled still adores the King of kings.

Or, if at home they stay,
Yet are they, day by day,
In spirit journeying through the glorious land,
Not for light Fancy's reed,
Nor Honor's purple meed,
Nor gifted prophet's lore, nor Science' wondrous wand.

But more than prophet, more
Than angels can adore
With face unveiled, is He they go to seek;
Blessed be God, whose grace
Shows Him in every place
To homeliest hearts of pilgrims pure and meek.

These last words, taken from Keble's lesson for
the day, I must repeat to myself, as my lesson.
It is a stormy Sunday, and I must not venture

out to church. I cannot enter into the blessing
that is promised to the two or three that are
gathered together. I must devote myself to a
solitary worship, and these lines may help to prepare me for it. What a contrast are the scenes
that they picture to the scene that shuts me in!
A cold rain patters against the window-panes, and
a sharp blast of wind hurries over the hills. How
different the cold New England landscape from
that spot

> " Where stately Jordan flows by many a palm,
>   Or where Gennesaret's wave
>   Delights the flowers to lave
> That o'er her western slope breathe airs of balm " !

I look out upon broad, brown hills, out of
which the summer green has died away, and the
cold mist-clouds shut up all warmth from the
sky.

"The blossoms red and bright" in these lines
allude to the rhododendrons, which, they say, cover the water's edge of the Lake of Gennesaret.
And the word *rhododendron* brings back to me
our own summer season, the gay flowers that
adorn its quiet nooks, and with them those that
light up the wayside. I forget a moment my win-
ter-imprisoning room, and feel again the breath
of summer air, and see again the summer rhododendrons, the rare flowers that came from their
hidden homes. Not only has this picture carried

me to the side of the river Jordan, to the Holy Land, but back again to my own home in the summer-time.

And if my thoughts have power to paint around me new scenery, they may have force to bring into my silent room the memory and help of friends to commune with me in my solitary hour. I must collect around me the writings of spiritual men and women, who from their written words can preach to me and lead me to prayer. With their help I may summon to my presence the presence of Him who is ever with us, and yet whom we seldom know how to approach fitly. He to whom this day is consecrated will draw near to me in my solitude, and help me to make it sacred to Him.

To-day I have no active duties to perform. I am shut out from visiting the poor or the friendless. George has left for church, and will be gone all day. I am alone in the house, and am not even called upon for the gift of a kind word. I am not even obliged to *appear* kind and gentle. If I have any evil thoughts, there is no one here for me to express them to. I have even no household duties to perform. The only duty that remains to me is to take care of myself, to watch over my own thoughts. I have come to one of the quiet places in the activity of life. A busy week lies before me, and now I am allowed

a few hours of concentration to prepare myself
for it. The outer warfare of life has ceased for
a while ; there is a short truce ; I may look back
upon the battle-field, and bury my dead. I may
summon up my army, and fit the survivors for
the renewed contest. Yes, there are dead resolutions to weep over, new hopes to encourage.

What, indeed, are the duties of such an hour ?
and what are its dangers ?

There is danger that on such a day I may con-
centrate into a few hours all that " conviction of
sin " that should serve to restrain me through
the duties of the week. Standing alone in the
presence of my own conscience, I may bow myself so heavily with compunction, that I shall find
a reaction in the busy days that are to follow.
What matter is it, that I do weep over the mis-
deeds of the last week, reproach the idle thoughts,
and bring my soul down on its knees to-day in
these quiet hours, — how will all this help me, if
with to-morrow's distractions there returns again
the old indolence, if the idle thoughts come back
again, and the heartlessness, and the sharp words
ready to wound others ? Now, in the presence of
myself alone and God, I am willing to confess all
these evil tendencies of my soul; but will not the
old vanity return to-morrow ? When I am in
the presence of others, I shall forget my own lit-
tleness, and wish to appear greater than my

stature. To-day, when I am alone, I can think with kindness of others, can even pityingly and shrinkingly draw a veil over their faults; I can forget how it is that these faults clash with mine, and find for them the excuses that I am so ready to spread over my own. But to-morrow the old selfishness will return; I shall give back an angry word for a supposed insinuation, wound a sensitive heart with a thoughtless act, neglect to bring the cup of cold water to the suffering, fall down quietly into the current of my own daily duties, not looking to either shore, to give or gather help! These words I write are a confession of that weakness that will again paralyze me to-morrow. I wish that I might preserve some 6f this humility when I come out from this silent chapel of to-day.

This must be the sin of those who live in convents, who pour out their souls in repentance in their quiet cloisters, and then have no opportunity to prove its healthiness by the good works that follow. This is the reason that the worship in the church should be more availing than the lonely worship at home. There we kneel side by side with others, and however in our solemn thoughts we strive to shut out all that is distracting, still we are conscious that others are kneeling by our side in spirit, or perhaps, like us, waiting for the entrance of the spirit of de-

votion into the soul. New duties are suggested
to us by the sight of others. In praying for our
own needs, we think of the needs of those around
us. The congregation is preaching to us; some
speak from their want, some from their excess.
Our solitary longing we see reflected in others;
we are led to resolve, not merely to work out our
own salvation, but, in the working week that is
to come, to help to bear the burdens of others.

Then the words of the preacher waken us to
the sight of some forgotten sin. We are not, as
at home, reading some selected sermon, that may
preach to us some favorite duty, but in the
church a man rises who may suddenly rouse us
to a new and unthought of field of action, that
before never had the power to charm us, but
which we now see truly demands us.

But in that church I am not. Neither audi-
ence nor minister preaches to me. No sermon
against vanity comes from nodding plume or
shining velvet, — no quickening to charity from
the sight of the poor, worn garment. I hear no
freshly spoken word of preacher to start me
from my indolence. With the temptation to
distraction and the desire to criticise others, I
lose, too, the influence that comes from the uniting of many in one great worship, I lose the
wakening inspiration from the sound of another's
voice. I can read printed sermons, the choicest

that ever were written, but my eye may wander heedlessly over the page : it is harder to shut out from the mind the *spoken* word. In the church, the tones of an earnest preacher rouse even a slumbering spirit. All alone here perhaps I may let my soul sleep. Instead of conviction of sin, I may sink into complacency.

For a different danger of this solitary worship is, that I may grow too satisfied with myself. Without a rousing word from without me, I may even flatter myself on my own humility! This bending towards God, this consciousness of my penitence, of my momentary freedom from sin, may make me pleased with myself, with my own progress. It is so easy to say over the beautiful words of some hymn of devotion, it is so easy to call myself a sinner, when no being but God can hear the utterance, when I am scarcely able to realize that even he is conscious of it. In my repose, while to be pure and noble and self-sacrificing seems so attractive, so lovely, I do not feel the burden of my own sin. It lies by my side, because I myself am not in action. Alas! if vanity and self-conceit steal upon me now, when other temptation seems far away, how will it be with me when my honesty in the presence of others is tempted? Can I be true then, firm and consistent, unmoved by the atmosphere into which I pass, pure and honest, at the same time patient and yielding? This day may become a day of selfish thought, rather than of self-renunciation, filled with idle fancies rather than prayer-fed resolutions. I do not wish to look, either, upon such a day as one of those long, dreary, stormy Sundays that are sometimes complained of. I should like to make it a true day of rest and strengthening to my soul.

For this reason I write down a record of my thoughts, that at some future stormy Sunday I may examine them, and find if they were healthful and life-giving, if they have brought to me any of that fervor that the walk to church on a sunshiny Sunday brings, and the meeting with the preacher and congregation of worshippers.

I will write down, too, the words of others, their prayers which I repeat too with my lips. This will serve for my Sunday service to-day, and perhaps for some future day. I begin with some solemn words of Thomas à Kempis.

OF THE EXERCISES OF A GOOD RELIGIOUS PERSON.

The life of a good religious person ought to be adorned with all virtues; that he may inwardly be such as outwardly he seemeth to men.

And with reason there ought to be much more within than is perceived without. For God beholdeth us; whom we are bound most highly to reverence wheresoever we are, and to walk in purity like angels in his sight.

Daily ought we to renew our purposes, and to stir up ourselves to greater fervor, as though this were the first day of our conversion; and to say, " Help me, my God, in this my good purpose, and in thy holy service; and grant that I may now this day begin perfectly; for that which I have done hitherto is nothing."

According to our purpose shall be the success of our spiritual profiting; and much diligence is necessary to him that will profit much.

And if he that firmly purposeth often faileth, what shall he do that seldom purposeth anything, or with little resolvedness?

It may fall out sundry ways that we leave off our purpose; yet the light omission of spiritual exercises seldom passes without loss to our souls.

The purpose of just men depends, not upon their own wisdom, but upon God's grace; on whom they always rely for whatsoever they take in hand.

For man proposes, but God disposes; neither is the way of man in himself.

If an accustomed exercise be sometimes omitted, either for some act of piety or profit to my brother, it may easily afterward be recovered again.

But if out of a slothful mind, or out of carelessness, we lightly forsake the same, it is a great offence against God, and will be found to be prejudicial to ourselves. Let us do the best we can; we shall still too easily fail in many things.

Yet must we always purpose some certain course, and especially against those failings which do most of all molest us.

We must diligently search into and set in order both the outward and the inward man, because both of them are of importance to our progress in godliness.

If thou canst not continually recollect thyself, yet do it sometimes; at the least once a day, namely, in the morning or at night.

In the morning fix thy good purpose; and at night examine thyself, — what thou hast done, how thou hast behaved thyself in word, deed, and thought; for in these perhaps thou hast oftentimes offended both God and thy neighbor.

Gird up thy loins like a man against the vile assaults of the devil; bridle thy riotous appetite, and thou shalt be the better able to keep under all the unruly motions of the flesh.

Never be entirely idle; but either be reading, or writing, or praying, or meditating, or endeavoring something for the public good.

About the time of the chief festivals, good exercises are to be renewed, and the prayers of holy men more fervently to be implored.

From festival to festival we should make some good purpose, as though we were then to depart out of this world and to come to the everlasting feast in heaven.

Therefore ought we carefully to prepare ourselves at holy times, and to live more devoutly, and to keep more exactly all things that we are to observe, as though we were shortly at God's hands to receive the reward of our labors.

But if it be deferred, let us think with ourselves that we are not sufficiently prepared, and unworthy yet of so great glory which shall be revealed in us in due time; and let us endeavor to prepare ourselves better for our departure.

" Blessed is that servant," saith the Evangelist St. Luke, " whom his Lord when he cometh shall find watching; verily I say unto you, he shall make him ruler over all his goods."

PRAYER FOR SOLITUDE.

O God, who at this moment art present to the congregation kneeling before thee, and to the silent worshipper in solitude, make me conscious of thy presence, that so I may bow my soul before thee. Thou art greater than any human thought can conceive of: with thy almighty power, help me to reach unto thee! Thou art more merciful than any earthly friend: forgive my many faults, and help me to rest upon thee! Thou knowest my past life, as well as what is to come: help me to tread in the path that lies before me! Thou hast surrounded me with blessings: help me to be grateful for them to thee! Thou hast appeared to me in sorrow: help me to remember that it was in the sorrowful moment I saw thee! I am too blind to see thy hand in all the changes of my life: wilt thou then help me to faith, that I may acknowledge thee!

I look back upon many hours of happiness when I was forgetful of thy presence, upon many of trial when my heart knew not how to turn towards thee. In the hours that are to come, let me be more conscious of thy presence, so that days and nights of sorrow or of joy need only speak to me of thee. Give me strength in my lonely moments, give me courage in the hour of temptation. Help me to help others, that in whatever I do I may act with thy inspiration alone.

May the good resolutions that I make this day grow stronger and become more fruitful as the days pass by. And when the hours of distraction come, let my heart never be distracted from thee. May I learn from the life and the words of Christ how I may find thee, that from these I may know how, and may venture to call thee Father, who art the creator and sustainer of all.

Help thou my unbelief, since I know not how to rise up to so great a good, and, with thy spirit helping me, may I learn what it is to be a child of God; which I would ask in the name and with the help of the Saviour.

2*

FROM THE NEW TESTAMENT.

Matt. vi.

No man can serve two masters; for either he will hate the one and love the other, or else he will hold to the one and despise the other. Ye cannot serve God and Mammon.

Therefore I say unto you, Take no thought for your life, what ye shall eat or what ye shall drink; nor yet for your body, what ye shall put on. Is not the life more than meat, and the body than raiment?

Behold the fowls of the air; for they sow not, neither do they reap, nor gather into barns; yet your Heavenly Father feedeth them. Are ye not much better than they?

Which of you by taking thought can add one cubit unto his stature?

And why take ye thought for raiment? Consider the lilies of the field, how they grow; they toil not, neither do they spin. And yet I say unto you, that even Solomon in all his glory was not arrayed like one of these.

Wherefore, if God so clothe the grass of the field, which to-day is, and to-morrow is cast into the oven, shall he not much more clothe you, O ye of little faith?

Therefore take no thought, saying, What shall

we eat? or, What shall we drink? or, Where-
withal shall we be clothed?

(For after all these things do the Gentiles seek;)
for your Heavenly Father knoweth that ye have
need of all these things.

But seek ye first the kingdom of God, and
his righteousness, and all these things shall be
added unto you.

Take, therefore, no thought for the morrow;
for the morrow shall take thought for the things
of itself. Sufficient unto the day is the evil
thereof.

A HYMN.*

O help us, Lord! each hour of need
  Thy heavenly succor give;
Help us in thought and word and deed,
  Each hour on earth we live.

O help us when our spirits bleed,
  With contrite anguish tore!
And when our hearts are cold and dead,
  O help us, Lord, the more!

O help us, through the prayer of faith,
  More firmly to believe!
For still the more the servant hath,
  The more shall he receive.

If, strangers to thy fold, we call,
  Imploring, at thy feet,
The crumbs that from thy table fall,
  'T is all we dare entreat.

But be it, Lord of mercy, all,
  So thou wilt grant but this;
The crumbs that from thy table fall
  Are light and life and bliss.

O help us, Father, from on high!
  We know no help but thee;
O help us so to live and die
  As thine in heaven to be!

---

* By Milman.

If we could but carry about with us the consciousness of the ever-present God, we might perhaps do without the solemnization of one day to
his service. We go about our week-day duties
forgetting him, as the busy man in the crowded
streets forgets the clear sky above him. Sometimes, it is true, God seems to have been scarcely nearer us on the day we pretend to devote to
him, than when we are about the world's business. Yet it is more deeply our fault, if we cannot bring him to our hearts in our devotion and
our worship. For it is easier to draw near to
him in contemplation than in action. We read
of mystics, of the old recluses, who spent their
lives in contemplation of God, swallowing up in
the thought of him all personal desires, all selfish impulses. Alas! often as they looked so
fixedly into their own souls, they may have found
there only the reflection of themselves, and, lost
in thought, have forgotten all the traces of God in
his creations. Yet in the silence of thought it is
easier to conceive of the greatness of God. As
in night the countless worlds appear that were
hidden in the daytime by the light of the nearer
world, the sun, so in silent thought come up the
memories of the countless blessings of God, that
are lost in the one great blessing that he gives
us, of action in life.

These quiet hours recall to us his greatness

and his love. We have time to dwell upon his
goodness. In the quick passing of every day
we do not find time to be thankful. We let
events go by as if they followed one another me-
chanically. And our life becomes mechanical.
Its duties are laid upon certain hours, and are
taken up without thought. We pass through
the routine of a week, and remember that our
hands have been occupied, while our hearts have
been moved with scarcely a single impulse. Or
else our affections have been selfishly employed.
We have not looked up from the round of our daily
occupations, nor been lifted by a single high aim.
Sometimes through the week we have been reminded of God, by some happy glimpse of nature,
or some awakening word of a friend. Or else, in
some moment of pain or agony, we have found
we must call upon Him, or have seen some sufferer who has found patience through love of him.
But seldom have we found him our strength
and support for our little daily trials. He seems
almost too great for us to come to him with our
little temptations and trials.   And yet it is these
little temptations that avail to stain the white-
ness of our character. It is our lesser trials
before which we grow weak and faint. It is the
duties of every day that we find so hard to perform. The greater duties, when they come, bring
with them a grand impulse, and carry us out into the fresh air.

How inspiring it is, when a fresh air does breathe over our daily duties, when some new awakening rouses us to a new life, and makes every morning like the first day in Paradise! It matters very little then what we have to do, — our zeal is strong to carry us through all. And we find our own earnestness reflected on those around us, and we no longer have any burden to carry, but are travelling because the way invites us! This is what we call life. Otherwise the passage of each day is monotony and mechanism. It is the same to the laborer who counts his hours till the time of rest shall come, and to the more weary man who tries to invent labor for his hours, that so he may buy rest for himself at the day's end. But life is more than this. It gives a charm to the necessary labor. It gives a freshness to the seemingly unoccupied hours.

But this life must come from God. We cannot work, even in this world, without him. When we involve ourselves in the interests of society, of business, of self, — however various we make them, however we number them, — we are losing our life so long as they shut out the thought of Him who is the source of life. One gay scene after another is but the repetition one of another, if we have not enlivened them all by a thought of something higher. The more we give our thoughts to our own self-interest, the more are we dulling our capacities for happiness, — we are contracting our hearts.

These thoughts have come into my mind on reading the text of a sermon before me, — " The Father is with me." I wish I could teach myself how it was that Christ felt always this presence of God, for so it was that he made his life a constant renewal, and his death but a sign of another life to come.

SERMON BY REV. W. B. O. PEABODY.

HITHERTO UNPUBLISHED.

" The Father is with me."—John xvi. 32.

'Have you never seen the time when you
felt so desolate that the presence of any being
would have been a relief to you? Have you
never seen the time when you have done some
unworthy deed which you could not have done if
you had felt that any being was near you?
Have you never gained some victory over your
own passions, and wished for some witness of your
triumph, some sharer of your joy ? Christianity
supplies these wants of the soul. It teaches us
that the greatest and best of all beings is always
near us, — all we need is to learn to feel His presence in our souls.

There is no safeguard of human virtue half so
powerful as the thought that a being is present,
nor does that thought lose its power when we are
told that a being *is* present, and that being is God.
Do we not fear him because we cannot see him
with our eyes ? If the simple presence of a human being has power over us, and the presence
of God has *no* power, there must be something
wrong in our souls.

There is something wrong in our souls, — this
want of spirituality is wrong, — it is wrong to let
our minds be so enslaved to visible things as to

3

think more of every created thing than of the God who made it. There is no such thing as being religious while we are strangers to God.

The spirit of religion consists in making the thought of God near, familiar, and welcome; and you can tell the amount of your own or any other man's religious improvement by ascertaining whether or not he loves to think of God. He who does not take pleasure in thinking of God has no claim to the name of Christian. It is true there are many in the Christian world who never think of God when they can avoid it, who pronounce his name often in profaneness, and never in prayer. They consider themselves Christians, they expect the Divine blessing, they hope to be saved; if so, they cannot be undeceived too soon. But let us learn from Jesus Christ how far he felt the presence of his Father,—from him we can learn our Christian duty.

Our Saviour is here telling his disciples that in a little while, in a few hours, the officers of power will be in search of him, and they will leave him alone, without a single friend to sustain him in the anxiety and suffering before him. He did not mean to reproach them with this desertion; it was but too natural that they should look upon their own danger with dismay. He meant rather to tell them that they need not upbraid themselves, for though all the world forsake him, he shall not be left alone; his Almighty Friend and Father will be with him still.

But while Jesus Christ used this thought of the Divine presence for his own support and encouragement, this was not the only reason for which he recommended it to them. He wished they might use it as a shield in temptation, because they were to be often and severely tried. He wished they might use it as a consolation in their solitude and despondency, when they too were tempted to say to God, Why hast thou forsaken me? He wished them to bear it with them, to inspire them in all their duties, — and this was the most important thing; to know that the eye of God was beaming in its kindness upon them, to know that it smiled encouragement upon their labor when lover and friend were far from them, to know that their least sacrifices and efforts were seen and remembered, would give them the animation they wanted as they went about doing good.

The reflection that we are not alone, but our Father is with us, is our safeguard in temptation; that he is with us, we know; that none of our actions escape his view, we know; that he sees our soul when balanced between the choice of good and evil, we know; — but these are among the things that we know without feeling them, and which it does no good to know without we feel them.   What avails it to us that there is a heaven, unless it serves to encourage us in our duties and sorrows? what avails it that we have a religion, unless we believe it so far as to be influenced by its revelations? what avails it to us that God is present, unless we act as if he were the witness of our lives?   It avails so little, that those who forget the presence of God are regarded as without God in the world.

But how are we to feel the presence of God? how can we make that which is not visible to the eyes distinct and visible to the soul?   How is it that the youth, who, distant from his parent's eye, with pleasures all around him soliciting his desires, with all things about him conspiring to drown the voice of his conscience and make him glory in his shame, — how is it that he is sometimes cut to the heart by the thought of parents who sit in solitude at home, depriving themselves of comforts for his sake, sacrificing their very lives that he may want nothing, while he is conscious that all he wrings from them is wasted in guilty pleasure? How is it that their written expressions of affectionate interest sometimes wound him as if they were written with fire upon his heart? how is it that sometimes the thought of their kindness makes him start from these delusions, burst the chains like a giant, and return to the path of duty?   Such examples are not uncommon among the young, and all who have seen them may know what a father's presence, even the thought of a father's presence, can do. Can it be that there is less power in the thought of God? I do not believe it. Sometimes God has been represented to us in youth in such a way that he has no place either in our affection nor reverence ; but when the parents have done their duty, — where we have been taught to look up to God as one who has an affectionate and never weary interest in our welfare, — where we have been used to regard him, not as a gloomy and stern avenger, but a kind and faithful friend, (all which he is,) — I believe that the thought of him has power to wound the heart as deeply as the mild upbraiding of a father's eye. But if we will not feel his presence, we shall not feel it, — it is a matter of choice ; if we will not feel it, we shall lose all the security which it would have afforded us in the various temptations of life, — we shall not feel it till this world is sinking before our eyes, when they are heavy with death, and when the feeling of his presence is a feeling of despair.

The reflection that we are not alone, but our Father is with us, is our support in sorrow. But his presence must be familiar to us, or it can afford us no consolation ; it is not the thought of one whom we have wronged and offended, one whose favor we have never tried to gain, that

3 *

can give us happiness in dreary hours. It is the thought of him whose kindness we have loved to acknowledge and remember, him whose friendship we have valued and endeavored to gain; and if in days of prosperity we have been thankless and forgetful of God, his presence cannot be grateful to us in adversity, however kind and cheering, for every word and look of an injured friend is a deep reproach to the guilty.

We not only lose the consolation which the presence of God might afford us, but, unless we are familiar with his presence, it seems like the presence of an enemy exulting in our pain. So darkly is God represented by those who know him not, that, when misfortune comes, they regard it not as a chastening, but as an injury; instead of asking what they have done to deserve kindness at his hands, what reason- there is why he should not send misfortunes severer still, they complain bitterly of his withdrawing his goodness when perhaps he has not heard one word of thankfulness from their lips in the whole course of their lives.

But how is it that a father's presence ever gives consolation? It is because the son feels that there is one near him who sympathizes deeply with his grief, one who is able to understand his feelings, one who is ready to aid him, tear for tear. The thing that makes suffering intolerable is the thought that it is nothing to them that pass by, that others are going about their business and enjoying themselves as usual, while our house is made desolate by grief; and to hear others rejoice in that suffering is more than we can bear. Even Jesus Christ, when he saw the smiles of malicious triumph, and heard the acclamations round his cross, felt for a moment as if all were against him, as if he was deserted even by his God.

If we will have a support in sorrow then, one which will sustain us when we have no other, we must make a friend of God. A friend to man he is, however unworthy; but we must feel his friendship, we must have an answering feeling awakened in our own breasts. Otherwise, though we are not alone, we shall feel as if we were alone; we shall endure all the sorrow of desolation when our friend is standing nigh. And who can say that he will remain with those who coldly disregard him? We know it is what we should never do for others, and we should ask ourselves what right, what reason, we have to expect it of God.

The reflection that we are not alone, but our Father is with us, is the best inspiration we can have in duty. And if our lot in life is a hard one, or if our interest in duty leads us to make great exertions, there will be many times when

we shall want all the encouragement which a
thought like this can give. Those who have
never done a duty from principle may not know
it; but there are times when, though the heart
retains its resolution, the weak nature faints and
cannot go through. Such times there were even
to Jesus Christ; divine as his resignation was,
there were times when he felt as if he could go
no farther, though the universe could not make
him retreat one step. In such a time you will
find it written of him that he withdrew into the
wilderness and prayed, — that he fell on his face
and prayed, while sometimes the drops wrung
from him by deep agony were flowing from his
brow; —

> "Cold mountains and the midnight air
> Witnessed the fervor of his prayer."

Our duty in life is as different from his, as the
fireside from the field of battle; our yoke is easy
and our burden light. But even in our duty,
when all goes well, when devotion is a pleasure,
when it is our enjoyment to do good, when we
feel that every day bears us onward as a wave to
that improvement which ends in heaven, it is
cheering to think that there is joy in heaven at
witnessing the growth of religious excellence in
any human heart. This happiness we may enjoy when we will, for if there is joy in heaven
over the sinner that repenteth, there is a calmer,

a less distrusting joy at witnessing the change from glory to glory which will, when the short labor of life is over, add another radiant spirit to the seraphs and sons of light.

But what is inspiring in the prosperous hours is necessary in those times of despondency from which no course of duty will ever be free There is a time when the heart sinks, when the confidence fails, when we feel as if we had labored in vain. There is a time when we seem with all our exertions forced downwards as by the rush of the stream, when we feel as if each coming year of life found us standing still farther from .God. There is a time when everything connected with the world, even its cares and duties, makes us weary and sick at heart. Then we can find encouragement in the thought of God, and of God alone. If all earthly things sink beneath us, we have left Him who alone has immortality; everything earthly is unsatisfactory, and there will be times when we shall feel it in our hearts. But we have no need to trust in the perishing world; and if we do, we do it in defiance of warning. When the doors of mansions of light are thrown open for us to enter, why should we insist on making our bed in the grave ?

Such is the security and support afforded us by the presence of God in life; but all these are hardly to be compared with the support it affords in death, — I mean to those who have not been strangers to God. It is as well to bring that hour before us, because it is one which we must all of us go through, — some of us very soon. It is well to ask whether we shall be sustained by the presence of God when the eye is closed to everything it has loved and treasured on earth, and the last breathings of affection have died away upon the ear for ever. All the past but the remembrance of our goodness or our guilt will perish from the soul; all the eternal future will spread itself out before us, — a dark and dreary wilderness to those who have left their affections behind them in the world, — a place of glory and joy to those who have prepared for the heavenly country. In all the wide reach of the universe, not a single being can be near to sustain us then beside our God. Let us, then, secure his favor, which is life; let us provide a stay and solace against that awful hour to which we all shall come.

Then we shall not be alone in death. The Father, our Father, will be with us; the gates of mercy will open to receive us; Jesus, the mediator of the new covenant, will welcome us to the many mansions, and we shall receive the crown of righteousness from the hand of God.

HOPE IN DEATH.

FROM THE GERMAN OF KLOPSTOCK.

How will it be with me then, O then!
When I, to rejoice in the Lord,
Shall fall asleep in Him!
No longer stained with any sin,
Set free from mortality,
Rejoice thyself, my soul!
Strengthen, console thyself,
Redeemed one, with the life
That thy God will give thee then!

I rejoice and I tremble!
The yoke of my misery presses me so,
The curse of my sin casts me down!
But the Lord makes easy my yoke;
Through Him does my heart grow strong:
It believes and rises again.
Jesus! Christ! Let me strive
To live to thee, — to die in thee, —
To inherit thy Father's kingdom!

Scorn then all terror of death,
My soul! 't is a path to look upon,
The way through the dark valley.
Let it be no more fearful to thee!
Unto the most Holy it leads,
The way into the dark valley
The rest of God
Is imperishable, abundant;
The redeemed may trust in him!

My Lord! my Lord! I know not the hour
That, when my eyelids shall fail,
Will gather me with thy dead.
Perhaps its night may surround me
Before I finish this prayer,
Or have stammered this praise unto thee.
Father! Father! into thy hands
Commit I my soul, —
Kind Father, into thy hands!

Perhaps my days will be many;
I am yet, perhaps, far from the goal
Over which the crown is shining.
Am I yet far from the goal?
This tabernacle of my mortality,
Will it be, but late, destroyed?
Permit, Father! my Father!
That good deeds, good deeds,
May accompany me
To the throne of Eternity!

How will it be, ah! how will it be with me then,
When I shall rejoice in the Lord,
Shall offer worship there!
No longer stained with sin,
A partaker of eternity!
No longer a child of earth!
Blessed One, let us sing to thee!
Bring praise and honor
To thee, who hast been, wilt ever be!

God only knows in what department we shall best advance. Our duty is to accept the situation best adapted for us, and use it to the best advantage as long as we live. Then, when we are called away, and enter another field of labor, it will be of little consequence upon what sort of materials we have wrought in this world. The test will not then be whether our hands have tilled the earth, built in wood or stone, pulled the ropes of a ship, written a book, painted a picture, or held the sceptre of a nation; but whether we have gained from these employments that power of mind, purity of taste, and uprightness and force of character, which will enable us to grapple with higher themes and more suitable occupations. Our gold, our merchandise, our lands, our civic honors, our poem, or our temple we cannot take with us; but we shall take the soul, which has been fashioned by our effort to gain these possessions, and to acquire and create this power and these works. And he who carries to the unknown world the noblest results from this, has lived the best, and had a genuine success in life. And whether that spirit be Shakespeare, Washington, or some faithful tiller of the ground or sailor upon the great deep, or man of various worldly cares, or woman unknown out of her well-ordered circle, God only can decide; but this we know, that we can serve him only by making the most of those opportunities his wisdom has contrived for our growth in the Christian life.

For God's method of education is the best, and we only go wrong and fall into confusion when we would alter it. When he creates an oak, he does not plant it in a hot-house, and send gardeners to water it, and shut off or let in the light and heat; but an acorn drops into the side of a hill, and by and by a green twig shoots up among the rocks, and through drenching and freezing, and scorching and blowing, and the sifting of the earth over it, and the "haphazard" of vegetable life, it fights its way along, season by season, till in a hundred years it shades the herdsman and the flock, and the wild storm becomes an anthem away up among its branches. Neither does he choose to rear us to manhood upon spiritual dainties, or in the conservatory of any transcendental theory, but gives us a soul, and a will, and a place to grow in the midst of his universe. And by living as he has appointed, — now standing with our faces scorched in fires of sorrow, now pacing over flats of monotonous labor, now twisting, and stooping, and clambering through rugged paths, now waiting in the dark for the appearing of one star, — by being all and doing all that he wills, do we grow up into the "perfect man, to the measure of the stature of the fulness of Christ." — *A. D. Mayo.*

Have patience with all things, but chiefly have patience with yourself. Do not lose courage by considering your own imperfections, but instantly set about remedying them; every day begin the task anew. For, in the first place, how can you patiently bear your brother's burden, if you will not bear your own? — *Francis de Sales.*

To live something more than one's self, — that is the secret of all that is great; to know how to live for others, — that is the aim of all noble souls.

Because thou sayest, I am rich, and increased with goods, and have need of nothing; and knowest not that thou art wretched, and miserable, and poor, and blind, and naked; I counsel thee to buy of me gold tried in the fire, that thou mayest be rich; and white raiment, that thou mayest be clothed, and that the shame of thy nakedness do not appear; and anoint thine eyes with eye-salve, that thou mayest see.

As many as I love, I rebuke and chasten; be zealous therefore, and repent. — *Revelation* iii. 17 – 19.

It is neither the austerities of the body nor the agitations of the soul, but the good emotions of the heart, which require and which sustain the

pains of the body and the soul. For there are
needed these two things towards our purification,
pains and pleasures. St. Paul has said that
those who will enter upon the good way will find
troubles and anxieties without number. This
ought to serve as consolation, since, being warned
that the way to heaven that we seek is filled
with them, we ought to rejoice at meeting such
signs that we are in the true road. But these
pains are not without pleasure, and are surmount-
ed only with pleasure. For as those who quit
God to return to the world do it only because
they find more sweetness in the pleasures of the
world than in a union with God, and because
this charm victoriously allures them, and, making
them repent of their first choice, renders them
the " devil's penitents," according to the phrase of
Tertullian, so we should never quit the pleasures
of the world to embrace the cross of Jesus Christ,
were there not to be found more sweetness in
contempt, poverty, self-renunciation, and in the
scorn of men, than in the charms of sin. And
thus, as Tertullian says, it is not necessary to fancy the life of a Christian a life of sadness. He
never quits pleasures but for others still greater.
Pray without ceasing, says St. Paul ; in everything give thanks ; rejoice evermore. It is the
joy of having found God that lies below the sadness of having offended him and the complete re-

newal of our life. He who has found a treasure in a field has such joy, according to Jesus Christ, that he sells all that he may buy it. The people of the world have their own sadness, and they have not that joy that the world can neither give nor take away, says Jesus Christ himself.

Let us not then give way to sadness, nor believe that piety consists only in a bitterness without consolation. A true religion, such as is found complete only in heaven, is so full of satisfactions, that its beginning, its progress, and its goal is filled and crowned by them. It is a brilliant light which it sheds on all that belongs to it. Is there any sadness mingled with it, and especially in its beginning, it is from us that it rises, and not from goodness itself; for it is not the effect of the piety dawning in us, but of the impiety that lingers with us still. Remove the impiety, and the joy will be without stain. — *Pascal.*

One of the most persuasive, if not the strongest, arguments for a future state rests on the belief, that, although by the necessity of things our outward and temporal welfare must be regulated by our outward actions, which alone can be the objects and guides of human law, there must yet needs come a juster and more appropriate sentence hereafter, in which our *intentions* will be considered and our happiness and misery made

4*

to accord with the grounds of our actions. Our fellow-creatures can only judge what we *are* by what we *do ;* but in the eye of our Maker what we *do* is of no worth, except as it flows from what we are. Though the fig-tree should produce no visible fruit, yet if the living sap is in it, and if it has struggled to put forth buds and blossoms which have been prevented from maturing by inevitable contingencies of tempests or untimely frosts, the virtuous sap will be accounted as fruit, and the curse of barrenness will light on many a tree from the boughs of which hundreds have been satisfied, because the Omniscient Judge knows that the fruits were threaded to the boughs artificially by the outward workings of base fear and selfish hopes, and were neither nourished by the love of God or man, nor grew out of the graces engrafted on the stock by religion. — *Coleridge.*

CHRIST'S LOVE TO US AN EXAMPLE FOR OUR LOVE TO OUR BRETHREN.

FROM THE GERMAN OF A. THOLUCK.

Think of the Son of God and man, whom the sea and the powers of nature obeyed;—to what did he turn the omnipotence of his powers? To establish a glorious kingdom? To collect all the splendor and all the riches of the earth around himself? Imagine that you should be gifted some time with such a power, that could rule heaven in its heights, and the abysses in their depths,—should you, my brother, turn it to such purposes as the Saviour did? Would *this* be nearest to your heart,—to go up and down in the midst of the want and the misery of the children of men, to show this divine, wondrous power in the healing of their infirmities? Would this be the joy of *your* life, too,—to walk among the blind, the deaf, the palsied, to become their Saviour and their helper? O where is there a heart like the heart of Jesus! His work was love,—love flowed from the hem of his garment. Christians, behold what a man was he! Yet what helps it, if the eye of the body becomes clear for the blind man, while the eye of the soul remains blind,— that your bodily ear learns to hear the words of men, while the spiritual ear remains deaf to the words of God,—that the dead in the body rise up from the dust of their graves, while the spiritual sleeper remains dead in the death of sin? It is said of him, " that he was moved with compassion that the multitude had no bread." O, far more is he moved when he sees that the world has not the bread of life! How did he go about to seek and to save that which was lost! Look with what company do you find him surrounded, the holy one and pure of God? Again and again you read, " with publicans and sinners." With the outcast, with the abandoned of the people, with just these does he take up his abode. O how earnestly did he woo each single soul, that he might not lose one of them that his Father had given him! " What man is there among you," he says, " having a hundred sheep, if he lose one of them, doth not leave the ninety and nine in the wilderness, and go after that which is lost?"—away through thorns and thistles, over the heights, through the valleys, till it is found; and when it is found, he lays it upon his shoulders, and brings it home with joy. Yes, faithful Saviour, this is *thy* picture, which thou hast thyself painted! Yes, we know it, so thou hast thyself sought for us, till thou hast brought us home to the fold of thy Father. See him in conversation with the Samaritan woman, who of us would have persevered with this very poor, very darkened soul? He offers her living water, and she thinks of the water of the well that stands before her.

But how he draws near her, how he penetrates the depths of her soul! See how he labors with a Peter, till the wavering reed is changed into a rock, till from his stirred soul presses the cry, "Lord, thou knowest all things,—thou knowest that I love thee!" See how he would have sued with love even the soul of his betrayer! So was he when he walked among us. Behold the man! But so too is he now, since he is glorified with the Father, and the promise fulfilled, "When I am lifted up, I shall draw all men to me." You who now are wandering in his pastures, and who in communion with the Lord receive daily mercy upon mercy, witness to the world how he has drawn near to your soul, how he has awakened you and lifted you through his Holy Spirit, till you at last lie at his feet, crying that his love has conquered, that, weeping bitterly, you bend like a child at his knees. This he has done for thee; *what hast thou done for him?*

Has he thus loved us, my brethren, how then ought we, following his example, love our brothers?

The first thing for us also, before we *do* anything for the need of our brethren, is that we must *suffer* with them, and before we suffer with them we must know their want and misery. Only the wants of the body, these we can easily acquaint ourselves with; for who is there who feels them not himself? But the need of the human soul! If you have yet known nothing of the need of the soul, the need of the soul is perhaps for many a wholly new ·thought! It will first dawn upon you when you have learnt to· understand that little word *sin*. There must have come in your own life hours when, in the light of divine truth, your own self-righteousness has appeared to you like a spotted garment, — when with trembling you have perceived that, if we are judged according to our works, no flesh will stand upright before God. You must feel your own fetters, you must know of those tears which spring from a longing for spiritual freedom, you must look into the abyss of your own heart.

But, my brother, do you belong to the class whom the Saviour pronounces blessed, — to the poor in spirit? Then you will not merely *be able* to suffer, but you *must* suffer with the need of the soul of sinful men. You see the broad street of which the Saviour says that it leads to destruction. Large, gay bands enter upon it, and in the ear of your soul sounds the heart-rending echoing shout of joy of some, with the heart-rending cry of sorrow from others; it sounds upon *your* heart when first your loving glance has fallen upon the needs of humanity; upon your heart there lies as upon the heart of the Saviour a world of woe; your soul is unspeakably sorrowful, and you fain would *help*.

Who among you feels his heart so pressed by

the need of his brother? I know it well, — so long as you do not feel your own need, you cannot sympathize with the need of your brother; and who is there who will confess the wounds of his own heart? Alas! most men pass by the plaintive cry of suffering humanity, and close their ears that they may not hear it. History tells us of an Asiatic prince who, that he might never more see the boundless misery of his suffering subjects, shut himself up for ever in his palace, extinguished the light of day, and by the glow of lamps, forgetting the misery that was without, went on gayly to his end. Such as he are you who until this hour have never felt the need of suffering humanity, not even your own! Can you then so completely forget the tears of your Saviour, that he wept for all humanity and for you?

Yet from our Lord has come to us, not merely an example of how we should *suffer* with our brethren, but how we should *help* them. "Even as he walked," said John, "ought we also to walk in the world." O you who have not yet learnt precisely what your vocation is in life, would you take up a glorious vocation, blessed beyond all measure? "As he walked in the world, so also ought you to walk"; as he went round among the sick and the poor of the earth, so also should you. It is true you cannot say to the blind, See! nor to the lame, Arise and walk!

But to each one of you has the goodness of God given many gifts, that you might be a preserving angel in the bodily wants of your brethren. The more our love grows, the more do we perceive our power to help. If in the beginning it seems to you that no gifts are lent you for your sorrowing brethren, O, believe me, the eye of love only fails you; with your love your power increases. And have you in the end nothing to give but the word of counsel and of consolation, and the silent, sympathizing pressure of the hand, and if you think that this is nothing for your sorrowing brethren, then you have never suffered yourself. But granting that there were no power lent you to dry the tears of your brother that are shed for the sorrows of this world, yet arise, since it is in your hands there rests the power to help the *need of his soul.* " Peter," said the Lord to his wavering disciple, " when thou art converted, strengthen thy brethren." " Simon Peter, lovest thou me, feed my sheep." O you who know how long Christ the Lord waited for you with long-suffering and with patience, until from the weak Simon, poor in faith, came forth a Cephas, a man of rock, to you are these words directed. Did the Good Shepherd go forth into the mountains and through the wilderness till he brought you home, who would not also go forth for his wandering brethren? " This I have done for thee; what wilt thou do for me?"

THE SECOND STORMY SUNDAY.

THE SURE WALL.

"God, when he takes my goods and chattels hence,
Gives me a portion, giving patience.
What is in God is God; if so it be
He patience gives, he gives himself to me."

HERRICK.

5

THE SECOND STORMY SUNDAY.

THE SURE WALL.

I STOOD by the window this morning and looked
out. It had been storming heavily through the
night, and I had heard the wind blustering loudly.
But all was still in the morning. Slowly and
quietly the snow was falling. Across the pathway from the door lay heavy drifts of snow, and
over these fresh snow fell. It fell like a white
mist, shutting out the distant landscape, like a
white curtain that shielded my window. Now
and then I could trace the softened outline of distant snow-covered hills, and then the veil would
close around me again. There was something
very impressive in the quiet and the solitude. A
sense of protection came over me, as I felt myself
shut in by this silently falling barrier. It all
recalled to me a story I had read, which I
cannot bring back clearly, but I can retrace its
impression.

It was a story of the sad times when the great

French army was making its retreat from Moscow. In a poor, low cottage, in a little village, was lying an invalid boy. This village lay in the course of the retreating army, and already the reports of its approach had reached the terrified inhabitants. In their turn, they began to make their preparations for retreat, for they knew there was no hope for them from the hands of the great moving mass of soldiery, which was seeking its own preservation, was reckless in its demands, and gave no quarter. Every one who had the strength to fly, fled, some trying to take with them their worldly goods, some to conceal them. The little village was fast growing deserted. Some burnt their houses or dismantled them. The old were placed in wagons, and the young hurried their families away with them.

But in the little cottage there was none of this bustle. The poor crippled boy could not move from his bed. The widowed mother had no friends near enough to spare a thought for her in this hurrying time of trouble, when every one thought only of those nearest to him and of himself. What chance in flight was there for her and her young children, and a poor crippled boy!

It was evening, and the sound of distant voices and of preparation had died away. The poor boy was wakeful with terror, now urging his mother to leave him to his fate, now dreading lest she should take him at his word and leave him behind.

"The neighbors are just going away; I hear them no longer," he said. "I am so selfish, I have kept you here. Take the little girls with you; it is not too late. And I am safe; who will hurt a poor, helpless boy?"

"We are all safe," answered the mother; "God will not leave us, though all else forsake us."

"But what can help us?" persisted the boy. "Who can defend us from their cruelty? Such stories as I have heard of the ravages of these men! They are not men, they are wild beasts. O, why was I made so weak, — so weak as to be utterly useless! No strength to defend, no strength even to fly!"

"There is a sure wall for the defenceless," answered his mother; "God will build us up a sure wall."

"You are my strength now," said the boy; "I thank God that you did not desert me. I am so weak, I cling to you. Do not leave me indeed! I fancy I can see the cruel soldiers hurrying in. We are too poor to satisfy them, and they would pour their vengeance upon us! And yet you ought to leave me! What right have I to keep you here? And I shall suffer more if I see you suffer."

"God will be our refuge and defence," still

said the mother; and at length, with low, quieting words, she stilled the anxious boy, till he too slept, like his sisters. The morning came of the day that was to bring the dreaded enemy. The mother and children opened their eyes to find that a "sure wall" had indeed been built for their defence. The snow had begun to fall the evening before. Through the night it had collected rapidly. A high wind had blown the snow in drifts against the low house, so that it had entirely covered it. A low shed behind protected the way to the outhouse where the animals were, and for a few days the mother and her children kept themselves alive within their cottage, shut in and concealed by the heavy barricades of snow.

It was during that time that the dreaded scourge passed over the village. Every house was ransacked; all the wealthier ones deprived of their luxuries, and the poorer ones robbed of their necessities. But the low-roofed cottage lay sheltered beneath its wall of snow which in the silent night had gathered around it. God had protected the defenceless with a " sure wall."

A silently falling snow often recalls to me this story. It shuts me in as if it were trying to protect me from outer enemies. And to-day its contrast has seemed especially opposed to the busy week that has gone before.

Another stormy Sunday, and I have been again alone. George is in New York. Joanna, with the perseverance of those of her faith, ventured to her church in the storm, but I did not dare to face it. All the plans that I formed yesterday with regard to going to church were changed by this unexpected storm, and I prepared myself again for a solitary worship.

I felt as if a new temple had been built around me of the snow; as if I ought to shut out from it every impure and unworthy thought; as if an Infinite Being were sheltering me. I tried to still within me all discordant ambitions, that I might be in tune with the silence of the day. To-day there has been no sound of the whistle of the steam-engine trying to force its way through the snow-drifts. Even the distant church-bells could not be heard through the deadening snow. I have not had so quiet a day since last Sunday. All has been turmoil and bustle, and I have had little time to think over my good resolutions.

I again invented for myself a series of solitary services, to occupy some of the quiet hours of the day. I read, devoutly and thoughtfully, prayer and hymn and sermon. In my lonely temple I tried to realize the close presence of the Most High.

It seemed indeed a very lonely, solitary service. I missed the sound of human voice. It was very impressive to me, yet after a while the silence seemed too deep. After my soul had offered its silent worship, I longed to give praise with my voice too, or to listen to the praising voices of others. I thought of the glorious music that accompanies the words, " I know that my Redeemer liveth ! " and I wished that I had the power to express such faith, in such grand changes of harmony. I called back to memory the wonderful voice that once had sung these words to me with convincing power; but memory brought them back silently, — there was no sound. I opened the piano and tried to hear, in the changing chords of the Prayer from Moses in Egypt, the varying voices of a congregation. And then I went back to silence again, to kneel before God.

The Lord is my Shepherd, I shall not want. He maketh me to lie down in green pastures, he leadeth me beside the still waters.

He restoreth my soul; he leadeth me in the paths of righteousness for his name's sake.

Yea, though I walk through the valley of the shadow of death, I will fear no evil ; for Thou art with me ; thy rod and thy staff they comfort me.

Thou preparest a table before me in the presence of mine enemies ; Thou anointest my head with oil ; my cup runneth over.

Surely goodness and mercy shall follow me all the days of my life ; and I will dwell in the house of the Lord for ever.

I have to recall the failure of my resolutions that I formed in the quiet of my last silent Sunday. I have to remember the passage of another week that has gone back to join many others as profitless.

How different will be our estimate of time,— the time that we have lived through, — when we shall reach the world that is no longer so measured! Memory now is dazzled by the present. Then we shall make a truer judgment of the worth of past events. In looking back upon a past week, now, we are scarcely able to judge which of our acts had itself a real worth. We look back with a sort of exultation upon some three hours' labor, that seems to us worthy of great praise. It may not, then, count so much to us as one moment's patience, or, alas! a moment's impatience. A hasty word or glance that broke forth from a moment of impatience will not merely leave its impression on the moment that follows, but on the eternity in which we shall have time to recall it.

We do not show our value of time by sitting down to count its sands as they pass, nor by regretting those that have past. We may make the moment that lies in our hand of value to ourselves or to others. We may waste it, by waiting, to wonder what we shall do with it. We *cannot* throw it away. Most frequently it comes to us labelled with its own duty or purpose; it needs only our earnestness to read this rightly and act upon it. Its value, of course, rests only in the way we use it. We cannot yet judge, ourselves, whether this will be because we have enjoyed that moment most, the sky and wayside flower; or because we have helped that moment a sufferer, shut up in a close street, out of reach of air or joy; or because we have that moment conquered some secret enemy of our heart, trampled down an evil passion, or turned away from some sorrow in our own soul, to join the happy chorus there is in God's creation. God, who has created a time for all things, knows best. We cannot judge. Yet at times we are supported by a courageous feeling at heart, that shows us when we have done the right thing at the right time. And at other times, we look back with a penetrating glance, and see more clearly than when the hour was passing,—see, sometimes with a shudder, when we have, and when we have not, acted simply, purely, and nobly. We see whether we have taken the gift of the moment joyfully and solemnly;—joyfully, because it is a gift; solemnly, because it is a gift of God's.

SERMON.

"But, beloved, be not ignorant of this one thing, that one day is with the Lord as a thousand years, and a thousand years as one day." — 2 Peter iii. 8.

There seems to be a contradiction in this statement, and yet we immediately see how it is reconciled.

We cannot understand the meaning of the words to be, that God beholds with serene indifference all the fluctuations in the ever-swelling tide of earth's joys and sorrows. We cannot understand by the statement, that a day or a thousand years are alike nothing to God; for this would be the same as declaring that the *events* with which a day or a century is crowned are nothing to him, which would amount to the same as saying that there is no such thing as Divine Providence.

We obviously understand, however, from our text, that, by the Eternal Being, events and actions are not measured according to the length of time which they occupy, but according to their moral significance; not by their duration, but by their quality.

It is upon the same principle that money is weighed in the scales of divine wisdom. It is not the vast amount which sinks down the scale; it is the two mites devoted to his cause by one who, when they are bestowed, has nothing left but faith in his God's protection.   She is the rich person in God's eye who has the wealth of heart to make such a sacrifice, while he who, even out of the abundance that he hath, refuses to give back aught to the great Being from whom he has received all, as he is seen from the battlements of heaven, appears stricken with poverty, covered with rags.

And so in regard to time.   Those ancient dynasties whose power has reached through long centuries, handed down from father to son,—men say of them, What a noble family! how glorious to be the founder of a race who should hold the throne for a thousand years!   Glorious!   How much longer in its influence than many such thousands of years, was that one day on which, in Judæa, that meek sufferer laid down his life for his friends!   And how must it have appeared to the Infinite Mind, who sees the end from the beginning!   And how much more space in the chronicle of eternity must one day which records the self-denying love of some unknown follower of Jesus occupy, than the thousand years' history of some line of pampered monarchs!

Let us then bear in mind, that mere duration does not appear to God as it does to us; that he is not oppressed by the contemplation of vast periods of time, nor unable rightly to estimate the opportunities of good provided for his children in one small day.

The passage of Scripture which we are considering contains its own divisions, and these let us seek to follow.

First, "one day is with the Lord as a thousand years." How awful is the thought! How significantly it forces on us the great idea of opportunity! For we are not to understand thereby that God, by special creative acts, can do in one day the slow work of a thousand years, or introduce at once new orders of creatures into existence, which thousands of years had rolled by without beholding, but .that, as he looks upon man, one day seems big with results which shall last through countless centuries. And what a reflection! You have discerned naught that is unusual in the day; you are willing that it shall leave you where it shall find you; but the sun, as it rose this morning, rose upon some who shall do this day the work of a thousand years. Some pious resolution made *and kept*, and the soul's future life, here and hereafter, a new thing for it; some earnest counsel given by parent to child, and the child turning short in his career, and from this day ever going upward, upward! some deed of Christian sympathy performed in the spirit of Him who made it lawful to do good on the Sabbath day, and the dawn of hope wakened in some despondent heart, — a dawn to know no night! And while you sit here, scarce taking in the thought that you are immortal, and I speak as if I forgot that this might be the last hour of our worship to some of us, there arc those even now somewhere on the earth who are hearing the voices of the sanctuary, as if they themselves were already in eternity, those speaking as if they were urging the great counsels of their dying hour. Sometimes it becomes plain in what way the providence of God may seem to exalt one day above a thousand years, by giving it a sun that never sets. Such a day was that in which the great German Reformer said to the friends who predicted his bloody death if he obeyed the summons of the Emperor, " If I knew there were as many devils at Worms as tiles on the houses, I would go." Such a day was that on which a youthful nation, hemmed in between the sea and the wilderness, as she broke from the chains with which a mighty kingdom was binding her, proclaimed her faith that all men are created equal.

But to see in any common day, as it passes, the opportunities of a thousand years,—opportunities waiting for us to improve them,—is a truth which it seems harder to realize. With what mysterious value it invests these fleeting moments! How solemn a thing does it seem to *live!* Within and around us, to realize that there are springs which, from the motion we impress on them, in one day, shall not cease vibrating for a thousand years! Never shall we do with true fidelity the work which God calls us to, until we awake to the significance of a single day. If we cannot see the immortal uses which lie hidden in *one* day, we shall not be likely to see those which lie hidden in many. We may speak of the dignity of human nature; but if, as we fasten our thoughts upon one human soul, we see no boundless capacities in it, our faith in the capacities of the *race* will hardly be a solid and animating one. And so, whenever we despise *to-day*, let us cease talking about the opportunities of life, let us give over dreaming of the great things which we shall do, " when we come to them."

We sometimes go through a series of events in one day which make it a long and memorable one in our lives. What a day that must have been to the inmates of that vessel which, not many years since, you may remember, within sight of our coasts was dragging her anchor, for eleven hours, through the wild waters and the grating rocks! How must the thoughts, the prayers, the anxious love of years, have been concentrated into the weary moments! And when that great anchor of the soul, once so sure and steadfast, no longer holds us firm,—when that drags heavily, displaced by the shock of successive fears, though they be condensed within the compass of hours,—how the anxious, throbbing life of years is crowded into such a day! Is it so? Can a messenger of God's afflictive providence thus stay the flight of time, so that the sun seems to stand still on Gibeon, and the moon in the valley of Ajalon? And shall the work with which life is full, the soul's immortal destiny, the hourly blessings which God is dispensing, be never enough to bid it pause in our earthly distractions? Shall we measure the length of the day only by the worldly excitements through which we rush, or by the tide of calamity which may set in upon us, and never by any deep, earnest meditations upon the great fact of our existence, the solemn thought of our accountability, the tremendous nature of the responsibilities which each single, solitary day as it passes summons us manfully to meet? O, let us be more intent, in this seed-time of our being, to permit each day to teem with the promise of its thousand years' harvest in a bright eternity!

And now let us turn to the second division of our subject. "Beloved, be not ignorant of one thing, that one day is with the Lord as a thousand years, and a thousand years as one day."

A thousand years as one day! How full of significance also is this reflection! Think of an existence to whose eternal being the thousands of years in the past, and those concealed from our eyes in the future, appear as but brief days! Consider, too, that it is your destiny as an immortal creature to see at length the period when a thousand years shall flit again before your memory as but a day! And what profiting thought shall we deduce from the reflection?

Do we not see, first, in a clearer light, the true nature of our earthly discipline? A thousand years but one day! Yet, when such a day comes back upon the soul's vision, what is there to leave an impress but the leading thought, the ruling purpose, which guided its long procession of hours? Could we but live more from week to week in the anticipation of that period when we shall measure time only by its results as left upon the character, we should not suffer ourselves to be so disquieted about things which ought to tempt superior intelligences to imagine that we believe we are but creatures of a day! How our varying duties and pleasures assume their true place, as we mark off our undying life by hundreds and by thousands of years! What we wore, what we ate, the flattery we received, the money we accumulated, how shall we find space to dwell upon these beguiling *circumstances* of our earthly being, in the period when, to memory, hundreds of years are condensed into hours? Look back even from your point of view to-day, look back ten years, and could you see again daguerreotyped with unerring minuteness upon your mind the little sources of annoyance which from day to day disturbed your peace, you would scarcely believe that the picture were a true one; you would look upon it with the compassion which the heart-breaking sobs of a child over the destruction of some plaything of the hour might excite. How could I, you would say, have anticipated so much unhappiness from that transient cause of uneasiness? Did I believe that to be vexed by that disquietude of a week was the sole end and purpose of God's calling me into being? And yet these thoughts, these rebellious emotions which come back before me, would make it seem as if I must almost have believed it.

But just so unworthy to engross your mind will the petty cares and vexations which cast their uneasy shadow over your brow now appear, as you look back on them ten and twenty years hence. How much more so, as you look back upon this short day of earth from the mysterious ages of eternity!

In the second place, the reflection that with the Lord a thousand years are but as one day, is adapted to inspire hope and courage in our endeavors to fulfil our Christian duty. Long and painful, at times, seem the efforts we need continually to renew in order to subdue an evil propensity, hopeless almost our attempts in any wise to catch the spirit of Christ's disinterested love. But what of the pains and the toil, with an enter-

prise in view so enduring? When the years of
life's pilgrimage retire into their true proportions
as compared with eternity, and appear but as
one day, who will then count the moments ex-
pended in a brave struggle with his self-indulgence, who lament that he did not more eagerly
follow deceitful phantoms by the wayside?

The two branches of our subject are indissolu-
bly intertwined. "Beloved, be not ignorant of
one thing, that one day is with the Lord as a
thousand years, and a thousand years as one
day." And how the truth which thus harmo-
nizes in these two statements ought to cheer those
who lament the yet unaccomplished triumph of
many a good cause! Let us take heart as we
remember that God has time in which to accom-
plish his will.

I commend the doctrine in the text to those
engaged in the instruction of the young, particularly those employed in their religious instruction, and I commend it to all who bear part in
the teachings of the Sunday school. We must
work, remembering that " one day is as a thousand years,"—that by speaking a *word* in season
we may save a soul from being put back a thousand years; and yet we must be kept from de-
sponding by recollecting that with God a thousand years are as one day,—that results cannot
be always immediately seen,—that he has other
means of influence besides ourselves.

"The eyes of them that see shall not be dim; and the ears of them that hear shall hearken." — Isaiah xxxii. 3.

* Of the bright things in earth and air
  How little can the heart embrace !
Soft shades and gleaming lights are there, —
  I know it well, but cannot trace.

Mine eye unworthy seems to read
  One page of Nature's beauteous book ;
It lies before me fair outspread, —
  I only cast a wishful look.

I cannot paint to memory's eye
  The scene, the glance, I dearest love ;
Unchanged themselves, in me they die,
  Or faint or false their shadows prove.

In vain, with dull and tuneless ear,
  I linger by soft Music's cell,
And in my heart of hearts would hear
  What to her own she deigns to tell.

'T is misty all, both sight and sound, —
  I only know 't is fair and sweet ;
'T is wandering on enchanted ground,
  With dizzy brow and tottering feet.

But patience ! there may come a time
  When these dull ears shall scan aright

---

* Keble.

THE SURE WALL.

Strains that outring earth's drowsy chime,
  As heaven outshines the taper's light.

These eyes, that, dazzled now and weak,
  At glancing motes in sunshine wink,
Shall see the King's full glory break,
  Nor from the blissful vision shrink; —

In fearless love and hope uncloyed,
  For ever on that ocean bright
Empowered to gaze, and, undestroyed,
  Deeper and deeper plunge in light.

Though scarcely now their laggard glance
  Reach to an arrow's flight, that day
They shall behold, and not in trance,
  The region " very far away."

If Memory sometimes at our spell
  Refuse to speak, or speak amiss,
We shall not need her where we dwell,
  Ever in sight of all our bliss.

Meanwhile, if over sea or sky
  Some tender lights unnoticed fleet,
Or on loved features dawn and die,
  Unread to us, their lesson sweet, —

Yet are there saddening sights around,
  Which Heaven in mercy spares us too,
And we see far in holy ground,
  If duly purged our mortal view.

The distant landscape draws not nigh
  For all our gazing, but the soul
That upward looks may still descry,
  Nearer each day, the brightening goal.

And thou, too curious ear, that fain
  Wouldst thread the maze of harmony,
Content thee with one simple strain,
  The lowlier, sure, the worthier thee ;—

Till thou art duly trained and taught
  The concord sweet of love divine ;
Then, with that inward music fraught,
  For ever rise and sing and shine.

A PRAYER.

O thou eternal and unchangeable God! the
same yesterday, to-day, and for ever; thou who
appointest the changes of the seasons,—the sun to
rule by day, the moon and stars by night,—wilt
thou still, in thy infinite majesty, accept the offering of praise from a humble heart? Help me to
draw near to thee, that so I may pray for what I
need, that I may be conscious that I am truly
near Him who giveth to him that asketh.

In the blessed quiet of this day, wilt thou help
me to purify my heart. Lead me to turn away
from all evil thoughts, to consecrate myself to
thee. Help me so to direct my thoughts that
they may strengthen all my principles, that they
may make clear the way that lies before me.
May I feel that I am not alone, that there is with
me One higher than I am, who can give strength
to my weakness.

Lead me in the way that opens before me the
coming week. Keep me from temptation. Deliver me from selfishness, from vanity. Make
me more careful of others, less thoughtful of
myself. Bless thou my friends in their coming
and their going, that we may always be near
each other in our love for thee.

And let the remembrance of the example of
Christ animate me to good works and to a holier

life. I ask in the name and as the disciple of
Jesus Christ, through whom I would ascribe all
honor and glory to thee.

I am so often longing to penetrate into that
"misty ground," that faith and not sight must
enter upon, and to question of that silent land
from which no answer comes to us, that to-day I
am going to read a sermon of Bretschneider, a
German preacher, that lies before me in the
German. This volume of sermons discusses the
many questions concerning the future state,
and this particular sermon is upon this subject:
"Why God has not permitted the souls of the
dead to appear to the living, in order to raise
the question of the immortality of the soul above
all doubt?"

SERMON.

BY DR. K. G. BRETSCHNEIDER.

The present alone shows itself clearly and plainly to man ; the past is dark to him, and the future concealed from him. The images of our own past life with each year disappear more and more. One object after another falls back from the light of certainty into the duskiness of that uncertainty which spreads itself over all past time, and at the point where our consciousness for the first time, like a spark of light, illuminated our being, is lost in deep night. The future is still more hidden from us than the past. The penetration of man can look forward, it is true, a very little way; but this is only a drop in the stream of future events, and all foresight ends with the grave. Beyond this, everything is hidden for us in the deepest darkness. We shall live, we shall meet with our reward ; this we know. But no mortal eye has penetrated that mysterious land of retribution, and never, never to the dead has a return to life been permitted, that they might inform us how it is beyond the grave. For all that credulity and superstition have reported, and frequently too, of the reappearance of the dead, has, on closer proof, been found to be either fraud or delusion. So fruitless has this been, that friends sometimes, while living, have made an agreement that he who should die first should appear again to the other, or give him some sign of his continued existence. Yet never has such a reappearance followed; the kingdom of the dead is fast closed, and no mortal breaks its mysterious seal.· This the unbeliever seizes upon with avidity; on this account he triumphs, and laughs at the hope of the believer, as a pleasing but groundless fantasy. Whatever there is most convincing that reason, that religion, has to bring forward, he believes he can overthrow with a single word. He says boldly, that if there were an immortality, at least one of the dead would appear again upon earth; and he declares openly that he shall hold the expectation of immortality as a vain hope, until one of the dead shall have arisen and returned to the land of the living.

Even the good and the believing cannot, at times, resist the wish that the dead would appear to the living, to make them certain of immortality, by their appearance and assurance of it, and to teach them what is the life after death. They flatter themselves that unbelief would thus be fully confuted, every doubt overthrown, the necessity of a virtuous life incontestably proved, and a general improvement of the human race be certainly brought about. This, too, was the hope of the rich man in the instructive parable in to-day's Gospel. But Jesus refuted this, and declared that neither the unbeliever would believe, nor the sinner lay aside his sin, even if the dead should appear, and could and should preach repentance. To convince you of this, my friends, may be difficult. . You believe, perhaps, that such appearances must needs bring about a great change. , But in truth there would be found neither more belief nor more virtue. We will now consider this, and for the strengthening of our own faith, and the weakening of such a common objection to the immortality of the soul, we will seek to convince ourselves of the truth of the assurance of Jesus.

"There was a certain rich man, which was clothed in purple and fine linen, and fared sumptuously every day; and there was a certain beggar named Lazarus, which was laid at his gate, full of sores, and desiring to be fed with the crumbs which fell from the rich man's table; moreover, the dogs came and licked his sores.

"And it came to pass that the beggar died, and was carried by the angels into Abraham's bosom. The rich man also died and was buried.

"And in hell he lifted up his eyes, being in torments, and seeth Abraham afar off, and Lazarus in his bosom. And he cried, and said, Father Abraham, have mercy on me, and send Lazarus, that he may dip the tip of his finger in water, and cool my tongue ; for I am tormented in this flame.

" But Abraham said, Son, remember that thou in thy lifetime receivedst thy good things, and likewise Lazarus evil things ; but now he is comforted, and thou art tormented. And beside all this, between us and you there is a great gulf fixed ; so that they which would pass from hence to you cannot, neither can they pass to us that would come from thence.

" Then he said, I pray thee, therefore, father, that thou wouldest send him to my father's house ; for I have five brethren ; that he may testify unto them, lest they also come into this place of torment.

" Abraham saith unto him, They have Moses and the prophets ; let them hear them.

" And he said, Nay, Father Abraham ; but if one went unto them from the dead, they will repent.

" And he said unto him, If they hear not Moses and the prophets, neither will they be persuaded though one rose from the dead." *

This parable of Christ's is one of the most instructive found in the Scriptures. It describes a luxurious rich man, who gave himself up wholly to the enjoyment of the senses, and

---

* Luke xvi. 19 – 31.

who followed the precept: "Let us eat and drink, for to-morrow we die." But he found it different in death from what he expected. He had five brothers as dissolute as himself, and given up to like evil ways. He begged that Lazarus might be sent to them to convince them; that is, by his appearance and his warning, convince them of the continued existence of the human soul, and the retribution of the good and the bad, that so they might repent. For he had the hope, that, at the reappearance of the dead Lazarus, or any other dead person, they would be so deeply shaken that they would reform, and believe in eternity. Yet Jesus declared that this wish could never be granted, and that its fulfilment even would be of no advantage. Certainly there are not few who wish that such an appearance of the dead might be possible, and who believe that it would have the weightiest consequences for the reformation of mankind, and the confounding of unbelief.

Yet why has God not permitted that the souls of the dead should appear to the living, to raise the immortality of the soul above all doubt?

Our Gospel gives us three reasons why God has not permitted this, where Jesus has declared such appearances to be, first, *impossible;* secondly, wholly *superfluous;* and thirdly, if they were allowed, *useless.*

In the first place, the Lord pronounces such an appearance impossible. For when the rich man expressed the wish that Lazarus might be sent to him to allay his sufferings, he received for an answer, that there was a great and insurmountable gulf fixed between the souls of the blessed and the sinful, — that no one could pass to the other, but each must remain in the place that God had set apart for his dwelling. If, then, it is true that spirits cannot leave the place of their reward or punishment, then it is also clear that they cannot return to the earth, their former dwelling-place, nor appear to mortal eyes in an invisible form. But what Jesus declares here as impossible, the reason also recognizes when it is turned earnestly to the subject.•

It is, in itself, impossible that the souls of the dead should be *seen* with our bodily eyes. The soul itself is a spirit, consequently is not visible to the eyes of the body. And allowing that it might be a wholly incorporeal being, but of the finest matter, even then it would still be as invisible to our eyes as the air, the wind, and so many other invisible, active powers in nature. Thus souls, separated from their bodies, could never become perceptible objects of our senses. Did we assume that the souls of the dead, when they entered the fields of immortality, were united to new bodies, that were recognizable by our senses, still these bodies, according to the laws of gravity, would be fettered to their dwelling-place, and could not forsake it to return to our earth. They would be then again in the condition in which they were placed here, where they, on account of their connection with the body, were fettered to this earth, and could not leave it to pass to any other sphere. Also, it appears impossible that a spirit that had passed on to perfection should ever have a desire, voluntarily, and from his own impulse, to come back to earth again, and to enter again into connection with a world so incomplete. There are exceedingly few men who have a desire to begin again their life upon earth. How could an immortal have a longing to return, — voluntarily to come back to the theatre of his earthly incompleteness? And did he desire it, and were it also possible that he could present himself to our senses, let us ask ourselves whether such a wandering upon our earth can be reconciled with the destiny allotted to the spirits of the blest, and whether souls could ever leave the state of retribution.

Considered on all sides, the reappearance of the dead seems something impossible. But, allowing that their *appearing* on earth were possible, yet the *knowing* them again were impossible. We should never be able to convince ourselves that it must really be their persons that we saw.

We might boldly ask of any one, who desires that the dead should appear again, to specify to us in what manner the dead can and shall convince us that *it is he* whom we have known in life, and through what means he can impart to us knowledge of his own state and that of the dead. It is the body by which we recognize each other here; but the body which the dead wore in life is mouldering in the grave. How could we recognize the souls of our friends? Perhaps they might unfold to us some peculiarities of their characters. But how insecure is such a sign, and how alike are all human beings in their principles, sentiments, and all that we call character! Or perhaps they might recall secrets that we are sure were only known to them. But how few men have such secrets! And who can assure us that a thousand other spirits are not familiar with our secrets? And who — and this is the most fearful question — who can assure us that other, perhaps hateful spirits, may not in this manner deceive us with vain hopes, or torment us with idle fears? Then, how could we recognize — *through our senses recognize* — that an appearance which presents itself to us is truly the soul of a dead man?

And how can such a spirit teach us of the future after death? Perhaps through words? But to utter words would require the organs of speech of the human body, which the dead no longer possess. They cannot speak in the human way, nor in tones audible to human ears! How can they, then, communicate with us? Will they perhaps originate thoughts and sensations directly in our souls, without our perceiving their presence with our senses? But how should we distinguish between these thoughts and sentiments and our own? How should we know it is the spirit of the dead that is coming in contact directly with our spirit? And could we call such a contact, always remaining in mystery, an *appearance* of the dead? And would it avail to convert the unbeliever, or strengthen our hope in immortality?

Thus, considered on all sides, is a reappearance of one who was dead, his recognition too, and the possibility of instruction from him, in itself impossible and not to be imagined. And with this, experience coincides, which has never been able to produce a single trustworthy example of such an appearance of the spirit. For all supposed experiences of this kind have in the end been recognized as deception or illusion. Even Jesus appeared after his resurrection to his friends, not in the spirit, but in the body; and it was by this that his trusted friends recognized him. If then the unbeliever, like the rich man in the parable, requires that the dead must appear to him before he can believe in immortality, and if the timid wish for such a reappearance, at least to destroy their doubts and to give to sinners a powerful impulse for repentance, then do they demand, do they wish for, something impossible. A demand for the impossible is wrongful, and such a desire for the impossible a folly.

But such a reappearance of the dead is, secondly, wholly unnecessary and superfluous; for we have, as Jesus says, or he allows Abraham to say, Moses and the prophets, whom we should listen to; that is, we have for the immortality of the soul so many weighty proofs, that it needs no further confirmation. It would be superfluous to discuss here circumstantially the proofs that reason and revelation present of the certainty of immortality. I have only this to offer, that these proofs must be completely satisfactory to us. Let us first look at the proofs of reason. With what right does the unbeliever refuse their issues, with what right does he demand a greater security for the recognition of the senses? A double power of comprehension is given to man by the Creator, — the senses which are possessed by the body, for the corporal objects of the visible world, and the reason, a power of the soul, for invisible things and for the truths of the understanding. Both of these powers are gifts of the Creator, with like intention, but for different aims ; both of them have a similar worth, both give a like certainty and deserve a like confidence. It must then be enough for us, if we have for the truth of a thought proofs of reason, and it is plainly a useless scepticism to desire for objects recognizable by the reason proofs of the senses. We might much sooner trust, nay, firmly believe, the verdict of the reason with regard to *invisible* things, rather than that of the senses with regard to visible objects. And as we require no proof from reason that the standing corn appears green, although some of infirm eyes may declare that it appears to them red or yellow ; and as we desire no proof from reason of the existence of very distant visible objects, although short-sighted persons may declare they cannot see them ; so little necessity have we to demand a proof to the senses of our continued existence after death, because some whose hearts are diseased by crime, or an evil conscience, or scepticism, will not confide in reason.

Yet the proofs of reason are not those alone to which we should listen. We have also proofs in the teaching of our Lord. We have countless promises in his divinely attested words ; we find in his own person, in the sublime work of that redemption that he brought about even in his death, and through which the entrance into a blessed eternity is laid open, — we find in his

glorious resurrection, and in his ascension to his
Heavenly Father, — the most complete surety
that we are immortal.   Why do we need further
witness ?   Can anything render it more sure that
men are destined for immortality, than that God
has sent his own Son to them ?   Can anything
assure us immortality more certainly, than that
Jesus founded a reconciliation, by which we are
saved from an eternal death, and consecrated to
an eternal life ?   Can a man of dust desire more
of his Creator than these securities, — this pledge
that we have in Jesus ?

Yet, if we would desire a proof of immortality
through our senses, we have indeed one which
more powerfully bears witness to us of immortality than even the mysterious appearance of
one dead.   This is the sight of the immeasurable
universe, and the countless glorious dwelling-
places which God has created for rational beings.
With deep wonder our eyes behold the countless
worlds spread abroad through the heavens, which
all bear outwardly some similarity to the earth
that we inhabit, and clearly are far more splendid and greater theatres of the majesty of the
Creator than the little globe on which we live.
But why, my friends, should we need further
testimony ?   Why must the souls of the dead
descend from the abodes allotted to them by
divine mercy to assure us that the precious say-

ing of our Lord Jesus is true, when he says, "In my Father's house are many mansions, — I go to prepare a place for you"? Do not our delighted eyes behold these heavenly mansions? Can anything from our own being convince us more strongly than their wonderful aspect itself?

With what right, then, do the unbelieving demand, and the wavering desire, that the spirits of the dead should secure to us a certainty of immortality? Have we not the strongest proofs, supported by the view of the visible heavens, which must leave us without a doubt?

Yet allowing that we might receive a confirmation of our hope in the appearance of the dead, such a reappearance would neither convince the unbelieving nor reform the sinful; in consequence, would be wholly *useless*. The unbelieving and the sinful say only too willingly with the rich man, "If indeed one arose from the dead, and preached us repentance, we would, we must believe; then should we surely repent." But Jesus declares this is a vain expectation. They hear not, he says, Moses nor the prophets, therefore they would not believe if one rose from the dead; that is, if the grounds which reason and revelation give us for immortality have no power over our hearts, then it would make no impression did one come from the dead, to appear to us, and preach to us. And in truth, my brothers, it is so. Neither faith nor virtue would gain any-thing by it; the unbelieving would not be con-verted, nor the sinful reformed. For, granting that it were possible the dead should appear to us, and teach us, yet we should never be certain of these appearances, — they would lose their power through habit, or the passage of time, and finally would rob our virtue of all which can give it a peculiar worth.

Never should we be wholly certain that we had not been deceived. We should always doubt whether they truly were the souls of the dead that had appeared to us. This lies in the nature of things. The apparitions of the dead would always retain something mysterious and incom-prehensible in their nature. We can think of no means, as we have before said, by which we could completely convince ourselves that indeed an ap-parition was the spirit of one dead, and nothing could offer us a security that such a spirit truly told us, or could tell us, the truth. Always would such an appearance leave room for scep-ticism; and even he who would willingly believe, could never bring his convictions to the necessary degree of certainty. What could we indeed ex-pect from such appearances? How could they disclose convincing facts? How could they con-vert the unbeliever and the sceptic, when they call in question, or completely reject, much more certain and convincing truths?

Yet, granting that it were possible to be sure concerning appearances of this nature, still would they lose all power over the heart, through habit and the passage of time. 'Do you doubt this? Let us, then, listen to experience. It is generally known and confessed, that the impression that great events produce at first, grows weaker and weaker, and at last disappears. You find examples of this, perhaps, in your own life. Now, should the dead appear but seldom, perhaps but once in a single generation, or but once to one man, the first impression would, it is true, be startling; but with each month, with every year, it would lose more of its power, and finally produce no more effect. But were such appearances something customary, they would have much less influence; for the most remarkable and extraordinary things become indifferent to us through habit. Knowledge alone — an acquaintance with the future, a perception of danger of sin — is certainly not enough, and does not make man prudent. What avails it, if the physician proves ever so clearly to the sensual man, that he is preparing for himself an early grave? What avails it, if the intemperate man, the glutton, the voluptuary, see countless examples of misery before their eyes, to which these vices lead? What impression does it make upon the spendthrift, when he sees that he is decreasing his riches daily, and when he can reckon the day that he shall become poor? What impression does it make upon the thief, the street-robber, though they see, daily, the gallows before their eyes, and can prophesy their own fate by the example of that of others? All this avails nothing, as experience shows. The first impression disappears by degrees, and is it often repeated, it loses still more its power. Those also who despise the voice of reason and revelation, as well as that of the wisest men and the clearest experience, would neither believe nor be made better, even if one rose from the dead. .

Imagine, my friends, that you were convincing a company of men who were born blind, of the truth that after death we are to enter into a new and more splendid world, because our Lord has assured us that in his Father's house are many mansions, and that he would prepare a place there, newer and happier. They would doubt, and reply: "How empty is this hope, with which you would console us! Where are the mansions of heaven of which the Lord speaks? Are they at hand? Why have we no perception of them through our senses? No, we cannot take hold on this hope, until we see and feel these mansions of heaven." Imagine further, that the eyes of those born blind should be opened to sight, and the splendor of the sun and the moon, and of the countless stars of night, should suddenly stream upon their eyes. Then would they fall down and worship; then would they say, " Yes, now my heart believes, for my eyes behold world upon world! Yes, we are indeed immortal!" But, my friends, how long would this impression last? To this give the answer yourselves. In a short time they would look upon the universe quite as indifferently as many an unbeliever and sinner who has beheld it his life long, — would even doubt like such a one, and need new proofs, as does many a man born with sight. Could you believe that it would be otherwise with the appearing of the dead?

But did such appearances truly produce the effect upon the unbelieving and upon sinners which we are so inclined to expect, then would our virtue lose completely all which gives it its peculiar worth. That Divinity which, in our reason, by revelation and the sight constantly presented of the world and of heaven, has given so many pledges of his goodness, desires, and justly, a confidence from us in his word, a belief in his promises, — that we should hold as true the word that he has disclosed to us in the Scriptures and by reason, and that we should through faith in these live holily and die consoled. The virtuous whose virtue, the good whose trust proceeds from such a faith, is a true child of God; his life is a

8*

true service of God, for through love of God and faith in him does he conquer the world, sin, and death. Without seeking with his eyes for the rewards of the future world, he is virtuous and trusts it to his Heavenly Father to give him his reward. Without beholding with his eyes the punishments of the future world, he flees the evil because he knows it is against the will of his Heavenly Father. And it is this faith that can make our virtuous acts pleasing to God, and gives them their worth in the eyes of men. But if the dead must first arise from their graves to confirm the word of God that is in us and the Scriptures, — if we would believe and follow, not the voice of God, but our own eyes and ears, — then would our merit sink away; our virtue is no longer a service to God, no longer the fruit of a childlike, a God-trusting heart.

If it is thus in itself impossible that the dead should appear again to the living; if such a re-appearance is wholly superfluous because the hope of immortality has elsewhere sufficient assurance ; and if it finally would neither convert the unbeliever nor better the sinner, and certainly have no weighty influence, — we see plainly how foolish is the desire for such an appearance, and how groundless it is to consider the want of it an excuse for disbelief in immortality. For to desire what is impossible, unnecessary, and useless, and to despise what is most worthy of belief and authentic, — this is either folly or wickedness.

No, my friends, we will not be guilty of this folly Our faith in a life after death has that degree of certainty which is good for us. It is strong enough, this faith, to animate us with a divine spirit, without making us unfit for the concerns of this life; powerful enough to lift us above the sufferings of this life, without making its joys distasteful to us. More light would dazzle our understanding, more certainty would rob us of this life's joys. *By faith should we live, and not by sight. It doth not yet appear what we shall be;* and it will not appear here. By hope and faith in God shall we train ourselves, and learn obedience. Happy those who understand this, and preserve their faith and virtue! What they believe here will they some time behold with their eyes; what they strive after, they will attain; what they hope for will become certainty. For never, never can it deceive, — the promise in us and that in the Gospel. Both come from God, and God is truth!

"In the day when I cried thou answeredst me, and strengthenedst
me with strength in my soul."— Psalm cxxxviii. 3.

Saviour! beneath thy yoke
 My wayward heart doth pine,
All unaccustomed to the stroke
 · Of love divine;
Thy chastisements, my God, are hard to bear,
Thy cross is heavy for frail flesh to wear.

"Perishing child of clay!
 Thy sighing I have heard;
Long have I marked thy evil way,
 How thou hast erred.
Yet fear not; by my own most holy name
I will shed healing through thy sin-sick frame."

Praise to thee, gracious Lord!
 I fain would be at rest;
O, now fulfil thy faithful word,
 And make me blest!
My soul would lay her heavy burden down,
And take with joyfulness the promised crown.

"Stay, thou short-sighted child!
 There is much first to do;
Thy heart, so long by sin defiled,
 I must renew;
Thy will must here be taught to bend to mine,
Or the sweet peace of heaven can ne'er be thine."

Yea, Lord, but thou canst soon
　　Perfect thy work in me,
Till, like the pure, calm summer moon,
　　I shine by thee, —
A moment shine, that all thy power may trace,
Then pass in stillness to my heavenly place.

"Ah, coward soul! confess
　　Thou shrinkest from my cure,
Thou tremblest at the sharp distress
　　Thou must endure, —
The foes on every hand, for war arrayed,
The thorny path in tribulation laid, —

" The process slow of years,
　　The discipline of life,
Of outward woes and secret tears,
　　Sickness and strife, —
The idols taken from thee one by one,
Till thou canst dare to live with me alone.

" Some gentle souls there are
　　Who yield unto my love,
Who, ripening fast beneath my care,
　　I soon remove;
But thou stiff-neckéd art, and hard to rule;
Thou must stay longer in affliction's school."

My Maker and my King!
　　Is this thy love to me?
O that I had the lightning's wing,
　　From earth to flee!

How can I bear the heavy weight of woes
Thine indignation on thy creature throws?

"Thou canst not, O my child,
    So hear my voice again;—
I will bear all thy anguish wild,
    Thy grief, thy pain;
My arms shall be around thee day by day,
My smile shall cheer thee on thy heavenward way.

"In sickness, I will be
    Watching beside thy bed;
In sorrow, thou shalt lean on me
    Thy aching head;
In every struggle thou shalt conqueror prove,
Nor death itself shall sever from thy love."

O grace beyond compare!
    O love most high and pure!
Saviour, begin,—no longer spare,—
    I can endure;
Only vouchsafe God's grace, that I may live
Unto his glory, who can so forgive.

ON FIDELITY IN SMALL MATTERS.*

St. Francis of Sales says that great virtues and fidelities in small things are like sugar and salt: sugar is more delicious, but of less frequent use, while salt enters into every article of food. Great virtues are rare: they are seldom needed; and when the occasion comes, we are prepared for it by everything which has preceded, excited by the greatness of the sacrifice, and sustained either by the brilliancy of the action in the eyes of others, or by self-complacency in our ability to do such wonderful things. Small occasions, however, are unforeseen; they recur every moment, and place us incessantly in conflict with our pride, our sloth, our self-esteem, and our passions; they are calculated thoroughly to subdue our wills, and leave us no retreat. If we are faithful in them, nature will have no time to breathe, and must die to all her inclinations. It would please us much better to make some great sacrifices, however painful and violent, on condition of obtaining liberty to follow our own pleasure and retain our old habits in little things. But it is only by this fidelity in small matters that the grace of true love is sustained and distinguished from the transitory excitements of nature.

---

* Fénelon.

It is with piety as it is with our temporal goods; there is more danger from little expenses than from larger disbursements, and he who understands how to take care of what is insignificant, will soon accumulate a large fortune. Everything great owes its greatness to the small elements of which it is composed; he that loses nothing, will soon be rich.

Consider, on the other hand, that God does not so much regard our actions, as the motive of love from which they spring, and the pliability of our wills to his. Men judge our deeds by their outward appearance; with God, that which is most dazzling in the eyes of man is of no account. What he desires is a pure intention, a will ready for anything, and ever pliable in his hands, and an honest abandonment of self; and all this can be much more frequently manifested on small than on extraordinary occasions; there will also be much less danger from pride, and the trial. will be far more searching. Indeed, it sometimes happens, that we find it harder to part with a trifle than an important interest; it may be more of a cross to abandon a vain amusement, than to bestow a large sum in charity.

We are the more easily deceived about these small matters, in proportion as we imagine them to be innocent, and ourselves indifferent to them. Nevertheless, when God takes them away, we may easily recognize, in the pain of the deprivation, how excessive and inexcusable were both the use and the attachment. If we are in the habit of neglecting little things, we shall be constantly offending our families, our domestics, and the public. No one can well believe that our piety is sincere, when our behavior is loose and irregular in its little details. What ground have we for believing that we are ready to make the greatest sacrifices, when we daily fail in offering the least?

It is very touching,— it brings both smile and tear, — to see the eternal hope, which always soars, like a white dove, from under the shadow of every disappointment, so white, so fresh, as if its wings were cleansed anew, in the darkness out of which it came; the hope that is like a courageous word, like a suddenly thronging thought of spring-time, like a walk in the cool air on an autumn mountain-side; the hope that something will yet be, that the ocean of futurity is yet filled with pearls for the successful diver, that nature is yet rich, and God lavish, as of old, and one's meed not utterly overdone.— *Studies in Religion.*

THE THIRD STORMY SUNDAY.

THE DAILY BREAD.

" God could have made all rich, or all men poore,
But why he did not, let me tell wherefore :
Had all been rich, where then had patience been?
Had all been poore, who had his bounty seen ? "

HERRICK.

THE THIRD STORMY SUNDAY.

THE DAILY BREAD.

ALL day long I have been sitting by the fire,
and, opposite me, that sad form! She is sleeping
now, and the tired body is leaning back for rest;
the poor, pale hands are folded, and a smile of
repose lies on the half-closed lips. She has been
telling me her story, — she, poor child, still so
much younger than I, who has yet lived through
a life of so much suffering!

I quite forgot the storm that has been all
day raging without, that has kept us both at
home from church to-day, — I forgot it all in listening to the trouble of her life. She came to
me yesterday; she is to leave me to-morrow, and
has administered to me to-day the religious service that I was not able to seek at the church.
I cannot write down all her words, nor linger
over all that she told me of her early life. Nor
can I write the quiet tone with which all was

9 *

told me, — the tone which showed the suffering that was so deep it could not yet be called a past suffering.

She said: "It was a very pretty home where I lived all my earlier years. And yet, at the time, my sorrow was not very great when I left it. For the sorrow had come before, when my father and my mother left me, one by one, and I was beginning to learn I was to live upon my own responsibilities. It is since then that I have looked back with sorrow upon my early home, and with regret. For though we lived so poorly, as some would think it, yet we lived comfortably. We did not know what want was, nor unkind treatment, nor harsh words.

"And since then I have learned to know what the beauty was that surrounded my old home. Small as the windows were, they looked out upon a broad landscape, and on sunrise and sunset. And the little door-yard was small, yet we hardly saw it was fenced in, since there was a grander boundary of mountains around us. But when I left it, there was neither father nor mother to say good-by to, and the few who had been my companions had gone, too, to seek their fortune in larger places, and I was willing to try mine also.

"I was going to meet my only brother, in New York. He was a carpenter, and had his own family to support; and I was to live with him, and support myself too, with my needlework. This was no hard work for me; it was what I had all my life been brought up to do. I had been known in our village, young as I was, as a skilful seamstress, and I was very willing to use my own hands for my support, and give my whole day to my work too.

"And at first we were all successful in our labors; we lived many years happily together. We were very busy, it is true. We had no time for amusements, we had no leisure, but we had each other, and we had steady work to do, — that was all we asked for. My work was steady indeed. I sewed all day, and had work to bring home for the evenings; so, though I loved my brother's children dearly, I had no time to play with them, and teach them to love me. Yet they did love me, without my teaching them. They welcomed me at night, had my supper ready for me, that I might lose no time, and then my lamp, for me to sit by it at work. And they knew how to work too, the older ones and the younger. They helped their mother, took care of each other; even the smallest could pick up the chips, and fetch little things to help the others.

"We were very happy then, though we had no time to stop and think so. We had no time either to make other friends; we were happy in

our work and in each other. And we were trying to lay up a little money, and talked over
plans of more comfortable days. I did not talk
indeed, for I used to talk little in those days.
The habit of sitting all day at my work without
speaking to any one had led me into the way of
shutting myself up in my own thoughts, of listening, perhaps, to others, but never replying in
words. It was not I who talked.

"It was Reuben, at night, when he was rest-
ing himself. He would tell over his plans, — of
how, some day, he would have laid up money
enough to buy the old homestead, the little house
under the great elm, — not of much value· to
anybody, but he would buy it, and set up a carpenter's shop in our own village. The children
liked to hear their father talk in this way, and it
was sometimes a Sunday evening's treat to talk
over what we would do when we bought the old
home again. But Esther, my sister-in-law, was
not so hopeful. She thought we ought to be
laying up money, indeed. We were very well
off, and we ought not to spend all the money we
earned now. For there would come worse days,
-days when there might be no work to be got, or
days of sickness, when there would be no strength
for the work,—when money could not be earned,
and·,would be fast consumed. What indeed
could we do, if any of us were taken with sick-

ness, unless we had something laid up in store for the medicines and doctor's bills? So the talk all ended in our all feeling that, while the strength lasted, we must work hard, from the strongest to the smallest, that we must not waste a cent of our earnings, and that we would try hard not to be sick, — perhaps then !

"So we worked harder and harder. When the extra holidays came, Reuben found extra work. Some of our neighbors would make excursions into the country these days, and spend some of their earnings in refreshing themselves with country air. And they might have been nearer right than we. Some would lounge away such time in the streets. But Reuben welcomed such days, because in them he could earn more money. And I would take in extra sewing. And Esther taught the children they might enjoy far more what they could earn those days, than what they would spend.

"Perhaps we were all wrong. But it is hard to know when to stop, when one is working to live. And in the crowded cities there are no lilies for the preacher to point to, and say, ' These toil not, neither do they spin, and yet Solomon in all his glory was not arrayed like one of these.' Nor could we see the free birds of the air whom the Heavenly Father feeds.

"Yet these days of toil were very happy in

comparison with the days of sorrow that came after; for we made a pleasure of our labor, and we had each other, and the children. For the children were always happy: they came home from school every day to work; but their work was what would be the play to other children, and their voices were always joyous, and their love always fresh.

" For Esther's forebodings were realized. The days of sickness came. Reuben first was taken with rheumatic fever, and the little savings were very fast exhausted for the necessities that were required for him. And the rest of us must all work harder now that his strong arm was powerless. And the days of anxiety on his account were still heavier. It was very hard to leave him all day, while I sat at my work. My work I could not leave, for every day it grew more and more important to the rest. It was a very sad winter. One of the children, my namesake, was taken sick, and she died. We had want and sorrow to struggle with, but still we tried to strengthen each other. And even that winter I could afterwards look back upon, and recall some of its happiness, because we could console each other. Sickness seemed to have brought us only nearer to each other. It made us more considerate of each other, more kindly to each other's failings.

" In the spring, Reuben got up from his sick-bed. But his power for work was very much gone. He had an offer to move down to one of the Eastern cities, — one which he could not neglect. It would be a good home for his family, and, hard as it was to find the money to move away with, it was accomplished at last. Reuben, at first, would have me go with him, but I would not consent. I had plenty of work where I was, and I did not think it safe to leave it. I did not tell him that I had begun to fear my own strength was failing. Yet I knew it was so. And I did not like to add a weak member to their family. I knew they would manage to get along, and that was all, and it would take me some time to get into regular work, and if then I should give way, I should be nothing but a burden to them.

" So they went away, and I was left alone. I felt too as if it were a very long parting. For when should we be well enough off to afford to visit each other, and when should we have the time to write to each other! I shall not tell you all about the time that followed. They were not sorrowful days. I became so used to my own lonely ways, that, as the time passed, it did not seem wearisome to me; though I think it was not well to have one day pass so like another, to have no one to speak to as I came home and went out. That too was my own fault. I shut myself up in my own little room when I was at home, and shunned all acquaintance. There were many other families living in the same house, and many of them would have received me kindly, but I avoided every one. In my lonely life, in this way, I lost my zest for work; I found I was not earning as much, and my strength was giving way. There was only one family with whom I was friendly; they lived in a room the door of which I passed every day as I went up to my attic. And frequently, as the door stood open, the mother spoke to me kindly as I passed. This was the way it began, then she asked me to come in, and rest myself as I went up stairs. Till, at last, I did go in; and finally I often stopped there, and even brought down my light in the evenings, occasionally, to sit and work there. There was only the mother and one son, with two daughters. The girls were a part of the time at work in places, and were not often at home. But the boy was always there. For he was an invalid, and a cripple, confined to his poor bed, and had been so for many years. And so, sometimes, I would sit there in the evenings, while the mother had gone out, perhaps with her day's washing, or to carry home her sewing. I could be a companion for Davie, some one whom he could talk to.

"And how he did talk! It was better to me than any book to hear him. For, as he was lying there, he had read many books that kind people had lent him, and he would tell over what he had read, I think, in a finer way than it was in the books. Such descriptions as he would give of far-away places that he had never seen! And yet it seemed as if he must be seeing them then, so bright and clear he made them all! And then he remembered the places he had seen in his well days, when he used, occasionally, to get out into the country. It brought back to me, then, all my early country days, and I did not know before they were so beautiful. And though I could not talk, though I had nothing to tell him that was happy and gay, and though my memory did not know how to paint pictures of any days that were happier, it could give him pleasure to talk to me. I could not answer nor reply, but I could listen.

"It grew harder for me to go up and down stairs, to go every day to my work; and my rent was raised, and I could not find a cheaper room, and the earnings grew smaller. Then came the hard days. At first, I did not dare to spend all my money, for I must save some for worse times; but by and by my savings grew smaller and smaller, — I was spending each day all that I earned.

" At this time I was working often by day in a large, handsome house in the upper part of New

York. I sat there sewing in a beautifully furnished room. It was a pleasure merely to sit there. It was Miss Ellen's boudoir, and it opened into larger and more beautiful rooms. All round me were comforts and luxuries. There was nothing there that was not beautiful, however useful it might be. The carpet and the chairs and the curtains must match. The little extinguisher on the toilette-table, with its peasant's cap, must match the peasant-girls on the pretty papering. Even the books, whatever they were inside, must lie in bindings that would agree with the colors of the room. There was a profusion of little luxuries on the tables, the use of which I knew not then, nor do I know now. As I passed through the house, I saw other rooms, all furnished in the same profuse and tasteful way. There were pictures and statues, and as I passed the breakfast-room door I saw the handsome silver that decorated the table. I dwell on all these, because in those days I dwelt on them, in the sickly state of my mind and body, O how minutely! I compared their excess with my want, this profusion with my destitution!

"I sat there one day at work the week that I believed myself starving! Yes, I had spent my last cent, and I had borrowed my next week's wages, and I had in my home but one crust of bread, that I was saving till I could do without it no longer! And my neighbors, Davie and his mother, they were in as evil a condition. I knew it, though they did not tell me. And still I had the strength to go to work, and, as I say, I sat in this room so filled with luxuries. O, it was heaped up with them, so that one could not single out a separate luxury for enjoyment. Like a large bunch of flowers, each one so gorgeous in color, yet each, as it were, so beautiful as to hide the other. I, who have perhaps lived in too great poverty of pleasure, have wondered sometimes if there were not more enjoyment in a single daisy.

"And there were beautiful flowers in this room, too, and handsome dresses were lying round. It was strange to sit in this profusion, and to be in utter want myself! There was profusion in everything,—in sights, in sounds, in pleasures of every sort.

"And Miss Ellen herself was tired of the pleasures even. There was a concert and a ball in the evening, and to go to both or either she must give up Miss Heron at the theatre. And she was not sure after all but she should prefer a quiet evening at Mrs. D.'s. A profusion of pleasures, and we had not one,—Davie and his mother and I! What would Davie not give to hear that concert, to hear music he had only dreamed of! Poor boy, he had nothing to give! Yes, in the midst of this excess of pleasure, at times I thought Miss Ellen sat as much in want as I! After all, we had each but one life to live,—I mean our own, whether here or in another world, and the fault and poverty in her own life was the same as that in mine; we were each living alone, each one too much to herself She little knew the excitement I was going through, so great I could hardly keep quietly at my work. I was to have a dinner. I was to stay that day, and they were to send me up a dinner! So full, so large it would be, it would serve me for two days, and my poor crust might be saved. The dinner came, too rich for poor famished me; yet I could venture to eat some of it. They sent me an orange, — that I could carry away to Davie.

"So that was not my starving day, though near upon it. Saturday night, as I went home after carrying some work, I passed the shops lighted up, — the confectioners' shops, daintily filled with glittering, tempting luxuries. I saw meat in the butchers' shops, I saw the loaves displayed in the bakers' windows. I lingered to feast my eyes, since I could satisfy myself no other way, — I with many others. Some of these went in to beg for food, and I watched them eagerly, and saw many turned away, some few treated kindly. I would have liked to have asked for something for Davie, and a selfish want almost led me to ask for myself. The worst day came on Sunday. I was not unwilling it should be so, for that day I might find some spiritual help. At least, so I thought at first; but perhaps my accustomed work would have more held up my body. I went to church. 'Give us this day our daily bread.' So did the preacher pray. And did I not, too, earnestly make this prayer, not only for myself, but for those other suffering ones? 'Our daily bread,'—O what a rich gift it seemed to me! Were those who could be always sure of their daily bread, were they conscious of what a gift it was? O no! so it seemed, for the preacher in his sermon went on to show that it was not *merely* the daily bread that was meant in these words. And so too, probably, thought the richly dressed ladies that sat in front of me, who never thought of praying for their daily bread, they who had never felt the want of it. They had indeed, perhaps, other wants.

"Not merely our daily bread! But what are we without it? Where is our strength, our faith, without this daily bread? Can we even have strength to pray, or faith in God, to pray without it? Ah! He who begged us to refuse not the cup of cold water to the little ones, and shared the bread among the suffering multitude,—when he told us to labor not for the meat that perisheth, yet he knew that this gift might be asked from God. 'Seek ye first the kingdom of God, and his righteousness. And all these things shall be *added unto* you,' he said.

"But that day I must pray for my daily bread. It was the *only* prayer I could utter in faith. Otherwise faith seemed dying out of me. It is little that I can remember of that day. For a little while I seemed upheld in the church by the sound of prayer and praise. I do not know how I reached home again, or how I managed to crawl up the stairs. Visions of plenty were floating before my eyes, — plenty that I could not grasp, — visions of repose in which I could find no soothing then flitted before me. Many strange days of unconsciousness followed. And when I woke to myself, I found I was being cared for. Davie's mother was watching over me, and then I heard that she had done for me what she had never done for herself. She had asked for help; she had gone to Miss Ellen to tell her of my case. And Miss Ellen had sent her doctor, and I had been treated with care, and they had brought me food. Miss Ellen had been so shocked. 'Dying of starvation! It was not possible! If she had only known!'

"'If she had only known!' Such words I have found myself since saying, when I have been in the condition to help others, — I, who have lived through want and starvation. I have found myself saying, 'If I could only know who they are that want my help!' That is the excuse of those who have the means to help others; and it is an excuse. For it was, indeed, partly my fault that I had not been willing to share my troubles, — that I had not been brave enough to tell them. O, it does require courage to say to the more fortunate, I have failed, — I am weak, — I need your strength! It was partly the fault, too, of those who should have asked me about them, — my employers. It is not enough for them to be just, or even generous, with their wages; they should give a little more, — some of their friendship. A kind, inquiring word would have opened my heart; it would have helped to give me strength against starvation even. We, working so hard, pining for free air, — it was not merely free air we needed, but freedom in thought, in conversation, in heart. We had no summers in the country, we had no winter-evening concerts; but some sympathy from those above us would have refreshed us, like the country breeze or the strain of music. And yet it is not my part to blame, for my fault lay that way. I had never cultivated the expression of my sympathy for others. I had always an unwillingness to open myself to others, — to give to or take anything from them.

"And this I felt when my more prosperous days came. For they did come. I was just regaining my strength, when I had an unexpected visitor. It was my uncle, my mother's brother, who had been away a long time, no one had known where. He had just returned from California, and he wanted to find some one to enjoy his money with him.

" So he had found poor me, who was little able to bring him joy or gayety. But it did please him to do me good,— to raise me out of want and destitution into comfort and comparative luxury. He allowed me, too, the great pleasure of giving. Then I found how hard on that side it was to give, and how one wanted more than money in knowing how to give. Even I, who knew so well what want and suffering were, found the difficulties in relieving it, for I had not been educated how to give kind words.

" O, there are many of us now suffering in the great cities who have no friend but our work,— who have never learned what it is to talk with others, what it is to be amused. It was very strange to me, to learn the art of pleasure. At the theatre, I saw people enjoy most the representation of suffering. At least, if they did not enjoy it, why would they have been there? I had lived too long in sorrow to be made happy that way. Could it give me any pleasure to see the fancied suffering of a young girl on the stage, dying, perhaps, of desertion and neglect,—I, who had looked upon the reality? I saw, at musical entertainments, artists who must have gained their power only through toil and suffering. I could think only of this, — I, who had not been educated to love music. Yet I liked the sound of simple music, — music that I could not fancy was the labor of any one, — that was uttered as if it gave pleasure to create it, not as if it were a means of livelihood, the drudgery to earn the daily bread.

"I did take pleasure in giving.! I did not care so much to make large charities, but I liked to give a little to a great many; and often I could remember the pleasure that some small, unexpected gift could excite in those who were just able to get along. I knew just where the want would weigh, and it was a great happiness to carry the relief.

"At first I made a mistake. I tried keeping my charities secret. I would see the pleasure I gave, without submitting myself to the gratitude. I saw this was a mistake, and remembered it was a pleasure to give thanks. I felt this when Davie's mother knew, at last, who it was had cared for her girls, and had brought Davie and herself into greater ease. I felt it in Davie's last glances before he died, in his mother's words of true thankfulness, in her pleasure that the last comforts that soothed him, some of the joys that helped him forget his pains, were owing to me.

"There was joy in meeting Reuben again, in seeing him freed from want, his children at school, and in bringing his youngest girl home for my own. It was not boundless wealth that my uncle wanted to share with us. We were helped by the 'little more' that is longed for by the very poor, the satisfaction of which disappears in the superfluity of the very rich. Many joys have gathered round me. Yet I see that the burden I bear now is not different from that I wore in my days of poverty; it is shutting up myself in myself, dreaming of doing good to others, sometimes helping them, but seldom by giving my whole self to them."

This was my sermon for the day, as we sat together before the fire, and the storm raged without. I heard more of the sorrows and struggles of my companion's life. Then she was silent. And I leaned back in the comfort of my chair, and thought of the contrast between poor and rich. I looked round upon the luxuries about me, and wondered what was my right to them, while want and suffering waited outside. I thought over my own weakness, my frequent thoughtlessness towards those who were dependent upon me, less happy in their circumstances than I.

And I bent my head in prayer. I prayed that

I might never forget my duty to those so near to me, might never shut them out from my sympathy, might never forget to treat kindly and thoughtfully those who might labor for me, — I could bring them pleasure and encouragement: I prayed that I might help the many laborers, the many desolate ones, with whom the earth is full; that I might bring the cup of cold water even, to one of the little ones.

What a great favor to ask! If God would but grant the power, to bring help to the weary, food to the starving!

For said Jesus, "Inasmuch as ye have done it unto one of the least of these, ye have done it unto me!"

In the afternoon my companion asked me to read to her, and begged that I would choose her two favorite passages in the Old and New Testament. This I did, and afterwards she wanted me to read her something more. I had a volume of German sermons, by Tholuck, and read to her some of the subjects of them, that she might herself select one. She chose a sermon on this subject: "Why the Christian should count temptation and trial as nothing but joy."

PSALM xlii.

As the hart panteth after the water-brooks, so panteth my soul after thee, O God. My soul thirsteth for God, for the living God: when shall I come and appear before God? My tears have been my meat day and night, while they continually say unto me, Where is thy God?

When I remember these things, I pour out my soul in me: for I had gone with the multitude; I went with them to the house of God, with the voice of joy and praise, with a multitude that kept holyday.

Why art thou cast down, O my soul? and why art thou disquieted in me? Hope thou in God; for I shall yet praise him for the help of his countenance.

O my God, my soul is cast down within me: therefore will I remember thee from the land of Jordan, and of the Hermonites, from the hill Mizar.

Deep calleth unto deep at the noise of thy water-spouts: all thy waves and thy billows are over me.

Yet the Lord will command his loving-kindness in the daytime, and in the night his song shall be with me, and my prayer unto the God of my life. I will say unto God my rock, Why hast thou forgotten me? Why go I mourning because of the oppression of the enemy? As with a sword in my bones, mine enemies reproach me; while they say daily unto me, Where is thy God?

Why art thou cast down, O my soul? and why

art thou disquieted within me ? Hope thou in God; for I shall yet praise him, who is the health of my countenance, and my God.

JOHN xiv.

Let not your heart be troubled : ye believe in God, believe also in me.

In my Father's house are many mansions : if it were not so, I would have told you. I go to prepare a place for you.

And if I go and prepare a place for you, I will come again, and receive you unto myself; that where I am, there ye may be also. And whither I go ye know, and the way ye know.

Thomas saith unto him, Lord, we know not whither thou goest ; and how can we know the way ?

Jesus saith unto him, I am the way, and the truth, and the life; no man cometh unto the Father but by me.

If ye had known me, ye should have known my Father also : and from henceforth ye know him, and have seen him.

Philip saith unto him, Lord, show us the Father, and it sufficeth us.

Jesus saith unto him, Have I been so long time with you, and yet hast thou not known me, Philip? He that hath seen me, hath seen the Father ; and how sayest thou then, Show us the Father ?

Believest thou not that I am in the Father, and the Father in me? The words that I speak unto you, I speak not of myself; but the Father that dwelleth in me, he doeth the works.

Believe me that I am in the Father, and the Father in me: or else believe me for the very works' sake.

Verily, verily, I say unto you, He that believeth on me, the works that I do shall he do also; and greater works than these shall he do; because I go unto my Father.

And whatsoever ye shall ask in my name, that will I do, that the Father may be glorified in the Son. If ye shall ask anything in my name, I will do it. . . . . .

Peace I leave with you, my peace I give unto you; not as the world giveth, give I unto you. Let not your heart be troubled, neither let it be afraid. Ye have heard how I said unto you, I go away, and come again unto you. If ye loved me, ye would rejoice, because I said, I go unto the Father; for my Father is greater than I.

And now I have told you before it come to pass, that when it is come to pass ye might believe. Hereafter I will not talk much with you; for the prince of this world cometh, and hath nothing in me.

But that the world may know that I love the Father; and as the Father gave me commandment, even so I do.

SERMON.

BY DR. A. THOLUCK.

When we meet again after a separation, we ask of each other how the time has been passing since we parted, and the answer is, " Well," if indeed it has gone by and no temptation has tried us. With envy do we look upon the happy ones near us whose tree of life the storms have never shaken; with joy do we look back upon a year where the little ship of life has glided gently on over smooth waves; and what would we not give if we could buy for ourselves such a future even to the end? This wish, indeed, to rest free from temptation, is not to be blamed. Man's nature shrinks and flies from what brings it sorrow and ruin. The Lord of our salvation prayed, " If it be possible, let this cup pass from me," and for us, his brethren, has he placed this prayer on our lips: " Lead us not into temptation." But though the Lord of our salvation prayed, " Father, if it be possible, let this cup pass from me," yet he must needs drink of the cup; and although we, God's children, pray, " Father, lead us not into temptation," yet is there temptation from within, temptation from without, temptation from below, temptation from above. Then must temptation and trial indeed have their good part; a treasure must lie concealed therein for those who know how to bear with them ; for from above, from the Father of lights, come naught but good and perfect gifts. This *light side* of temptation let us reflect upon in our devotions of to-day, and at the urgency of the Apostle James in the first chapter of his epistle to the disciples of our Lord : —

"My brethren, count it all joy, when ye fall into divers temptations."

Do you understand this, you upon whom God's hand rests heavily ?   Do you understand this, children of the world, fearful of sorrow, who are happy when you can cry, " Let us make use of life while it is here " ?   " Count it all joy," cries the Apostle, " when ye fall into divers temptations."   With what he says here a Paul can sympathize when he cries, " We glory in tribulations also " ; and again, " A godly sorrow worketh repentance to salvation not to be repented of.   And the Apostle Peter : " Beloved, think it not strange concerning the fiery trial which is to try you, as though some strange thing happened to you, but rejoice inasmuch as ye are partakers of Christ's sufferings, that, when his glory shall be revealed, ye may be glad also with exceeding joy."   And the Epistle to the Hebrews : " For whom the Lord loveth, he chasteneth, and scourgeth every man whom he receiveth.   If ye endure chastening, God dealeth with you as with sons; for what son is he whom the Father chasteneth not?" You see the Scriptures give a different view of sorrow and affliction from that of the carnal man. The Christian, it is true, prays, in a consciousness of his weakness, "Father, lead me not into temptation"; but when temptation does come, the joy of victory flushes his brow while his eyes overflow with tears.

How it is that the Christian counts his temptation as nothing but joy, — let this be the subject of our to-day's consideration. We answer this question when we say, first, he knows whence it comes; secondly, he knows whither it leads.

He knows whence it comes; — from the Father of our Lord Jesus, Christ, from the all-powerful, all-wise, all-good Creator of heaven and earth. O that those who bear the name of Christians certainly knew all this! — then a half of the burden of their temptation were taken from them. They *know* it perhaps, all who dwell far over Christendom, but do they *believe* it also, believe it with undoubting confidence? That there is an Almighty Power that upholds the world and brings forth the little dust that is called man, this they believe indeed. They hear the all-powerful storm that rolls along the wheel of an immeasurable creation; they hear the step of a giant spirit that strides through the generations of men, and see that irresistible hand that here calls a world from nothingness, and there extinguishes a sun. But what kind of a power this is, what thoughts or aims the unknown Almighty Spirit has, — that his power is the power of *fatherly wisdom and love*, — this is too difficult for them to believe. O, and this unbelief, indeed, can make every sorrow insupportable, entering like a little drop unobserved in an ocean. But its waves pour forth from unknown sources, and lead towards a goal that no one knows.

There are indeed some strong spirits, who with such a faith, when temptation and adversity press upon them, as upon an armed man, are not crushed, but remain standing, like the traveller who covers himself from the raging storm in his mantle, and plants his foot firmly upon the earth. *Resignation*, so they call the iron shield which they oppose to the arrows that are hurled upon them from distant, unknown heights. Cold and iron, as their hearts, is their consolation. They are often met with in life, these mailed men, whom the fiery trial of the Lord, instead of melting, has changed to stone ; but can it be otherwise, when the power which must try man in the crucible of affliction is not recognized as the power of a fatherly wisdom and love ? O those of you who have taken to heart the voice of that Son who has made manifest to us the Father,—the Father, whom no one has seen but the only-begotten Son who has rested in his bosom,—fall down with blessed thankfulness that ye know that all our temptation is ordered by the wisdom of a father, and is guided by a fatherly love! It is ordered by the wisdom of a father, and guided by a fatherly love; for "we know," says the Apostle, "that all things work together for good to them that love God, to them who are the called according to his purpose." The Scriptures lead us back to the very origin of eternity before the world's foundation. Then did the Father lay down his purpose to glorify and justify as many of those who became flesh who would receive the word unto blessedness. Could you, Christian brethren, of yourselves, rise to the thought that far on in eternity, when the day of judgment will be held, and the former heaven and earth shall be no more,—that all which then will be fulfilled in you has already, before the foundation of the world, been before the eye of God, to whom, as the Scripture says, all his creatures have been known from eternity, and who has chosen you in Christ Jesus! But so says the Apostle, "Whom he did predestinate, (that is, before the foundation of the world,) them he also called; and whom he called, them he also justified; and whom he justified, them he also glorified."- Do you know this, Christian soul, you

know also that each one of your temptations,
every hour of sorrow, has been ordered in the
eternal plan of that spirit of peace that a divine
wisdom and love feels towards you. From eternity down, the hour·is counted when your temptation shall begin; so is the hour counted when it
shall pass away. So are all the bitter drops reck-
oned that shall fall into your cup; so is the
measure weighed out how far the scale of affliction shall sink, and it will fall not a finger's breadth
farther! O what a thought, consoling beyond
all measure, that the Apostle utters, — " He will
suffer no one to be tempted beyond that he is
able "! There are moments in life when indeed
the pain and agony of temptation reach such a
point, that one may think, " Is there one drop
more in the cup, I am lost! " Ye who neither
know nor believe in the Father of the Lord Jesus
Christ, — wherefore do ye know that this drop
will not fall? The very anxiety that it might
fall, — and all were then over with you, — this
alone agonizes the soul! O, blessed is the Christian who can believe in the word of inspiration, —
" God will not suffer you to be tempted beyond that
ye are able"! You know with confidence, however
great struggle the Lord gives, he gives as much
power; however great the trial, he gives as much
patience. It sounds to you no longer wonderful
when the Apostle cries, " My brethren, count it
all joy, when ye fall into divers temptations."

Why he should consider it as joy, the Christian knows; for he knows not merely whence the trial comes, but *whither it leads him.* Diversely as the rounds of the ladder may be placed, it is the declaration of the Holy Scriptures, that tribulation is a heavenly ladder, which reaches from earth, where suffering is born, to heaven, in whose blessings it is lost. For Paul says to us, " We glory in tribulations also; knowing that tribulation worketh patience, and patience experience, and experience hope, and hope maketh not ashamed." And lest any one should doubt of this, God himself has impressed his seal upon it, a convincing seal, — " Because," Paul continues to say, " the love of God is shed abroad in our hearts by the Holy Ghost which is given to us." Let us then consider how temptation leads us to that issue, by which our hope maketh not ashamed. That wound must be very deep, that requires the deep cut of the surgeon to heal it. Is this true, how deep must the wound be from which mankind suffers, when we see in what strong expressions the Scriptures speak of the necessity of temptation and sorrow for the purification and perfecting of man! " He that findeth his life shall lose it, and he that loseth his life for my sake shall find it," says the Saviour. " He that taketh not his cross, and followeth after me, is not worthy of me." " For every one shall be salted with fire, and every sacrifice shall be salted with salt." Death, the cross, the salt of fire, are the gateways to be entered by every new man who is newly born and fleshly created after the image of God. It were easy indeed, many times, to fancy that there might be smoother ways. Shall not the gentle sunshine which falls upon the rocky valleys of our earthly life, shall not the stream of good and perfect gifts, that, like the torrent from the mountain-top, pours down unceasingly from the Father of lights, — shall not these be able to soften a hard heart? We have moments in our inner life, hours of a thankful heart tender and ashamed like that of a child, when it seems inconceivable that this is not the case. But, in fact, it is not the case. In the pillars of fire by night must God appear to man, in the cloudy pillar by day he passes by unmarked. Tribulation first teaches us to know ourselves; it first teaches us to pray. Therefore does the Christian congregation sing : —

> " Cross, I greet thee from my heart !
>   Enter, welcome guest !
> Pain of thine will bring no smart,
>   Thy burden is my rest !

> " Christ stands always by his own,
>   His love stands near their fears,
> By the pathway where the cross
>   They bear with dropping tears."

Therefore does the Christian congregation believe it, when the Apostle cries, " Count it all joy, when ye fall into divers temptations."

Temptation and trial teach us to know ourselves. " There was a man in the land of Uz, whose name was Job; and that man was perfect and upright, and one that feared God, and eschewed evil. And there was a day when his sons and daughters were eating and drinking wine in their eldest brother's house. Then came the Sabeans and slew the servants with the edge of the sword; then fell fire from heaven, and burned the sheep and the servants; then came the Chaldeans, and carried away the camels; then came a great wind from the wilderness, and smote the four corners of the house, and it fell upon the sons and daughters, so that they died. Then Job arose and rent his mantle, and shaved his head, and fell down upon the ground and worshipped, and said, Naked came I out of my mother's womb, and naked shall I return thither; the Lord gave, and the Lord hath taken away; blessed be the name of the Lord. In all this Job sinned not, nor charged God foolishly."

And who of you thinks not now, that he has seen into the inner soul of this good man? But, friends, within the inner shrine of a man's heart lies an *innermost*, and that was not yet disclosed.

" And Satan answered the Lord and said, All

that a man hath he will give for his life. But put forth thine hand now, and touch his bone and flesh, and he will curse thee to the face. And the Lord said to Satan, Behold, he is in thine hand; but save his life. So went Satan forth from the presence of the Lord, and smote him with sore boils from the sole of his foot unto his crown." Then, then first is the innermost soul unclosed, and you behold him upright towards God. O you who foolishly do not desire to know anything of any dark abyss in your hearts, and who fancy your shoulders are strong enough for even the trials of Job, " Ye have not yet resisted unto blood, striving against sin,"—so the Apostle cries to you.

No, a dark recess does every man bear in his heart. From this in the hour of trial rises, first, a *doubt* of God's word and promise, then a murmuring against God's will and decree, and deep, deep in the innermost shrine hides at last the worm that whispers, "Bid God farewell!" And it is true they are not the thorns of an outward sorrow that make the hours of temptation so bitter for the Christian. O, much sharper and more biting does the anguish feed upon his soul, that the angels of faith, hope, and love forsake him, and that instead he hears the rustling of the wings of the Prince of darkness,—that in his own heart, which would so willingly worship, there must enter doubt, murmuring, and perverseness towards his God, — this is his sorrow. And so long as just this sorrow and pain have not passed away, so long is help still here. But if this pain dies away, if the soul becomes indifferent to doubt, murmuring, and pride, then all the stars in heaven disappear; then is it wholly night, and morning twilight comes perhaps never again.

In such trials by fire does the Christian learn what he is himself. The opinion that many have expressed is just, that they are the most faithful and the truest servants whom God is wont to try with such severe fires of temptation. But who but these could bear such trial? Have you not yet been carried into such depths and abysses? O, look not upon that of which the holy ones of God speak, as the mere vain image of a dream, but thank the goodness of God, who verifies to you that he tries "no one beyond that he is able." Will you indeed begin, as the Saviour calls it, to "put on the power of the kingdom," — would your Christianity grow more earnest, — then will the time of the trial by fire come for you also; but fear it not, — then, then will you experience, with all the disciples of the Lord, that the Apostle says with truth, "My brethren, count it all joy, when ye fall into divers temptations."

Did we, indeed, in the fire of this temptation, learn to know nothing but ourselves, and the greatness of our power of being tempted, this were something to be complained of. But we learn also in the heat of our temptation to know God, his righteousness, his pity, and his power.

We learn to know his righteousness. It is true, evil upon earth is not distributed according to the measure of personal guilt. In a certain measure, each one must partake of the suffering from the guilt of the community, and bear his part of it. Therefore, indeed, is the trial which brings us most sorrow at times not self-incurred. Yet with the evil which he has not called upon his own person, the Christian goes back to his innermost recess, and there becomes aware what he has committed himself. It teaches him, that the sin which can have such evil in its consequences is especially a detestation to God; and while he feels this freshly, he bows himself in the consciousness of that which in himself is displeasing to the holy God. Yet how many cases there are when the trial which comes upon him comes through his own guilt! O how often they are the sins of youth, which return to rest upon the gray head with a burning heat! O often it is a concealed guilt, that no man but yourself—only God — knows! Men come and show you their sympathy, and weep over you as unfortunate; but you know of the worm that gnaws within, and weep over yourself the repentant tears of guilt. So long as your sin did not bring you to judgment, you know how to speak of the forbearing love of God; now you know that the Apostle's saying is true, "Be not deceived, God is not mocked," and "Our God is a consuming fire." O young men! let me for this cause warn you, "Flee the lusts of youth"; they may otherwise fall upon your head when it is gray, and may bring forth the account when you have but one more step to the judgment.

In the midst of the proofs of his righteousness, God allows his pity and his power also to be recognized in tribulation. Friends, how many hundred times do we repeat, that all that we have are the gifts of his goodness; but do we inwardly feel what we say once in a hundred times? Were we inwardly conscious of this, O friends! at every fresh breath we draw from our breast giving us the feeling of life, — did we inwardly recognize it at every glance at the beauty of nature, at the very sight of our home, or farm, or wife, or child, or all that we can call our own, — then our hearts had long ago become temples of God. A man in whom each healthy pulsation, each free breath, awakens the tone of a prayer of thanks, must, under such a constant devotional sounding of bells and singing of praises within, be built up freshly as a man of God. To *say* that all is a gift of God, and to *feel* it inwardly, — these are two different things, between which often an immeasurable gulf is fixed. . On the bed of sickness, when the stifled breast cannot draw a single breath, do you first become inwardly conscious that each fresh draught of breath is a gift of God! When the death-angel stirs his wings over the soul that is dear to you, do you first learn to know inwardly that this soul was a gift of God! In temptation, when the time of blessedness in faith, the time of peace in the sonship of God, appears to you like a past dream which you can with difficulty recall, — then first do you inwardly know that each drop of the peace of God is a gift of God! For this reason we have seen sometimes Christians whom the Lord has led in their lives through very severe trials, who have borne in the end so tender a heart, that at every blade of grass and at every kindly ray of sunlight their eyes overflow on account of the undeserved pity of their God.

With this pity you can also experience his *power*. Sometimes it happens that you lie in an abyss, and even the smallest thread is taken away from you on which you can seize and rise again; and not before you are inwardly conscious that no other hand than that from the clouds can help you, does it bear you upwards to the heights. Then do Christians learn what it is to trust to nothing transitory, then they learn " to hope when there is nothing to hope, to hold on to the invisible as though they beheld it."

In such trials the soul learns to *pray*. Alas that man himself is obliged to learn *prayer* through trial! What would you think of the child who must first learn by blows to thank and to pray to his father? With invincible power, like the stream that has been withheld, should prayer break out from the heart of every child of man. Joyous and blest should we exult, that we may venture to speak to Him whom the heaven of heavens cannot contain, and lay our little cares upon the great heart of the Creator of the world. Do you know how I think it would appear if a mortal could not venture to pray? As if the wide, clear sky of heaven above us through which the eye penetrates as into the sanctuary of God, were covered and hidden with garments of the grave. Both in height and width would the prospect be wanting. O how indescribably narrow would it be for man! Now we are permitted to pray, and lo! we forget it, and the scourge must first be brandished over us before we think of it. Yes, it is terrible to say that in truth there are men in Christendom who pray only when there is a storm in the heavens. And scarcely has the thunder ceased to resound, when the lips are still, and remain still till a new thunder-bolt rings again. It is a terrible experience that only the lightning-shafts of heaven are the ladders by which prayer climbs upward to heaven, when it could and should rise by every beam of sunlight that has trickled down from heaven! But so it is, man learns his dependence upon God and his own guilt first when God appears in the pillars of cloud by night, and I dare to say it certainly of all of us, that trial has first taught us to pray with fervor. If then, as the body is dead without the beating of the pulse, so the soul is dead without prayer; and if we do not learn to pray without trial and temptation, O how then could we do without them? Who then would not sing to the cross:

> " Cross, I greet thee from my heart!
> Enter, welcome guest!
> Pain of thine will bring no smart;
> Thy burden is a rest!"

How shall we not grant that the Apostle is right, who cries to us, " Count it all joy, when ye fall into divers temptations " ?

But while I now place before you the blessings of trial and temptation, I remember, at the same time, those for whom what is meant by that little word " trial " has remained so far unknown. You believe what I have been preaching to you; you are inwardly conscious of it; you have till now learnt to know neither the Lord nor yourselves intimately; you feel earnestly, " My stony heart must be crushed: O that He would cast me to the ground three times with his all-powerful arm, that so I might become weak and like melting clay in his hands!" You who are convinced that you need some lightning-bolt to rouse you, some earthquake to shatter the old temples of idolatry, — what must you do? What does to-day's sermon teach you? Shall you pray, shall you entreat, "O Lord, why so long-suffering? Chasten me in thine anger! Haste and send thy lightning and thy thunder!" I know there are blameless hearts who are many times alarmed at the continued sunshine over their heads. You know the story of Polycrates, of the ring that in despair he sacrificed to the waves of the sea, that he might in one point be *unhappy*. It is a story full of meaning. There are those among us to whom such thoughts are not unusual.

And yet, beloved, the Gospel of Jesus Christ offers not the example of Polycrates. It forbids you to hold the scales in your own hand, but rest them rather in God's hand, who can weigh out how much your shoulders can bear, because it is written, "God is faithful, who will not suffer ye to be tempted above that ye are able." If then his thunder-bolt is silent above you, while you upon your knees would pray for it, O dear friend! be only sure that you have not known the fortitude of your own shoulders. Take joyously the happy days that He sends you, as the proofs of his forbearance, and be thankful. Praise and thanks be to God! We Christians know not a God who is jealous of the gifts that mortals enjoy! We only know of a Father in heaven, from whom " cometh every good and perfect gift, with whom is no variableness, neither shadow of turning." But, my brothers, we are so placed that with regard to trial and suffering not one of us need to be at a loss. It is here, without your needing to seek for it. Could you only take hold of the great idea, that we are all members of one body, and that not a single member can be sick without the whole body suffering with it, then you need not be anxious for trial. My dear friends, why do you not make the *trials of your suffering brethren your own?* Know you not these words : " Who is weak, and I am not weak ? Who is offended, and I burn not ? " Know you not Him who, though in the form of God, took upon him the form of a servant, and humbled himself even to death ; because he, as he himself said, had not come into the world " to be ministered unto, but to minister " ? O that we only rightly understood how to make the sorrows of our fellow-men our own, — their outer trial, their inmost suffering, — then should we truly have not the power to complain of our want of tribulation. Arise, then, you who are longing for tears, for necessity, O go forth to-day and seek out the weeping ones with whom you can weep,—you will not have far to go! Yes, if generally among us Christians the weeping and the rejoicing with each other were only more common, then were all the measures of suffering and sorrow more equally allotted among us. And this might easily come to pass, could we truly picture one body in Jesus Christ, and become one the member of the other. While you suffer also in the sufferings of others, you will then also become strong, my beloved, so that your own shoulders will be able to bear the burden of sorrow; and if you have thus become strong, the Lord will not remain behind with his wholesome discipline.

O God, come near our hearts and soften them with a love for the suffering! Give us each day our daily bread,—not for ourselves alone, but that we may feed with it the starving. In trial and temptation thou wouldst bring us near to thee: help us to find thee then! Let not the trial in our own hearts make us forget those who suffer from earthly wants, but may the cry of the desolate that is sent up to thee reach our hearts also! In the midst of outward prosperity, and the sunnier life that thou hast given us, we brood over our selfish troubles, and weep the failure of our poor ambitions. O waken us with a sympathy for the poor and lonely whom thou hast given us to lead into more cheerful ways! May they teach us our duty here, that we may carry into the by-ways where want and sorrow are dwelling, some of the joy that we have found in the rich gifts that thou hast showered upon us!

Bless our homes with the ever-present thought of thee! Come into our solitude, and strengthen us when we come out from the quiet of prayer, that we may not forget our love of thee, nor of thy children!

PRAYER.

FROM THE GERMAN.*

O God, thy goodness far extends,
   Far as the heavens above are spread,
But still in mercy ever bends,
   And gently watches o'er my head.
My Shepherd, Lord, my rock, my hill,
   My prayer accept, attend my word;
For I will wait before thee still,
   Till my poor prayer by thee is heard.

I ask not for abounding wealth,
   The treasures of this world below,
But what thou givest, joy or wealth,
   To feel that all to thee I owe, —
Wisdom, an understanding heart,
   To know thee, and thy own dear Son,
Who came thy love and truth to impart,
   To know myself, an erring one.

I pray not for repose or fame,
   Much as for these men toil and sigh,
But for a pure and spotless name,
   To lose not, if I live or die.
My glory let my duty be,
   My glory in thy holy eye,
While love and smiles from pious friends
   To cheer my heart be ever nigh.

---

* Gellert.

For these, O God, I humbly pray, ·
  Not for a lengthened life below,
Humble, if prospered be my day,
  Brave, if in danger's path I go.
Give me but these, for in thy hand
  My times are held ; thy love alone
Sustains my soul ; and let me stand
  Hopeful in death before thy throne.

THE FOURTH STORMY SUNDAY.

FORGIVENESS.

" God, lift me from the power
    Of flesh corruption ; how shall I
  Bear to be borne along with stainless flower
    And fleecy cloud on high !

" God, lift up unto me
    The sinning heart of human-kind ;
  How can I flutter down the skies, and see
    Their errant souls and blind !

" Or wrap me in the light
    That folds thy glory's outer zone ;
  Be thou the sole horizon to my sight,
    Content in thee alone. "

H. ALFORD.

13

THE FOURTH STORMY SUNDAY.

FORGIVENESS.

THE sun rose clearly this morning, on a broad
field of pure ice. The hills and the fields were
covered with the white, crystal surface. The
trees were laden with brilliant hanging icicles.
I went to the door, and opened it to look out,
and feel the clear, frosty air. I said to myself:

> " Some butterflies of snow may float
>   Down, slowly lingering in the mote ;
>   And silver-leaved and fruited trees
>   Lose not a jewel in the breeze.
>   Frost-diamonds tremble on the glass,
>   Transformed from pearly dew,
>   And silver flowers encrust the grass
>   That gardens never knew."

But while I stood looking out, a heavy wind
rose, bringing dark storm-clouds, and before the
end of an hour, again a thick snow was falling ;
and by the time the bells were ringing for church,
the roads were quite too impassable for me. And
again I was alone.

One can easily see that a solitary life would lead to selfishness. Saintine wrote a story to prove that the lonely Robinson Crusoe, though he might have passed through hours of repentance, reached at last a state no higher than that of the brutes. His solitary life made him lose his humanity; his want of duties to others made him forget the duties owing to himself. The utter deprivation of society, the being denied sympathy or conversation with another, extinguished all other wants and needs but the physical ones. Instead of being refined, he was brutified; and the late visitors to the solitary island saw its inhabitant flying in terror from the unaccustomed sight of men.

This is not the romantic idea of a Robinson Crusoe life, but it may be a true one. We can see somewhat of the same effect, in a modified degree, with those who live a partially lonely life. They may not lose their refinement of character, because they can carry into their solitude books and a refining education of the mind. But what they gain in individual strength they lose in self-control, in the power of governing themselves for the sake of yielding to others. We detect in them a selfish fondness of their own ways, an unwillingness to give up to others in the little details of life. And it is the willingness to yield in these smaller details that shows the influence of a Christian spirit. It is an opportunity for discipline that one who lives in the midst of his own marked-out ways is ignorant of.

We return to our homes, tired with some -day's exertion, and find others dependent upon our hearty sympathy, upon our good spirits. We have no time to sit down and nurse our ill-humor. A dispirited word of ours will throw one, two, or more into melancholy, or set them into a state of irritation and discord. We must exercise a direct self-control, thrust away the selfish spirit that would arise, that would lead us to retire within our own troubles, in a fancied hope of rest.

Or we go to see a friend sometimes, when we are in depression ourselves, and want a sympathizing, kind word to excite us. Our burden has grown too heavy for us to bear alone, and now we are going to ask for the assisting hand of a friend. But we are unexpectedly ushered into a sick-room. Instead of finding comfort and cheerfulness, we are asked to bring it. We must suddenly control our own sadness in the presence of one who is not able to bear the expression of it. Our own selfish trouble must give way before the trouble of another, and we must give the very solace that we asked for.

There are very many who will say, that these demands upon our patience have done more to dissipate our selfish troubles than any dwelling upon them, or brooding over them in our quiet thoughts. The effort for exertion has sent away the languor, and given us strength. In the end, we are grateful to the little interruptions that have only disturbed idle dreamings or selfish plans. We have gained the power of being equal to the present moment, which is a glorious victory, even though that demand seemed petty, and the renunciation it required seemed great.

Sometimes we ask, What right have others to make such demand upon our time, even upon our temper? We question if it is not an infringement upon our liberty. Let us ask ourselves, in turn, if we had this precious liberty of acting unbound by our duties to those around us, should we not use it in limiting ourselves? We should, for instance, scarcely make a better use of our time. It is very probable that we should give the time we have saved from the demands of friends to idleness, to vanity, and to morbid selfishness. And as for our temper, we may be very sure it is of poor metal, if it will not stand the trying, and, sound as it may be, it is of little use if it is kept constantly in the sheath. A few days passed in solitude may convince us of this. There is very little time gained. The lesser, daily acts of life grow up into greater ones, and require more thought and time. Excitements that seemed stale and powerless enlarge, in the absence of greater ones, into the great excitements of the day, and take their turn in dissipating the thoughts and consuming the time. The hours that are not shut in, and marked by duties that must be paid to others, become common ground, and by and by a waste. Many moments are lost in indecision, many in indolence. More than all, there is wanting the zest that comes from the presence of others, the excitement of seeing others work, as well as their co-operation. We are willing to do quickly what we do for the sake of another, or we finish our own work quickly, that we may be ready to help others.

We are thrown in with many people, some of whom we have chosen for our companions, and some have been thrust upon us. The question arises, Have we duties to perform towards all of these? Must we show kindness, must we even give up our valued time, our well-laid and conscientiously approved plans, for the sake of others who happen to be near us, — whom we cannot love, whom we may not even esteem? Those who are filled with a truly Christian spirit are not troubled by this question. They have a love, differing in intensity towards those around them, but sufficiently deep to give them a kindly feeling to all who approach them. It is no constrained smile with which they greet even the least agreeable of those who come within their circle. They offer the cup of cold water, without prompting from any but their own thoughtful hearts, even to the very least of the little ones. Whether they are led so to do by the thought that "beings so dear to God, the friends of Jesus, should be treated by us with gentleness," we cannot tell; we only see that their love comes without restraint, that its expression is free.

But there are others who have not reached so high a plane, who say conscientiously, that they do not think people indifferent to them have a right to claim their time, and infringe upon their plans. Yet they are willing to acknowledge the beauty of that sacrificing nature, that is willing to give up even cherished time and plans, even a beloved ten minutes' ill-temper and spite, for the sake of those who can give them nothing in return, who have not even thanks for them, or an agreeable word or glance.

Some say that such concessions are impossible, and require a want of truth. "How can I express what I do not feel?" one says; "I do not love these people, and if I made them think so, I should be untrue." Untrue to what? To your own false nature! Do we call a watch true that is five hours behind the time, even if it keeps its minutes and its seconds exact? You have no right to say that you do not love any one suf-

ficiently to treat him or her with kindness. If
one of " these people " comes within your door,
interrupts you even with his presence, your sense
of truth does not lead you to push him out of the
door; even your forbearance goes as far as to
offer him a chair! Why not let it lead you a
little farther? If he were asked which he would
prefer, he might answer, he would rather be
thrust from the door than suffer from your stint-
ed politeness, your cold indifference. Your love
of truth does not lead you to treat him with
blows; why should it lead you to make him suffer from your coldness? It is your duty to feel
kindly towards all who come within your circle,
certainly according to the degree of your influence. And if you have not this feeling, it must
be cultivated. After the soil is well prepared by
prayer to God that he will send a Christian spirit,
the seeds of kindly deeds must be sown, and the
increase will come. This doctrine I am often
obliged to preach to myself. We are thrown
into such superficial relations with others, we
are so often shown only their outside, that our
duties grow very involved and uncertain. The
way becomes clearer, the more we are in the habit
of thinking that, besides the outer forms of politeness, there is due to every one we meet with a
kindly feeling. It becomes the easier, the more
we find ourselves prompted by a true Christian

spirit. And the nearer we draw to others, the more easily do we find something worthy of love, something that comes back in return for what we give, something in response to us, which encourages and helps on our effort.

I have seen, lately, a discussion upon the words of the Lord's prayer, " Forgive us our trespasses, as we forgive those who trespass against us," questioning if we do not promise in these words more than we can perform. In my mind, there is no difficulty in reading these words literally. Is not every sincere prayer to God as it were a compact with him, in which we would promise to strive to do our part in reaching those blessings for which we pray? Even the prayer, " God be merciful to me a sinner," is a confession of sin, which is at least an approach to repentance. Alas! " the heartlessness of our prayers is the source of our other infidelities." We pray not to be led into temptation, and pass directly into the scene where we know temptation lies in wait for us. We ask that God's kingdom may come upon earth; but as soon as our lips have closed upon our prayer, we open our minds to all earthly thoughts. We pray ourselves for daily bread, and forget directly those who are suffering for need of it. Yet, at least at that moment when we are asking God to forgive us our trespasses, can we be sufficiently forgiving to our debtors.

If not, we may well leave our gift at the altar, and first " be reconciled to our brother, and then come and offer our gift." 'But if our prayers were hearty, if we often approached God to pray to him for his forgiveness, the more often should we be conscious of our own debts, the more willing to forgive our debtors. The forgiving spirit, instead of being momentary, like our consciousness of our own guilt, would be so constant with us, that we need have no dread in saying, " Forgive us, *as* we forgive those who trespass against us." It would be a mockery to come to Him to ask for that forgiveness, if our hearts were rankling with ill-feeling towards those indebted to us. At least, in our moments of prayer, let us sweep out and garnish our hearts, to strive to make them more pure, more fit for the invited presence of God.

CHARITY THE LIFE OF FAITH. *

"Marvel not, my brethren, if the world hate you. We know that
we have passed from death unto life, because we love the brethren."
— 1 John iii. 13, 14.

The clouds that wrap the setting sun,
   When Autumn's softest gleams are ending,
Where all bright hues together run,
   In sweet confusion blending, —
Why, as we watch their floating wreath,
Seem they the breath of life to breathe?
To fancy's eye their motions prove
They mantle round the sun for love.

When up some woodland dale we catch
   The many-twinkling smile of ocean;
Or, with pleased ear, bewildered watch
   His chime of restless motion;
Still, as the surging waves retire,
They seem to gasp with strong desire;
Such signs of love old Ocean gives,
We cannot choose but think he lives.

And he whose heart will bound to mark
   The full bright burst of summer morn
Loves too each little dewy spark
   By leaf or floweret worn;
Cheap forms and common hues, 't is true,
Through the bright shower-drop meet his view;

____

* Keble.

The coloring may be of this earth,
The lustre comes of heavenly birth.

Even so who loves the Lord aright,
　No soul of man can worthless find
All will be precious in his sight,
　Since Christ on all hath shined;
But chiefly Christian souls, for they,
Though worn and soiled with sinful clay,
Are yet, to eyes that see them true,
All glistening with baptismal dew.

Then marvel not, if such as bask
　In purest light of innocence
Hope against hope in love's dear task,
　Spite of all dark offence.
If they who hate the trespass most,
Yet, when all other love is lost,
Love the poor sinner, marvel not;
Christ's mark outwears the rankest blot.

No distance breaks the tie of blood;
　Brothers are brothers evermore;
Nor wrong nor wrath of deadliest mood
　That magic may o'erpower.
Oft, ere the common source be known,
The kindred drops will claim their own,
And throbbing pulses silently
Move heart towards heart by sympathy.

14

So is it with true Christian hearts :
  Their mutual share in Jesus' blood
An everlasting bond imparts
  Of holiest brotherhood.
O might we all our lineage prove,
Give and forgive, do good and love,
By soft endearments in kind strife
Lightening the load of daily life !

There is much need, for not as yet
  Are we in shelter or repose ;
The holy house is still beset
  With leaguer of stern foes ;
Wild thoughts within, bad men without,
All evil spirits round about
Are banded in unblest device
To spoil Love's earthly paradise.

Then draw we nearer day by day,
  Each to his brethren, all to God ;
Let the world take us as she may,
  We must not change our road ;
Not wondering, though in grief, to find
The martyr's foe still keep her mind,
But fixed to hold Love's banner fast,
And by submission win at last.

SERMON BY REV. W. B. O. PEABODY.

HITHERTO UNPUBLISHED.

" Love your enemies." — Matt. v. 44.

I shall ask your attention to these words, not because they are not familiar, for the subject has been often presented. I do it to guard against the limitations of the meaning of the command by which the spirit of the charge is often explained away. We are all in danger of suiting the precepts of Christianity to our lives, instead of conforming our lives to the precepts, — instead of raising ourselves up to the standard required, we lower the standard to our own levels; a most dangerous proceeding, since it not only prevents our doing what is right at the time, but prevents our discerning what is right in future: in truth, the heaviest curse of all wrong-doing is that it depraves the judgment, it makes us blind to the difference between right and wrong, and thus puts repentance out of our power.

To prevent our falling into dangerous error on this very practical subject, let us weigh the terms employed in this injunction of our duty.

Our enemies, who are they? And the answer probably would be, Our enemies are those whom we are conscious of hating; those whom we know we strongly dislike are the persons who are here recommended to our regards. But no. If this definition were just, we should all say that we had no enemies; for no man is ever conscious that he hates another. He knows that he has no satisfaction in meeting another man. He knows that he thinks contemptuously of him; he knows that his feeling towards him is something quite different from interest or regard. But he does not admit, he does not know indeed, that the savage passion of hatred has any place in his breast. But watch his eye when it turns toward or turns away from his neighbor, — you will see hatred in its contemptuous glances; hear his words concerning him, — they are words of scorn and aversion; observe his actions, — you will find that they all express in the most decided manner that bitter hatred which he is not aware he feels.

Some would say, — in reply to the question, Who are our enemies? — they are those who have injured us, and they certainly are included in the meaning of the words. But that meaning is not broad enough to embrace the whole. There are some who have never injured us, some who have never crossed our path, for whom we entertain feelings of dislike. In fact, it is easier to forgive those who have injured us, than those whom we have injured. We do sometimes see those who are kind to men from whom they have suffered wrong; while it is unusual indeed, perhaps impossible, to find one who is ever thoroughly reconciled to the man whom he has injured; so that the word enemy includes those to whom we have done injury, as well as those who have injured us.

But we shall see who are the enemies here spoken of better by watching our own feelings, and the unguarded expression of our feelings, than in any other way. Is there any one whom it is unpleasant to you to meet? He is the enemy whom you are charged to love. Is there any one of whom you are tempted to speak bitterly, contemptuously, or in words of slight regard? He is the enemy whom you are commanded to love. Do not look far for the subjects of this kind feeling. There is deep hostility often without any declaration of war. A man's foes may be those of his own household. He may be provoked by the different opinions of one, or the cold selfishness of another; the calculating malice of some, and the thoughtless folly of others; the inconsiderateness of childhood, or the infirmity of old age; — these and a thousand other influences directly about him may be producing in him those feelings of enmity which we are sternly cautioned against indulging. If there are any, then, at home or abroad, near or distant, who awaken in us unpleasant feelings, we must not say that our feelings are just, for these are the enemies whom we are commanded to love ; — here is our field of duty.

The next most emphatic word in the command is *love*. " Love your enemies;" and here the deceitful heart steps in, and says that it cannot really be meant that we should love them. To love is a strong affection, and it cannot be supposed that it shall extend to a great variety of objects; it is reserved for our nearest friends; it cannot be expanded to embrace the whole human race in its arms. In reply to this it is only necessary to say, that the word *love* means something, — something must be done within us in order to discharge the duty. So then we are not to feel released from the obligation because we cannot give the same measure of affection to all. We are certainly required to love our enemies, and yet the authority that enjoins it is not one that requires unreasonable things.

In order to determine what this duty is, we must refer to particular cases in which the duty is to be discharged. If, for example, I feel strong resentment at any one on account of injuries he has done me, I must not only suppress, I must dismiss that feeling. I must so far get rid of it as to give him the same interest which I felt before he injured me; that is, I must not suffer the wrong he has done me to affect my bearing toward him. I must render no protest, under no name whatever indulge a passion which would prevent my regarding him as a brother of the family of man. It is not said that I must make no distinction between him and my nearest friends, but that I must act as if I had received no injury at his hand.

In the same manner are we to reason with respect to all toward whom we have any unpleasant feeling. Whether they are at home or abroad, near or distant, we must make it our business to change that feeling into a friendly one, so that instead of being painfully alive to their faults, as we now are, we may be able to see some merits and virtues in them; and where we now are tempted to make sharp comments on their failings, we may take pleasure in what there is good about them; and if they are such that charity can say but little in their favor, we may at least keep silence, and leave them to be condemned by other tongues than ours. For this purpose we must watch the words that spring readiest to our lips; and if we find them indicating any unkind feeling towards those of whom we speak, we must look to ourselves; whatever their faults may be, our own hearts are not clear, and all diligence must be applied to reform the bad passion within us before we sit in judgment on other offenders.

If then I have rightly explained who are meant by our enemies, it is not difficult to see wherein this duty consists; all those towards whom, or concerning whom, we have any contemptuous feeling; all those with whose conduct we are displeased, either with or without reason; all those whose malice or folly offends us; all those whom we are disposed to shun,—are the objects of this duty. Such persons are always near us and about us; they may be inmates of our dwellings, they may be connected with us by the ties of nature. But wherever or whoever they may be, we must make it the chief business of our lives to stifle, suppress, and root out this feeling before it grows and spreads, and casts its deathly influence over the better affections; for any such feeling is like deadly nightshade to the soul.

And now comes the practical question, Can we love our enemies? Can the duty be done?

And the first impulse of the heart is to rise up and say, It is impossible; the duty cannot be done. But let us reflect what part of our nature it is from which the reply proceeds. Is it from the conscience? Does the conscience, after having been deliberately consulted,— does the conscience say that it is impossible? No, the conscience has not been consulted; it was the voice of passion that answered; and the whole meaning of it is, that, with our present feelings, we cannot perform the duty. This is very likely. But what does it prove? Not that the duty is beyond our reach, but only that our present feelings must be altered; we must be renewed in the spirit of our minds, and then we may find that the obligation which now seems so far beyond us will be comparatively easy to perform. But have we a right to pronounce any duty impossible? Does not God know what we can do, and how much we can bear? Impossible the duty cannot be; for it has been done. Jesus Christ has done it; some of his followers have done it; and where there is a true heart and a right spirit it can be done again.

Perhaps the chief reason why this duty is often thought impossible is this. We think of changes in others, rather than of a change in ourselves. We say, if they would be kind and considerate, if they would lay aside their selfishness, we would give them a place in our regard. And this means, that if there were nothing to forgive, we could forgive them; we could bear with them, if there were nothing to bear. But this is not the way with Christian duty. But this will not do; if we wait for all to be such as we should naturally love before we consent to regard them, it is like waiting in a journey for the rivers to run by, before we consent to cross them. We must take mankind as they are; and if, as we are now, we cannot love them, *we* must be changed; we must have more of the spirit of our Master, more of the spirit without which we are not for heaven, and heaven ĩs not for us. For to pronounce a duty impossible is only saying, in other words, that we are not disposed to do it; it is a full acknowledgment that our religion has made no change within.

But now the question arises, How shall we bring ourselves to this duty? And clearly the reason of our not doing it now is, that we do not *love* to love our enemies; that is, we love better to indulge our present feelings than to make the effort required to change them, we love self-indulgence better than duty. And the only remedy is to change the present purport and purposes of our lives; to seek first the kingdom of God; to put ourselves under his authority, so that his will shall be ours, so that we shall steadily cherish such feelings as he enjoins and approves, so that we shall not permit a single feeling which he condemns to have place in our hearts if it can be dislodged by our exertions and our prayers. When this is our purpose and endeavor, it will succeed; resist the devil, and he will flee from you. The reason these evil spirits harbor within us is, that they find we have no serious desire, no steadfast determination to drive them away.

The way to learn this duty is a plain one to those who are disposed to walk in it. It is this. If there are those towards whom you have unpleasant feelings of resentment, dislike, or suspicion, — if there are those towards whom you are coldly indifferent even, — for all these are enemies in the sense of inspiration, — instead of keeping away from them, you must make it a point to meet them, to be familiar with their presence, and all the while to make an effort to exercise the feelings of kindness toward them. Be ready to speak to them, if they are not ready to speak to you; let your bearing towards them be influenced, not by their manner towards you, but by your Christian feeling and your sense of duty. Give no utterance to the feeling which their selfish coldness awakens in you; resolve that, so help you God, you will be true to the spirit of the Master, and you will carry your point in yourself, if not in them. They, too, will be softened, even if they do not become all you would wish to have them. But however it may be with them, you will find a new sunshine in your heart; the perpetual gloom that now scowls in your horizon will disappear; the peace which passeth understanding will prevail in your breast.

Such is the duty of loving our enemies, and such the way in which it may be done. Many are those toward whom our feeling is to be changed; near and distant, at home and abroad, we find perpetual subjects of this duty. Let us resolve to perform it, looking unto Jesus, who endured all manner of hostility and coldness, and answered not again; or rather, only answered injury with kindness, and enmity with love.

> " He is our pattern; may we bear
> More of his gracious spirit here;
> And may we trace the steps he trod,
> Which lead to Virtue and to God."

FIRST EPISTLE TO THE CORINTHIANS.

Chap. xiii.

Though I speak with the tongues of men and of angels, and have not charity, I am become as sounding brass or a tinkling cymbal. And though I have the gift of prophecy, and understand all mysteries and all knowledge, and though I have all faith, so that I could remove mountains, and have not charity, I am nothing.

And though I bestow all my goods to feed the poor, and though I give my body to be burned, and have not charity, I am nothing.

Charity suffereth long and is kind; charity envieth not; charity vaunteth not itself, is not puffed up, doth not behave itself unseemly, seeketh not her own, is not easily provoked, thinketh no evil; rejoiceth not in iniquity, but rejoiceth in the truth; beareth all things, believeth all things, hopeth all things, endureth all things.

Charity never faileth; but whether there be prophecies, they shall fail; whether there be tongues, they shall cease; whether there be knowledge, it shall vanish away.

For we know in part, and we prophesy in part; but when that which is perfect is come, then that which is in part shall be done away.

When I was a child, I spake as a child, I

understood as a child, I thought as a child; but when I became a man, I put away childish things. For now we see through a glass darkly, but then face to face; now I know in part, but then shall I know even as also I am known.

And now abideth faith, hope, charity, these three; but the greatest of these is charity.

PRAYER.

I pray to thee in faith, O God, my dependence! for when naught else can help me, thou forsakest me never. Thou art ever near to sinners, O God, our best portion! before we cry to thee thou art with us, bringing joy and salvation. Thou knowest, O Lord, what casts us down; nothing can escape thee; before even the sigh is uttered to thee, thy help is already given us. In many a bitter night of misfortune, in pressing danger, thou hast watched over us like a father, and art ever with us. I trust in thee, my shield, in the truth of thy love, which goeth forth ever, and is fresh every day. Thou willingly redeemest thy children from every pain with a Father's care; and does any sorrow wound our hearts, thou turnest it to our gain.

Thou measurest to us in love and kindness

what is best for us ; thou rewardest, O Father, not according to our desert. So I come into thy presence, with joyous confidence, and know thou forsakest not thine own who look up to thee in faith. My heart and soul are ever thine ; what thy love decrees must always be the best; thou orderest all things well. Not what I will, what thou willest, be done; wisdom dwells alone in thee, in my wish is often folly and crime. Therefore, all that I have and am, my joy and my sorrow, with the humble spirit of a child, do I lay in the heart of the Father. Thy will shall be my will; I live and die in thee, confident and joyous; I sleep and wake, for thou art ever near me.

"Her sins, which are many, are forgiven; for she loved much; but to whom little is forgiven, the same loveth little."

He to whom much is forgiven is not he who has sinned much, but he who feels that the difference among men is not so great as we foolishly imagine, and that one has little glory above another, because they all fail of that glory which they shall have in the presence of God ; in short, it is he who feels in his own sin the sin itself, the sins of the whole world, who waters the feet of the Saviour with his tears, who pours out the perfumed ointment of the thankfulness of a humble heart. He to whom little is forgiven is not he who has sinned little, — for who could stand up, and say in truth, I am he! — but it is he who has made little account of sin, without knowing it, perhaps, because he would not be indebted too much to the mercy of God in Christ. The Pharisee who invited Jesus to his house was such a one ; but in the hypocrisy of a cold heart, he still doubted whether he were a true prophet, and was anxious lest too much honor should be shown to the Saviour in his house.

We are forgiven, and therefore we love ; we ourselves forgive, and for this reason we love ; and for both these reasons are we loved by our brethren. Is the forgiveness on both sides abundant, then is the love abundant ; is it little, then

the love must be little and lukewarm. Yes, that
much is forgiven us because we have loved much,
that we love little if little is forgiven us, this must
we feel in all relations of life. Look upon the
dearest and the closest, upon the relations between husband and wife, children, brother, and
sister, — those ties by which God has touched
our hearts in a peculiar way, and which awaken
in us our warmest love. Who are they who, in
these relations, can rejoice that they have sinned
little, and that little is forgiven them? Ah, think
of life, how it is, with all our changing dispositions, our little injustices, our struggle never
to be overcome with selfish humors or weak indolence ; and you must confess that to him only is
little forgiven who has loved little, who satisfies
himself with what can be measured out by some
external standard. But he who demands all that
the spirit can give in its fulness, which truly only
the spirit of love can estimate, — he who from
his own impulse extends to every one all that
God has given him, — in short, he who loves
much, — O how often will he find reason to cry
out for patience and forbearance, how deeply will
he feel that to him much must be forgiven ! But
because the inner principle of his loving spirit
makes the deepest impression upon all who live
with him, — because before this inward principle
all unevenness becomes smooth, all disturbance

15 *

disappears,— for this very reason he finds patience and forbearance, and much is forgiven him because he has loved much.

And so is it also with all the less close relationships among men. He who flatters himself that he stands in nobody's way, that he injures no one, neglects nothing which is laid down in the laws of a moral way of life,— it may well be that he is forgiven little according to his own interpretation; but he also loves little. On the other hand, he who goes forth actively, kindly, to work with *living* purpose in the life of men, for how many sins of omission, how many moments of slow indifference, of cold reserve, must he reproach himself! But if men feel how powerful are his efforts, how much he loves, and loving offers to others, to him will much be forgiven.

Let us think how the forgiveness of Christ worked upon those dispositions that were subject to it, so that those whose closed eyes he opened, whom he healed from heavy infirmity, even those whom he waked from the body's death, could not be so near to him, cling to him so thankfully, nor enjoy such lasting love, as those to whom he could say, Go, thy sins are forgiven thee. So also with us. All benefits and gifts which we can scatter are less powerful to strengthen the bond of love than this gentle sympathy with the inward spirit, this strengthening forbearance, this

reconciling support and consolation for the repentant and fallen. That was the most beautiful
praise of the Saviour, uttered by the prophet of
the Old Testament: "The smoking flax shall he
not quench, the bruised reed shall he not break."
O how many like these weak ones do we see
around us! Let us bind fast with tender hand
the broken reed, — let us breathe into the expir-
ing flame the breath of love, that it may live
anew; so may we come nearer to Him, and feel
how blessed are those who deserve to be called
his brothers, and that we with truth can cry,
"Forgive us, as we forgive." — *Schleiermacher*.

How carefully should we cherish the little virtues which spring up at the foot of the cross,
since they are sprinkled with the blood of the
Son of God.

These virtues are humility, patience, meekness,
benignity, bearing one another's burden, conde-
scension, cheerfulness, compassion, forgiving injuries, simplicity, candor; all, in short, of that
sort. They, like unobtrusive violets, love the
shade; like them, are unstained by dew; and
though, like them, they make little show, they
shed a sweet odor on all around. — *St. Francis
de Sales*.

"A bruised reed shall he not break, and the smoking flax shall he not quench."

Why hast thou, for our earthly gloom,
    Thus left our Father's hall?
" Not for the righteous am I come,
    But sinners to recall."

What bear'st thou from yon desert nook,
    Upon thy shoulders bound ?
" A sheep who left my Father's flock,
    Whom I have lost and found."

What is it wakes the angelic mirth,
    'Mid sons of God in heaven ?
" 'T is some poor, sorrowing child of earth,
    Who is of God forgiven."

What makes the gracious Father rise,
    And hasten from his seat ?
" 'T is one in distance he descries, —
    A long lost son, to meet."

O Thou who seest our secret prayer,
    And every inmost grief,
Teach us on thee to cast our care,
    And find in thee relief.

I read to-day a sermon of Cudworth's, who preached in the day's of the Commonwealth and of Charles II. It measures six times the length of the printed sermons of the present day, showing greater perseverance in both preacher and hearer than in these latter days.

EXTRACT FROM RALPH CUDWORTH'S SERMON

UPON THE CHRISTIAN'S VICTORY OVER SIN, THE LAW, AND DEATH.

Some there are who will acknowledge no other victory over sin, but an external one; that by which it was conquered for us, sixteen hundred years since, by Christ upon the cross; when he spoiled principalities and powers, and made a show of them openly, triumphing over them in it, " and when he redeemed us from the curse of the law, being made a curse for us." And, doubtless, this was one great end of Christ's coming into the world, to make a propitiatory sacrifice for the sins of mankind; not only that he might thereby put a period to those continually repeated and ineffectual sacrifices of brute beasts, and the offering of the blood of bulls and goats, which could not take away sin, nor propitiate his Divine Majesty; but also that he might, at once, give a sensible demonstration, both of God's high displeasure against sin, and of his placableness and reconcilableness to sinners returning to obedience; and therefore to that end, that the despair of pardon might not hinder any from repentance and amendment of life, he promulgated free pardon and remission of sins, through his blood, to all those who should repent and believe the Gospel.

But it is a very unsound and unwholesome interpretation of this salutary undertaking of Christ in the Gospel, that its ultimate end was to procure remission of sin, and exemption from punishment only, to some particular persons still continuing under the power of sin, and to save them, at last, *in* their sins, that is, with a mere outward and carnal salvation; it being a thing utterly impossible, that those undefiled rewards of the heavenly kingdom should be received and enjoyed by men in their unregenerate and unrenewed nature.

For a true Christian, that has anything of the life of God in him, cannot but earnestly desire an inward healing of his sinful maladies and distempers, and not an outward hiding and palliation of them only. He must needs passionately long more and more after a new life and nature, and the divine image more fully formed in him; insomuch, that if, without it, he might be secured from the pains of hell, he could not be fully quieted and satisfied with such security. It is not the effects and consequence of sin only, the external punishment due unto it, from which he

desires to be freed; but from the intrinsical evil
of sin itself, from the plague of his own heart.
As he often meditates with comfort upon that
outward cross to which his Saviour's hands and
feet were nailed for his sins, so he impatiently
desires to feel the virtue of that inward cross of
Christ, also, by which the world may be crucified
to him and he unto the world; and to experience
the power of Christ's resurrection within him,
still to raise him further unto newness of life.
Neither will he be more easily persuaded to believe, that his sinful desires, the malignity and
violence of which he feels within himself, can be
conquered without him, than that an army here
in England can be conquered in France or Spain.
He is so deeply sensible of the real evil, which is in
sin itself, that he cannot be contented to have it
only histrionically triumphed over. And to fancy
himself covered all over with a thin veil of mere
external imputation, will afford little satisfactory
comfort unto him that hungers and thirsts after
righteousness, and is weary and heavy laden with
the burden of sins, and does not desire to have
his inward maladies hid and covered only, but
healed and cured. Neither can he be willing to
be put off till the hour of death, for a divorce
between his soul and sin; nor easily persuaded,
that, though sin should rule and reign in him all
his life long, yet the last parting groan, that

shall divide his soul and body asunder, may have so great an efficacy, as, in a moment also, to separate all sin from his soul.

The true Gospel righteousness, which Christ came to set up in the world, does not consist merely in outward works, whether ceremonial or moral, done by our own natural power, in our unregenerate state, but in an inward life and spirit, wrought by God.

But there is a second degree of victory over sin, which every true Christian ought not only to look upon as possible, but also to endeavor after, and ceaselessly to pursue; which is "such a measure of strength in the inward man," and such a degree of mortification or crucifixion of our sinful lusts, as that a man will not knowingly and deliberately do anything, that his conscience plainly tells him is a sin, though there be never so great temptations to it.

Wherefore, I demand, in the next place, why it should be thought impossible, by the grace of the Gospel, and the faith of Christ, to attain to such a victory over sin? For sin owes its original to nothing else but ignorance and darkness; every wicked man is ignorant. And, therefore, in that sense, another maxim of the Stoics may have some truth, also, that men sin against their will; because, if they knew that those things were indeed so hurtful to them, they would never do them. Now, we all know, how easily light conquers darkness, and, upon its first approach, makes it fly before it, and, like a guilty shade, seek to hide itself from it, by running round the earth. And, certainly, the light of God, arising in the soul, can with as much ease scatter away the night of sinful ignorance before it. For truth has a cognation with the soul; and falsehood, lies, and impostures, are no more able to make resistance against the power of truth breaking forth, than darkness is able to dispute with light. Wherefore, the entrance in of light upon the soul is half a conquest over our sinful inclinations.

Again, though sin have had a long and customary possession in the soul, yet it has no just title, much less a right of inheritance. For sin is but a stranger and foreigner in the soul, an usurper and intruder into the Lord's inheritance. Sin is no nature, as Saint Austin and others of the Fathers often inculcate, but an adventitious and extraneous thing; and the true and ancient nature of the soul of man, suffers violence under it, and is oppressed by it. It is nothing else but the preternatural state of rational beings; and, therefore, we have no reason to think it must needs be perpetual and unalterable. Is it a strange thing, that, by the hand of a skilful musician, a jarring instrument should ever be set in tune again ?   Doubtless, if an instrument of music were a living thing, it would be sensible of harmony as its proper state, and abhor discord and dissonancy as a thing preternatural to it. The soul of man was harmonical as God at first made it ; till sin, disordering the strings and faculties, put it out of tune, and marred the music of it ; but, doubtless, that great *Harmostes*, who tunes the whole world, and makes all things keep their times and measures, is able to set this lesser instrument in tune again.   Sin is but a disease and dyscrasy in the soul ; righteousness is its health and natural complexion ; and there is a propensity in the nature of everything, to return to its proper state, and to cast off whatever is heterogeneous to it.   And some 'physicians tell us, that medicaments are but subservient to nature, by removing obstructions and impediments ; but nature itself, and the inward Archæus, released and set at liberty, works the cure.   Bodies, when they are bent out of their place, and violently forced out of the natural position of their parts, have a spring of their own, and an inward strong propension to return to their own natural posture, which produces that motion of restitution, of which philosophers endeavor to give a reason.   Now, sin being a violent and preternatural state, and a sinner's returning to God and righteousness being that motion by which the soul is restored to its true freedom and ancient nature, why should there not be such an elater or spring in the soul, (quickened and enlivened by divine grace,) such a natural *conatus*, of returning to its proper state again? Doubtless, there is; and the Scripture seems sometimes to acknowledge it, and to call it by the name of spirit, when it speaks of our free-acting in God's ways, from an inward principle. For the spirit is not always to be taken for a breath or impulse from without; but, also, for an inward propension of the soul, awakened and revived in it, to return to its proper state, as it is intellectual; and then to act freely in that state, according to its ancient nature.

Lastly, we must observe, that, though this inward victory over sin be no otherwise attainable than by the spirit of Christ, through faith, and by a divine operation within us; so that, in a certain sense, we may be said to be passive recipients; yet we must not dream that our active co-operation and concurrence are not also necessarily required. For as there is a spirit of God in nature producing vegetables and minerals which human art and industry could never be able to effect; a certain nutritive spirit within, as the poet sings, which yet does not work absolutely, unconditionally, and omnipotently, but requires certain preparations, conditions, and dispositions in the matter which it works upon; (for unless the husbandman plough the ground and sow the seed, the spirit of God in nature will not give any increase;) in like manner, the Scripture tells us that the divine spirit of grace does not work in the souls of men absolutely, unconditionally, and irresistibly, but requires in us certain proportions, conditions, and co-operations; forasmuch, as it may both be quenched, and stirred up or excited, in our souls. And indeed, unless we plough up the fallow ground of our hearts, and sow to ourselves in righteousness, as the prophet speaks, by our earnest endeavors, we cannot expect that the divine spirit of grace will shower down that heavenly increase upon us. Wherefore, if, by the spirit of Christ, we would attain a victory over sin, we must endeavor to fight a good fight, and win a good race, and to "enter in at the strait gate"; that so, overcoming, we may receive the crown of life. And thus much it shall suffice me to have spoken at this time concerning the first particular, *the victory over sin.*

We cannot now but take notice briefly of some errors of those who, either pretending the impossibility of this inward victory over sin, or else hypocritically declining the combat, make up a certain religion to themselves out of other things, which are either impertinent and nothing to the purpose, or else evil and noxious.

For first, some, as was intimated before, make to themselves a mere fantastical and imaginary religion; they conceit that there is nothing for them to do but confidently to believe that all is already done for them; that they are dearly beloved of God without any conditions or qualifications to make them lovely. But such a faith as this is nothing but mere fancy and carnal imagination, proceeding from that natural self-love with which men fondly dote upon themselves, and are apt to think that God loves them as fondly and as partially as they love themselves, tying his affection to their particular outward persons, to their very flesh and blood; — thus making God a being like unto themselves, that is, wholly actuated by arbitrary self-will, fondness, and partiality; and perverting the whole nature and design of religion, which is not a mere phantastry and historical show, but a *real* victory over the *real* evil of sin; without which neither can God take pleasure in any man's person, nor can there be any possibility of happiness, any real turning of the soul from darkness unto light, from the power of Satan unto God.

Again, some there are, who, instead of walking in the narrow way which Christ commends, of subduing and mortifying our sinful appetites, make to themselves certain other narrow ways of affected singularity in things which belong not to

life and godliness ; outward strictnesses and se-
verities of their own choosing and devising ; and
who persuade themselves that this is the strait
gate and narrow way of Christ, which leadeth
unto life. Whereas, these *are* indeed nothing
else but some particular paths, and narrow slices,
cut out of the broad way. For, though they
have an outward and seeming narrowness, yet
they are so broad within that camels with their
burdens may easily pass through them. These,
instead of taking up Christ's cross upon them,
make to themselves certain crosses of their own ;
and laying them upon their shoulders, and carrying them, please themselves with the conceit that
they bear the cross of Christ ; while in truth and
reality they are frequently too much strangers to
that cross, by which the world should be crucified
to them and they unto the world. Some place
all their religion in endless scrupulosities about
indifferent things, neglecting in the mean time
the more weighty matters, both of law and gospel ; straining at a gnat and swallowing a camel ;
that is, not being so scrupulous as they ought to
be about the substantials of religion and a good
life. For, as we ought not to place the chief of
our religion in the mere observance of outward
rites and ceremonies, whilst, in the mean time,
we hypocritically neglect the morals and substantials, which may deservedly be branded with the

name of superstition; so, we ought to know that it is equal superstition to have such an abhorrence of indifferent things as to make it the main of our religion to abstain from them. Both of these argue equal ignorance of the nature of God, as if he were some morose, humorous, and captious being; and of that righteousness in which the kingdom of God consists; as if these outward and indifferent things could either hallow or defile our souls, or as if salvation and damnation depended upon the mere using or not using of them. The Apostle himself instructs us, that the kingdom of God consists no more in uncircumcision than in circumcision; that is, no more in not using outward ceremonies and indifferent things than in using them.

Wherefore, the negative superstition is equal to the positive. And both of them alike call off men's attention from the main objects of religion, by engaging them overmuch in small and little things. But the sober Christian, who neither places all his religion in external observances, nor yet is superstitiously anti-ceremonial, — as he will think himself obliged to have a due regard to the commands of lawful authority in adiaphorous things, and to prefer the peace and unity of the Christian Church, and the observation of the royal law of charity, before the satisfaction of any private humor or interest, — so he will be aware of that extreme, into which many run, of banishing away, quite out of the world, all the solemnity of external worship, the observance of the Lord's day, and the participation of the Christian sacraments, under the notion of useless ceremonies.

To conclude: unless there be a due and timely regard had to the commands of lawful authority, in indifferent things, and to order, peace, and unity in the Church, it may easily be foreseen, that the reformed part of Christendom will be brought to confusion, and at length to utter ruin, by crumbling into infinite sects and divisions.

Wherefore, laying aside these, and similar childish mistakes and things which are little to the purpose, let us seriously apply ourselves to the main work of our religion; that is, to mortify and vanquish our sinful natures, by the assistance of God's Holy Spirit, through faith in Christ; that so, being dead to sin here, we may live with God eternally hereafter.

THE FIFTH STORMY SUNDAY.

THE CHILDREN.

"Lo, to Thy kingdom here below
We little children bring,
For to that kingdom such we know
The meetest offering.

Let naught allure them from Thy word,
Or tempt their spirits frail;
Keep thou their steps, O blessed Lord!
Nor let our loved ones fail."

THE FIFTH STORMY SUNDAY.

THE CHILDREN.

AGAIN a stormy Sunday! This is the fifth Sunday that I have been prevented from going to church by the heavy storm. What, indeed, shall we do, we weaker ones, who cannot venture into the storm to find our Sunday food? If I could only penetrate through the heavy drifts down the hill as far as Mrs. Blake's house, how gladly would I do it! But George says that it is impossible. Poor Mrs. Blake! She was telling me only yesterday of the troubles that these stormy Sundays had brought her, with her family of children. It was so impossible to find any Sunday quiet. All the week she has days of noise and interruption, and is quite dependent upon the rest of the Sunday services for thought, for worship, and for help from the words of the preacher.

"People," she said, "talk to me of the *quiet* of a Sunday at home, in preference to church worship, and have even wished they might pass it like other days. But I should like to have them find the quiet in a house with three boys from five years old to twelve, and a baby, and three such girls as Isabel and Mary and Clara! Neither would they like it any better to pass it like other days. Six are enough of that kind. I am preaching to the children all the week, and it is a comfort to go where I can hear some one preach to me, and think of my own sins, and pray for patience! Discipline I may have enough of, to be sure, all through the week; but I need teaching, to learn how to turn it in the right direction. I need the day of rest to recall to myself what rest is, to put my thoughts in order."

I hoped, if there were another stormy Sunday, I might go to Mrs. Blake's to help her through the day with the seven children. But as I cannot reach her, I must help myself with her account of her last stormy Sunday.

Isabel stood by the window, disconsolate, watching the storm. I am afraid that her disappointment was the deeper, because she could not wear her new furs that her grandfather had sent her for a birthday present the day before. I am sorry to confess it; but Isabel has so much taste about her dress, that perhaps I cannot wonder if she gives too much thought to it. Clara was sorry that she could n't go out, because she had studied her Sunday-school lesson so very carefully the night before. Generally her Sunday lesson is left till the morning, and then very hurriedly learned ; but this time she had taken particular pains with it, and now she said, " It 's of no use ; I shall forget it all before next Sunday." Mary, poor Mary, looked sorrowfully out of the window too. She has been, indeed, a prisoner all winter, and a stormy day only gives her less to regret without. But a stormy Sunday, with all the children shut inside the house, would be rather a trial for her aching head. She already looked pale and anxious.

Now what should I do ? Should I declare a truce, and tell the boys that they might play their games just as they would other days ? For more than one reason, — even if one good one were not enough, — I should not have wished to do this. Though I do not like to have the children connect a feeling of constraint with the Sundays, I would rather give them early the habit of making it a different day from others. I would like them to learn it is the day on which they are to do the *best* things, — " not merely to *wear* my best things," suggested Clara, when I was once expressing this.

And even if I had yielded my cherished feelings on the subject, that I might get along the easiest way I could, there was Mary's headache to be thought of, and she could not bear the noise attendant on the jubilee of "playing on Sunday." And Isabel and Clara were old enough to prefer a quiet time for reading to the noise of the children.

Harry was permitted to try and shovel away the snow that was banking up the porch, so that his father need not lose his way to the house when he came home. All the smaller boys wanted to go out too. The storm was quite too high for the little things; the wind would have blown them off the hill. But this they were not willing to believe, and so arose uproar the first. The baby was waked by the noise. The breakfast things were to be washed and put away, for Bridget insisted upon her privilege of going out, in spite of the storm, and had started off a little earlier on account of it. It was a moment of discouragement. Perhaps it was no great wonder that I looked round and saw only the dark side of everything, — that I thought Isabel was troubled by the disappointment of her vanity, that I gave Clara no better motive, that I saw in Mary irritation and peevishness.

But one should go down into such great depths only to rise up again. I saw that my own discouragement was only adding to that of the others, making Mary gloomier, Isabel and Clara more discontented, and the boys more restless.

" Come," said I, when Harry had given up and come in, " we will have services, and a ' meeting' at home. But we shall not any of us be ready for it, unless everybody helps. Harry must take the baby, and Clara must get some pillows, and arrange the sofa for Mary to lie down. And Isabel and the boys and I will clear away the breakfast things."

Presently, I had more hands and feet offered me than were necessary, and some were more in the way than in service. But we only broke one plate among us, and the work was done at last. Then Horace and Willie were very busy in arranging the chairs to look like a " meeting," and Isabel was willing to take the baby. She is very successful in taking care of the baby, and lets him pull about her curls as he pleases. Horace took his place in his chair, as if he were promising to be quiet, but a little naughty gleam stole out of the side of his eye.

But I told the children,—though they seated themselves round me, as though I were the preacher, — that we were not in a church, and would not have services as if we were in a church ; that we had no preacher here to teach us, but, instead, we would try and preach to each other, and each one of us would say something, and take a part in this meeting. I said that we would begin with the youngest, and that Willie should read us a hymn, from Mrs. Barbauld's Lessons, the book in which he reads at school every day.

Isabel did not think much of Willie's reading, and she gave more attention to the baby. But we all thought the reading was better than we expected from the little fellow. And after he had read a few verses, Mary read the rest for him.

"Can we raise our voices up to the high heaven? Can we make Him hear who is above the stars? Yes: for he heareth us when we only whisper; when we breathe out words softly with a low voice. He that filleth the heavens is here also.

"May we that are so young speak to Him that always was?

"May we that can hardly speak plain, speak to God?

"We that are so young, are but lately made alive; therefore, we should not forget his forming hand, who hath made us alive. We that cannot speak plain should lisp out praises to him, who teacheth us how to speak, and hath opened our dumb lips.

"When we could not think of him, he thought of us; before we could ask him to bless us, he had already given us many blessings.

"He fashioneth our tender limbs, and causeth them to grow; he maketh us strong, tall, and nimble.

"Every day we are more active than the former day; therefore every day we ought to praise him better than the former day.

"The buds spread into leaves, and the blossoms swell to fruit; but they know not how they grow, nor who causeth them to spring up from the bosom of the earth.

"Ask them, if they will tell thee; bid them break forth into singing, and fill the air with pleasant sounds.

"They smell sweet; they look beautiful; but they are quite silent; no sound is in the still air; no murmur of voices among the green leaves.

"The plants and trees are made to give fruit to man; but man is made to praise God who made him.

"We love to praise him, because he loveth to bless us; we thank him for life, because it is a pleasant thing to be alive.

"We love God, who hath created all beings; we love all beings, because they are the creatures of God.

"We cannot be good, as God is good to all persons everywhere; but we can rejoice, that everywhere there is a God to do them good.

"We will think of God when we play, and when we work; when we walk out, and when we come in; when we sleep, and when we wake, his praise shall dwell continually on our lips."

Horace was very restless while Willie was reading, and grew red when Willie made any mistakes; but he listened quietly as Mary finished reading the hymn.

He did not know very well his own Sunday-school lesson, which I asked him to repeat. " It was something about being afraid of God," he said. I should have preferred it, had the lesson taught something about the love of God rather than the fear. Children sometimes learn from these words, " the fear of God," to look upon him with such dread, that they would like to shut him out from their happier moments. In this way they would like to avoid the thought of God; and when they grow up, are obliged by study to learn to love him. We talked **a** little about it, and I tried to show to Horace, that, if he were a good child, he need not be afraid of the presence of God.

Am I wrong, I wonder, in teaching him such a lesson? Perhaps this restless boy, who may always be rushing into the roads that lead to temptation,—perhaps he will need some greater curb than I am aware of. Alas! who am I to guide such a mind as his? Commands often make him defiant, requests often make him malicious, and, young as he is, he has learnt some boy notions of making fun of sentiment. Tender words seldom seem to impress him, as far as I can tell. All day he is busy with boyish games. When he is reproved for his mischievous deeds, he looks up with wonder at the reproof, sometimes with a smile of superiority, as if he had already — he, the little fellow — thought over the consequences, and were willing to bear the risk.

I read next a prayer from a little book of prayers belonging to the children.

" Great and glorious God, who hast made the sun in the skies to give light by day ; thy throne is in the highest heaven, yet thy goodness takes notice of thy creatures on earth, and thou hearest when children pray to thee.

" Look down, O Lord, and pity me; for I desire to be heartily sorry that I have so often offended thee, by breaking thy commandments ; and when I am serious, I am grieved to think that I should be so ready to break them again. O God of mercy ! punish me not as my faults and follies deserve, either in this world, or in the world to come. But when thou bringest pain or trouble upon me, let me be patient under it, and grow better for it. Send thy good spirit into my heart, to subdue my evil inclinations, and form me after the likeness of thy Son, Jesus Christ. Preserve me from the danger of evil company, and let me choose and love the company of the wise and good ; nor suffer me to waste those hours in

idleness or play which are allotted for my learning or work. Keep my heart from malice and
from evil thoughts. Preserve my tongue from
lying and slandering, and all evil words. With-
hold my hands from fighting and stealing, and all
evil actions. Guard my feet from running into
mischief. Let me dwell with my companions in
peace and love, and be ready to help them at all
times. Let me not dare to sin against thee in
secret, remembering that I am always in thy
sight. Grant me sufficient food and raiment
while I live. Increase my strength daily. Secure me from sickness and from death in my
younger days, that I may do some service for
thee on earth ; and when I die, and my body is
carried to the grave, may my soul be taken up to
live for ever with thee and with thy Son, Jesus
Christ.

" I praise thee, O Lord, for all the blessings I
have ever received, for they all come from thee.
I give thee thanks for my rest the last night, and
that I find myself in peace this morning. I bless
thee for my sight and hearing ; for all my senses
and my powers of mind and body ; and, above all,
for the words that tell me the life of Christ, and
for all the helps that I enjoy in order to the salvation of my soul. Let me so carefully fulfil all
my duties every day, that I may come with delight to worship thee when the evening returns.

Heavenly Father, accept all my prayers and praises, through Jesus Christ, thy well-beloved Son. Amen."

The children were very quiet as I read this prayer, and then Harry said to me his Sunday-school lesson. He had learned this very well,— some answers to questions upon the New Testament. He has a good memory, and these answers, which he had learned last Sunday, he remembered very well. He has a careful teacher, too, at Sunday school, who requires that he should learn the meaning of what he is saying, — a very necessary thing for Harry, since he so easily learns the words. His lesson was upon the passage where the mother of James and John came to Jesus, to ask that her sons might sit upon his right hand in his kingdom. And Jesus asked them if they would be able to drink of the cup that he should drink of, and be baptized with his baptism. And James and John had promised that they would be able. And Harry had been told by his teacher to study the lives of James and John, to see if they had performed this promise. And he had found out how James was the first martyr among the twelve Apostles, that he was killed by Herod in Jerusalem; that John suffered long for the sake of Jesus, and in his long life never forgot his love of Christ. While he had studied about these he had thought of Judas, who died a miserable death in agony and remorse, because he had betrayed his Master, and had sold him to his enemies for a few pieces of silver.

Then Mary repeated a hymn she knew, which is by Keble, on this subject.

ST. JAMES'S DAY.

Sit down and take thy fill of joy
  At God's right hand, a bidden guest:
Drink of the cup that cannot cloy,
  Eat of the bread that cannot waste.
O great Apostle! rightly now
  Thou readest all thy Saviour meant,
What time his grave yet gentle brow
  In sweet reproof on thee was bent.

"Seek ye to sit enthroned by me?
  Alas! ye know not what ye ask;
The first in shame and agony,
  The lowest in the meanest task, —
This can ye be?　And can ye drink
  The cup that I in tears must steep,
Nor from the whelming waters shrink,
  That o'er me roll so dark and deep?"

"We come; thine are we, dearest Lord,
  In glory and in agony,
To do and suffer all thy word;
  Only be thou for ever nigh."

" Then be it so: my cup receive,
   And of my woes baptismal taste;
But for the crown that angels weave
   For those next me in glory placed,

" I give it not by partial love;
   But in my Father's book are writ
What names on earth shall lowliest prove,
   That they in heaven may highest sit."
Take up the lesson, O my heart!
   Thou Lord of meekness, write it there;
Thine own meek self to me impart,
   Thy lofty hope, thy lowly prayer.

If ever on the mount with thee
   I seem to soar in vision bright,
With thoughts of coming agony,
   Stay Thou the too presumptuous flight;
Gently along the vale of tears
   Lead me from Tabor's sun-bright steep;
Let me not grudge a few short years
   With thee toward heaven to walk and weep.

Too happy, on my silent path,
   If now and then allowed, with thee
Watching some placid, holy death,
   Thy secret work of love to see;
But oh! most happy, should thy call,
   Thy welcome call, at last be given:
" Come where thou long hast stored thy all;
   Come, see thy place prepared in heaven!"

Then, as performing my part of the service, I read the following sermon of Dr. Arnold's:—

CHRIST'S WARNING TO THE YOUNG.

"Then Jesus, beholding him, loved him, and said unto him, One thing thou lackest: go thy way, sell whatsoever thou hast, and give to the poor, and thou shalt have treasure in heaven: and come, take up the cross, and follow me. And he was sad at that saying, and went away grieved; for he had great possessions."—Mark x. 21, 22.

There came a young man to Christ, to ask him what he should do to inherit eternal life; and Christ named to him some of the ten commandments, to which the young man replied, "All these have I observed from my youth." Then says the Evangelist, "Jesus, beholding him, loved him." This is, as it were, the first part of the story, and surely this case is very like our own. Are not we here come avowedly to learn of Christ, to be brought up in Christian truths and principles, for this life and for life eternal? And if Christ were to ask us of our knowledge and of our practice, surely a large proportion of us would be able to answer that they knew the main truths of the Gospel and the main distinctions between good and evil; and many of us might go further, and say, not indeed that all their common and most obvious duties they had followed from their youth up, but at least that they had followed many of them, and desired still to follow them; that from much-evil they had been accustomed to shrink, and purposed and hoped to shrink from it still. And so great is the tenderness of our Lord Jesus Christ to all his people, and especially to the young, that when he sees any of you so living as I have described, living, that is, respectably and amiably, guilty of no gross sins, and doing many duties, loved by your friends, and affectionate to them in return, it is not too much to say that Christ loves you; that his eye is upon you with a loving anxiety; that he regards you with nothing of severity nor of threatening, but with an earnest desire that you may become wholly his, and be loved by him for ever.

So it is then, so we may venture to apply it, that we stand before Christ to-day. Jesus, beholding us, loves us. His voice to us is nothing harsh, but full of gracious encouragement; all that there is of good in us he acknowledges, and regards with approbation and love. But let us hear his words, for he speaks to the young man who had just declared that he had constantly kept his commandments, and whom as he beheld him he loved: " One thing thou lackest: go thy way, sell whatsoever thou hast, and give to the poor, and thou shalt have treasure in heaven: and come, take up the cross, and follow me." What is this when addressed to us? will he, does he, find that there is one thing which we lack also, and which he bids us without delay to gain? Or might he say to us that we are all clean, all his true servants, going on from good to better, and lacking nothing at all but that ripeness which added years will not fail to give us? If our consciences will not suffer us to believe this, then it must be that Christ is saying to us, "One thing thou lackest"; there may be many things which we lack, but there must at least be one.

Now the one thing which he sees wanting in so many of us is expressed clearly in the latter part of his words to the young man in the Gospel. He tells us, " Come, take up the cross, and follow me." The words are figurative, we see, when he says, " Take up the cross," and we may ask what the figure means. But we know that, in the Latin language, the term *crux*, or *cross*, had been long used to express generally any great pain or evil; and the words *crucio* and *cruciatus* derived from it are yet used only generally; they do not express literally the pain or suffering of crucifixion, but pain and torment simply. And this manner of speaking had come into use, because the Romans used the punishment of crucifixion commonly, not only towards slaves, but towards criminals generally of their subject nations, unless they were persons of high condition. So that when our Lord tells the young man to take up his cross, it meant exactly, " Bear thy pain or thy suffering, whatever it may be, and follow me." And so he had said in another place, " He that taketh not his cross and followeth after me, is not worthy of me," — meaning the very same thing ; he who does not submit willingly to his pain or suffering, and continue to follow after me notwithstanding the pain, he is not worthy of me. In both places we see that the taking up the cross is joined with the following after him; in both places the cross means the same thing, — *cruciatum* rather than *crucem*, — pain, suffering, burden, evil hard to bear, let the particular kind be what it may.

Now to take one of those seeming contradictions in the Scriptures, of which I have spoken so often, as containing some of the Scripture's most useful lessons, let us put side by side our Lord's words, " Take up thy cross and follow me," and his other words, " My yoke is easy and my burden is light." In one place he seems to call his followers to the most painful service, in the other to tell them that their pain will be nothing at all. What is now called our cross, that strong term signifying the extremity of pain and suffering, is again called an easy yoke, and a light burden. Take them out of their right order, and they are falsehood and death; take them in their right order and according to Christ's mind, and they are truth and life.

He calls us to take up our cross and follow him. We were following him, not taking up our cross; we were following him where to follow him was easy, and it is many times very easy. We loved those who loved us; we were glad to please them; it is good and right so to do, but surely not very hard or painful. ·We abstained from low vices, vices disgusting and discreditable; good and right also, but surely involving no severe sacrifice. We were good-natured and good-humored when we were pleased and happy; a right temper and an amiable one, but still there is no bearing our cross in this. He beholds us, and loves us, but he calls us to something of a more real service. He says, " You have followed me where it was easy, and you have done well; but now prepare for something far more trying, — I call you to follow me where it is hard. Be quite sure that there is in you, somewhere or other, a temper or an inclination which does not suit my law. Follow me in this point, and you will know what it is to take up your cross; follow me always, and this point, and many such points, will be found in you." It is easy to be temperate in meat and drink when you are neither hungry nor thirsty. It is easy to speak truth

when the truth is convenient and creditable. It
is easy to work when the work to be done is pleasant, and when you are strong; but to be temper-
· ate always, to speak truth always, to do our appointed work always, this is ·not easy, this is to
bear our cross. And here, in how many points
is your cross very near to you, the pleasant fault
to be shunned, the painful duty to be done, the
scornful smile to be endured and unheeded, the
unkindness to be borne without irritation or desire to return evil for evil, the regulation to be
kept when it may be broken without detection,
and apparently with no worse fault than the simple breaking it: all these things, and such as
these, which run through your lives daily, which
you well know from past experience, which are
coming or come to you again this half-year, as
they came the last,—these are the things with regard to which Christ tells you, " One thing thou
lackest; come, take up thy cross, and follow me."
Now may I venture to alter the words of what
next follows in the Gospel, while I faithfully keep
its spirit: " They were sad at that saying, and
went away grieved; for they were young and at
school." Even so it is, and·even such is sometimes the very actual language which may be
heard: This is too hard for us; it is not possible
to be fully such as we should be at school; there
are things, not right we know, but which we can-

not help doing; there are things, right we know, but which we cannot here set ourselves to practise; the principles and practice around us must in some degree be ours; we have followed Christ in many things from our youth up, and hope still to follow him, but this hard saying, to follow him where it is very painful, to shun the fault which all practise, to do the duty which all neglect, this we cannot do. And even so it is continually; they go away grieved, for they are young, and they are at school.

"Then Jesus looked round about and said, How hardly shall they that are young enter into the kingdom of God! It is easier for a camel to go through a needle's eye, than for a young man to enter into the kingdom of God. And they were astonished out of measure, saying among themselves, Who then can be saved? And Jesus looking upon them saith, With men it is impossible, but not with God, for with God all things are possible." This is the very real Scripture of the passage as applied to you. What hindered the young man in the story from taking up his cross was his riches; what hinders you, so at least we hear it sometimes said, is your being young and being at school. This is the excuse urged, the extreme difficulty of making the sacrifice required in your actual circumstances, just as the young man found it so difficult in his actual circumstances to sell all that he had. His cross was surely not lighter than ours, but much heavier, but he could not take it up, and he went away grieved, much grieved that he could not be good easily; that the two things which he loved, his duty and his comfort, and which had long been united, were now divided; both he could have no longer, yet it grieved him to part with either. He went away grieving; and surely with a far deeper grief did our merciful Lord look after him as he went away, and see him whom he had loved, him whom he had hoped to love always, now turning to destruction. But did he call after him and say, " Turn back, thou young man, for I love thee still, and if thou wilt not follow me taking up thy cross, follow me without it, when thou wilt and where thou wilt, and no farther." Alas! nothing of the kind. His own way led to Calvary, thither his Father's will called him. He was to bear the cross for us all, not figuratively, but literally. Thither he must go, and thither must those follow him who would be with him for ever. Wherefore he looked round about on those who still remained with him, and said, " How hardly shall they that have riches," — " they that are young and at school," he says to those to whom that is their difficulty, — " how hardly shall they enter into the kingdom of God!" His disciples were astonished at his words, and they are often astonished still; nay, they say, "Youth surely is an excuse, the young cannot serve him fully." But he says again, "And therefore it is easier, if this be so, for a camel to go through a needle's eye, than for a young man to enter into the kingdom of God." Then say we in astonishment beyond measure, "Who then can be saved?" But he answers, "With men it is impossible, but not with God, for with God all things are possible." Yes, if that rich man had not turned away from Christ, but had run up closer to him, and had thrown himself at his feet, crying out and saying with tears, "Lord, I will follow thee; help me to follow thee whithersoever thou goest,"—then surely his gracious Saviour would have beheld him and loved him far more than at first, and would have given him the strength which he needed, and that which was so hard would have been done, and the rich man would have entered into the kingdom of God. The application lies at the door. You have heard Christ's call, to take up your cross and follow him, to serve him always in all things, in small and great, in thought, word, and deed, there most carefully where it costs you most pain to do it. But do not go away grieving, because you are young, and because you are at a place where temptations are many, and faithful steady service of Christ will cost you many a sacrifice. Turn not from him, but to him much rather, with earnest prayer that he who bore his most painful cross for you will enable you to bear your light one for his love ; that he will help you daily, as your trial will come daily ; that his strength may be made perfect in your weakness. And then, though the thing be harder than that a camel should pass through a needle's eye, yet shall it be done. The young and they that are at school, with all their carelessness, with all their difficulties from without as well as from within, they shall enter into the kingdom of God, for so some have entered, and so shall some enter again, and so may all enter who do not turn away from their cross, but ask Christ's grace to help them to bear it.

Harry listened with some interest. Little Willie had fallen asleep, his head in Mary's arms. A part of the time Horace was restless. I think a part of the time he made a horse of his shoe, and used the strings for reins. But he was more quiet than I expected.

Then I took the opportunity, while the baby was asleep, to hear Isabel's Sunday-school lesson. It was in " Lessons on the Parables of the Saviour." Isabel did not know her lesson very well, but I made all the children find the Parable that was the subject of the lesson, in the eighteenth chapter of Luke.

"And he spake this parable unto certain which trusted in themselves that they were righteous, and despised others.

"Two men went up into the temple to pray, the one a Pharisee and the other a publican.

"The Pharisee stood and prayed thus with himself: God, I thank thee that I am not as other men are, extortioners, unjust, adulterers, or even as this publican.

"I fast twice in the week, I give tithes of all that I possess.

"And the publican, standing afar off, would not lift up so much as his eyes unto heaven, but smote upon his breast, saying, God be merciful to me a sinner.

"I tell you, this man went down to his house justified rather than the other; for every one that exalteth himself shall be abased, and he that humbleth himself shall be exalted."

I asked all the children in turn the questions in the Lesson upon this Parable, that they might give what answers they knew best. Harry knew all about the Pharisees and the scribes. When I asked, "Who were those haughty persons that thought themselves righteous and despised others?" Horace said there were a great many at Sunday school, and began to name over some names. Harry laughed, and said he knew of some there too. There was Flora Temple, and some others, who swept by as if there were nobody fit to speak to. And some of the teachers, too, thought themselves righteous, and despised others. He was glad he was not like them!

Clara interrupted Harry, and said, "Take care! you are beginning to be thankful that you are not unjust, as other men are."

Mary said that Miss Grace, who used to be her Sunday-school teacher, used to say that people who prided themselves upon their liberality, often shut themselves up in pride, thanking God that they were not like these other men, and forget-. ting the limits they themselves put upon other people.

But this Harry and Horace did not understand. They had begun to talk of the different people they did not like at school and at Sunday school, and were brought back to the lesson with diffi- culty. On the whole, they gave very good answers to the questions. The subject was insincerity and hypocrisy. And that is what children see through very quickly, and from their own im- pulses despise. Grown-up people, who are not in the habit of being with children, are hardly aware how they fall, in the estimation even of a little child, when they are detected in an untruth. To be in the presence of children is more a test of truth, than to sit constantly opposite a mirror would be. They detect the least deviation, they insist on a clear statement.

Clara's lesson was upon a chapter in the Acts of the Apostles, which they are reading by way of preparation for reading Conybeare's Life of St. Paul. It was in the third chapter of Acts, and she told how Peter and John healed the lame man at the gate of the temple, with the words of Peter: "Silver and gold have I none, but such as I have give I thee." Clara's teacher had told her scholars to bring her some account of others who had imitated Peter and John, and had given not merely silver and gold, but all that they had, for the good of others. Clara had chosen, without consulting anybody, to write a little Life of Elizabeth of Hungary. She was led to do this, because some one, a little while ago, had given her a picture of Elizabeth of Hungary, which represented her holding open her apron filled with roses. And she had been told the legend,— that this princess was filled with such a passion for charity that she gave away all that she had to the poor, until at last her husband forbade her to give any more. But when she heard of the sufferings of the poor people who were famishing around her castle, she could resist no longer, and went out with her apron filled with bread and food from her table, to give to them. On the narrow pathway down the hill from her castle she was met by her husband, who spoke to her roughly, and seized her, and asked her why she had disobeyed his commands. At the same time he opened her apron, and found it filled only with roses! This legend had made Clara anxious to know the real history of Elizabeth of Hungary. We read the little Life that Clara had written, though she would not stay and listen to it, but went to rock the cradle, and to take care of the baby. It was very prettily written, such as a young girl would be likely to write, — with many sentimental words, perhaps, but simply written too. Harry liked it; so did Mary and Isabel.

Then we sang one of the children's hymns, while Isabel played upon the piano, and baby, who had waked up, seemed to like the music.

Mary asked me if I would read a story she had written for the children. "Partly for the children," she said, — and I think partly to help herself. It was called

THE WATCHMAN.

You know how my watch stands at night in the pretty watch-case that papa gave me at New Year's. It hangs in the tower of a little castle, and at the door of the castle stands a little watch-

man, as if to guard the entrance. Every night
my watch hangs in the tower, by my bedside,
where I can see it if I lie awake, and often in
the daytime it rests there too, when I am not
well, and must lie on the bed. It entertains me
sometimes, even when I am in pain, to see how
the hours go by, and I never forget the pleasure
I had at first, when the little watch was first
given me.

The other night I had been lying awake a long
time, very tired of thinking, very tired of lying
awake, wondering if I never should sleep, when,
because I had nothing else to do, I suppose, I
began to listen to the ticking of my watch. It
seems to you, perhaps, that the ticking of a
watch has a great deal of sameness in it, one
tick being very much like another. But then it
sounded to me very like words, as if the watch
were very busily talking, and with the watchman
below. It did not give the watchman much
chance to answer, but ran on, a word a second,
till I fell asleep : —

"Down in the kitchen ! Think of my spending the day in the kitchen ! I did think, when
I heard of it, you might have drawn your sword
in my defence. For, pray, what are you put
there for, except to guard me and my dignity ?
When I heard Mrs. Blake ask Miss Mary to lend
cook her watch, because the kitchen clock had

stopped, I had really half a mind to stop myself. I have done such things when I was younger. At that Christmas party, a year or two ago, when I knew our dear Mary would like to stay for a few more dances, I stopped precisely at nine. And it was hard work, too, for the music set all my cogs going, and I should have liked well enough to have kept time to her feet! Then it was I made her late for the train, when she was coming away from Ferndale. I knew she would like to stay to the afternoon picnic, if she had only a good reason. But those were youthful follies! Now we have a dignity to keep up, and we succeed. Lady's watches! How they are sneered at! I am sure the women keep up with the times more than the men.''

"Pray don't get upon the woman's rights question," interrupted the watchman.

"But down I went to the kitchen, and was on my good behavior. I was determined to set an example for that kitchen clock. It is always behind time, and the potatoes always come on to the table underdone, and dinner at least half a minute behindhand.

"I created an excitement in the kitchen, I can tell you. As I hung over the mantelpiece, the tongs tumbled forward upon their head to see me. An ill-bred pair, those tongs. I observed they were constantly falling out. The

gridiron stood upon its hind legs to grin at me.
And some turnips on the kitchen table absolutely
claimed relationship with me! A difficult place,
you will agree, to maintain one's self-respect,
and go on with one's duties systematically. My
springs were constantly jarred by the voices and
loud laughs of the cook and the chambermaids.
I hope that kitchen clock is made of sterner stuff
than I! I was truly thankful I had my hands
before my face all the time, to hide my blushes.
The iron pots and kettles made such a coarse
noise, too, as they were lifted off the fire, it set
my teeth all on edge. Such unpunctuality, —
never boiling up at the right moment! If one
could only impress upon people what it is to be
a watch, the importance of regulating the time
for others, there would not be so many lost minutes in the world!

"But I suppose there are alleviations in the lowest condition of life, and I was not insensible to
them. The smell of the steak came up refresh-
ingly from the fire, and it was done and taken up
just at the right moment, thanks to my punctual-
ity, which really imposed upon the cook. The
eggs at breakfast were done to a point. You observe that, when time is well regulated, everything
else falls into order too. So cook had time to set
her kitchen to rights, which I have not seen for
many a day. This consciousness of an influence

does something to spread a charm of self-satisfaction over the roughest lot!

"But the marked moment of my morning was when the cook's niece came in. She struck me as soon as I saw her, — a pretty, curly-haired child, with such an air of neatness about her! She discovered me as soon as she came in. 'O, what a pretty little clock!' she exclaimed. Now this touched my vanity! To be a *clock*, that always has been the summit of my ambition. To be able to strike now and then, and express one's self in a way that is listened to. Everybody respects the striking of a clock, and stops to hear what it says, while one might tick on for ever without any notice being taken of it! The notice is taken when we stop ticking. How ungrateful that is! No one praises our regularity, but everybody is ready with their blame if we rest a minute, or our wheels are out of order once in a while!

"But to be a clock in a church-tower, that is what I have sighed for! I like this little tower we rest in because it shows *in little* what I would like to be. Think how grand to strike so that a whole town would hear, — everybody listening! To peal out 'one' o'clock in the middle of the day. Not a word more! Think what restrained power! To stop just at that. Majestically it sounds forth, and all the workmen are listening, and they stop work awhile. It is the middle of the day, and the weathercock on top of the spire shows that the sun is beginning to drop down to its setting. Everybody wonders if he has done half his work, for the last part of the day has sounded out its first hour.

" Then how grand to peal out twelve at midnight, when nobody else is speaking, when there is not a voice to be heard anywhere, — no other voice but this! It marks the middle of the night for the wakeful that are longing for morning, and it startles the guilty wanderer. Nobody else ventures to speak so loud just then. The church-clock has it its own way. But it does its duty ; it would not strike a stroke less, and more none but an Italian clock would think of.

" Then for each separate hour somebody is listening. Some are waiting impatiently for it, some are dreading its approach ; others it wakes up from their busy toil, or out of their indolence. Yet to some one just that hour is dear, and the voice of the clock seems just then musical as timely. Clocks and watches have to thank railroads for giving them more respect than they had in former days. In running to a railway station, nobody cares for a better companion than his watch. And how many eyes are cast up to the church-clock from hasty travellers, who have not time to consult their private watches!

" But my experience of to-day has taught me

a lesson. I am satisfied with my own lot. There are lower positions than ours, and harder fates. I must be thankful for what I do enjoy. And I have learnt content from those whom I thought worse off than I. That kitchen clock is really respectable. It would not look well in the parlor, but I am convinced it does as well as it can. After all, we are all of us dependent upon some one who winds us up.

" I can remember, in my younger days, when Miss Mary and I went about visiting this one here, and that one there. What a gay life we led! We thought it a useful one too. We fancied we were doing a great deal. Now she has to lie still, doing nothing sometimes all day long. And I, too, have to keep quiet; yet I feel that it is just as important to be regular with my time, as when we felt we must be at a certain place precisely at a certain hour. Perhaps, after all, that was not as important as we thought it. Perhaps the duties we performed then were not so great in value as the patience we practise now. I used to tick on as regularly as I could, but so taken up with what was going on, that I never thought about the hours till some clock struck them for me. Now I watch the hours as they go by, and learn the value of a single minute.

" At first, this seemed a weary business, but now that we learn it is our business, we try not to do it wearily. I am thankful that I am still wound up regularly every night, and never have to stand still from forgetfulness; and it is a pleasure to keep my time regularly and truly, and cheerfully too. Nobody can accuse me of an indolent expression in my ticking ——"

The voice went on, and I could not tell if it were the watch speaking, or I thinking, — thinking that I, too, ought to be grateful, even if I were dependent upon others for my "winding up." I cannot go about of my own will, much more than my little watch. But I need not envy the days when I used to go about as the rest of you do, for I have still my own time to keep, with patience and regularity.

And I have such a pleasant home to rest in, and cared for by friends, and cheered by children's voices. And my watchman? I went to sleep offering up my heart and soul into the care of Him who slumbers not nor sleeps.

———————

After we had listened to Mary's story, which the children heard, laughingly at first, and afterwards interestedly, Harry took a book to read, " Tom Brown's School Days at Rugby."

Horace took Willie up to Mary's watch-case to see if the watch would say anything to them. and then came down, and asked for a book to show Willie some pictures. They had a noisy time over these, but not an angry time, as these two boys do sometimes when they are left together. Horace is too fond of teasing his little brother, but to-day he seemed more subdued, and exerted himself to entertain Willie. Meanwhile I had a few minutes' quiet talk with Mary.

Mr. Blake came home at noon. There was such a storm, the church was to be closed for the afternoon. We did not have a very quiet afternoon. The children were restless, baby and all; the baby would not leave me, and Willie was tired, and Horace troubled him. Towards the end of the afternoon, Harry came to ask me if I would not read something more to him; he should not care if it was a sermon, and he was tired of reading by himself. The baby was so unwilling to leave me, that I persuaded Isabel to read to Harry, and they went into a corner, and read another of Dr. Arnold's sermons that I chose for them, one that had some striking pictures in it, which I thought might touch a boy.

CHRIST'S CRUCIFIXION.

" And the people stood beholding." — Luke xxiii. 85.

It was our Lord upon the cross whom they were beholding, and they who so beheld him were the mixed multitude which, with all sorts of feelings, poured out of the walls of Jerusalem to see the spectacle. And so it is still; Christ is crucified among us daily, and the people stand beholding.

They stand beholding, an infinite variety of persons with an infinite variety of feelings, even as the multitude who then stood around his cross. There was his mother, and there was his beloved disciple; there was the centurion; there were the women of his acquaintance, and the women of Jerusalem generally; there were the Roman soldiers, there were the common Jews, there were the rulers and chief priests and scribes, beholding as they thought the accomplishment of their work. These beheld him, standing around or at a little distance from his cross. Nor were there wanting others who beheld him, themselves being to mortal eyes invisible, the angels of God, who looked with awe and adoration upon that infinite display of God's love. They too are beholding him now, crucified as he is again daily amongst us.

We may, if we will, apply this in two ways;

we may apply it to ourselves, this present congregation, at this present season, beholding, so to speak, the representation of Christ crucified in the services of this week, and in the communion of next Sunday. In this sense it may be said, " The people stand beholding him." Or again we may apply it to ourselves, still to this present congregation, in another sense; as beholding Christ crucified, not in the historical representation of it given in the Scriptures, and read out to us in the Church services; but actually, according to the language of the Epistle to the Hebrews, in the sins which his people are daily committing; we standing and looking on the while, and regarding it very differently some of us from others.

And lastly, if I may so speak, we behold Christ crucified in yet another sense: we each are guilty of sin, we each look upon ourselves thus sinning and having sinned with a great variety of feelings; our minds do not always keep the same temper; in one and the same heart, as various moods prevail, there is sorrow, there is seriousness, there is indifference, there is even hatred and scorn; another aspect of the words contained in the text, " And the people stood beholding."

Now, in the first place, let us apply the words to ourselves, and to the services of this week. Already the sufferings and death of our Lord have been brought before us in the Lessons, and in the

Gospel of this day; then on Wednesday, when we usually assemble in this place, they will be brought before us again; and yet again on Friday. We know that the Gospel for every day in this week is taken from the Scriptures which describe our Lord's death; the Epistle and some of the Lessons also more or less exclusively relate to it. The mere outward and formal difference of this week cannot escape the observation of the most careless; we cannot but distinguish it from other weeks. Therefore the representation of Christ crucified is set before us: we stand beholding, more or less attentively indeed, and with more or less of interest, but we all stand beholding.

Amongst those who stood round his actual cross, there were, as we have seen, great varieties. There was our Lord's mother, and his beloved disciple John, and there were the chief priests and scribes; there were thus the very extremes of love and of hatred. Each of these in anything like the same intenseness cannot be supposed to exist here: who of us loves him as his mother and as St. John loved him? Who of us hates him as the chief priests hated him? But between these extremes were there not still great differences? The women of Jerusalem weeping with compassion; the centurion observing seriously and fairly; the Roman soldiers car-

ing for nothing but to get each man their share
of his raiment; the scornful multitude who said,
"Let be, let us see whether Elias will come and
save him." Have we not amongst ourselves resemblances at least of all these? Have we not
some who feel that he suffered for us? Have we
not some who think seriously? have we not some
who think only of what outward good things they
get from him, food and clothing, and pleasure of
every sort? nay, have we not some also who have
heard and have listened and will not heed, — who
know what sin is, yet sin deliberately, — who put
conscience aside, and turn away from Christ's
Spirit in defiance? Some of all these kinds of
persons, God only knows how strongly bearing
the character of any or in what proportions to
one another, are surely here this day, beholding
the Church's yearly representation of Christ crucified. Let each ask himself, which character is
his own.

But one thing I will say. Those whom I compared to the Roman soldiers, to the soldiers who
were sitting beneath the cross casting lots for our
Lord's raiment; those whom I fear I must suppose to be a large portion of our number, who
sit here to-day, and will sit here on Wednesday,
and on Friday, utterly unconcerned in what is
going on, thinking only as they think always, of
something to be enjoyed, or some pleasant thing

to be done, or unpleasant thing to be avoided,—
of something, in short, very near them, in their
hands, or within their near view, something worldly, something in which God and God's service
have no part at all;—all these persons have by
no means the same excuse for their indifference
which the Roman soldiers had for theirs.   Christ
is not to them wholly unknown, as he was to those
soldiers; their teaching, let them have derived
ever so little good from it, has been far more than
ever fell to the lot of those poor Romans.   We
have noticed from time to time, in the course of
our common studies, how miserable was the moral education which could be gained at that time
among the heathens, even by those whose circumstances were most favorable.   What do we think
it must have been for the common soldiers of the
legions? what had been the lessons of their childhood or youth, what the experience of their manhood ? Not in vain, depend upon it, were holy
names spoken to you from your earliest years;
and you were told of God and Christ, and heav-
en and hell ; and were taught to pray,—ay, and
have prayed sometimes, I doubt not, even the
very most careless and most ignorant of you all.
Nor yet is it in vain that these same lessons are
still repeated to you here ; let it be repeated ever
so imperfectly, ever so scantily ; let it be that such
teaching is but as one little drop amidst streams

of an opposite power, still you cannot get rid of the fact that you have had more than a heathen's teaching; the very walls of this building, meeting your eyes as they do every day, are themselves a witness; your sin in sitting in perfect carelessness as it were beneath Christ's cross, and thinking only of your earthly pleasures and inconveniences, must be far greater than the sin of those soldiers who cast lots for Christ's raiment.

And now let us apply the text in its second sense. We stand beholding Christ crucified, not to-day only, nor Wednesday, nor Friday only, nor beholding him in the Scripture representation of what he suffered once on Calvary; but every day beholding him crucified afresh,—I speak the language of the Epistle to the Hebrews,—crucified afresh in the sins that are committed amongst us; committed amongst us, I am saying now, not committed by ourselves individually. I am considering how we look upon the sin which is done daily within our sight and knowledge by those amongst whom we are living. Again, have not we resemblances of those different sorts of persons who stood around the cross? I should be very sorry to think that no one beheld Christ thus crucified with sorrow, that none so much as beheld with serious attention. Can it be really that the many sorts of evil, the want of positive good being one of the very worst of all, which present themselves to us every day, should be to all of us a matter of absolute indifference? Consider that, so far as we are not such a society as Christ's people will be hereafter in heaven, so far sin is corrupting us, and dishonoring our Lord. Of course I know that there are some things in which, without any fault of ours, our condition cannot be what that of Christ's people will be when they are with him. So far as bodily pain affects us, brought on by no fault of ourselves or others, so far as sickness makes us uncomfortable, or the innocent troubles of our friends, or their being taken away from us, so far I grant Christ's truest people on earth will ever be different from his people in heaven. But set aside these things, and what differences remain are surely differences caused by sin; differences caused by want of faith, want of hope, want of purity, want of truth, want of meekness, want of love; differences caused by unbelief, by indifference, by greediness; by falsehood, by pride, by hardness and the love of giving pain, by slothfulness and selfishness. Can it be that we see ourselves so different from what Christ's people should be, and that not one of us thinks seriously about it, not one of us grieves for it? It is but too certain that many do not care about it in the least; nay, it is to be feared that here we have really something like the very feeling of the chief priests and scribes, who looked on upon the sight of Christ crucified, and rejoiced at it. I am afraid that some almost take a pleasure in the state of sin which they see around them, at least that they would and do oppose and view with suspicion and dislike all attempts to make it better. Even to this hour, after so many years' experience, my astonishment at this is as fresh as ever; I wonder, and ever shall wonder, I hope, not that there are some who do evil, but that there are so many who do not hate it when done by others. I can understand our being over-indulgent to our own faults; I can understand that self-love should get the better of conscience; or that, a great temptation being before us, we should be found often to yield to it. But that sin should not be hateful when there is no self-love to blind us; that evil should not be abhorred even when no temptation is present; this does seem to me very wonderful and very shocking. It seems to show an habitual and deliberate turning away from Christ, which really reminds one of the rancor of the chief priests, or at any rate of those who said, " We will not have this man to reign over us." It says that the common state of our minds is one of apostasy; that when no particular temptation is present, in cool blood, as it were, and constantly, we look upon Christ crucified among us, and we

20*

are absolutely without a single wish that it should not be so.

It is but too certain that, as long as we care not to see Christ crucified by others, so long we shall never be careful not to crucify him ourselves. This was the last point which I spoke of: how differently at different times we behold him crucified as it were in our own hearts by our own sin, sometimes, I trust, being penitent, and sometimes being serious, but more commonly, I fear, being careless, and sometimes being hard and wilfully rebellious. Now it may be that one who hates evil very sincerely may yet sometimes, under strong temptation, yield to it: he may grieve to see Christ crucified by others, and yet may crucify him by his own sin. This is not hypocrisy, but human weakness, which does not bring its practice fully up to the level of its principles, even though it holds the principles most truly. But who will care for evil in himself, being tempted to it, when he does not care for it in another, where he has no temptation to make him tolerant of it? Who will scruple to commit a sin himself when he has occasion, if he sees the sin committed by others with entire indifference? Who will shrink from lying, or from any other sin, in his own person, if these things give him no disgust when he sees them in another? It is quite certain that he cannot hate them, and not hating sin, it is quite certain that he cannot love God.

"The people," says the Evangelist, "who came together to that sight, beholding the things which were done, smote their breasts and returned." The soldiers were indifferent, the chief priests triumphant; but the general feeling was sorrow; when they had seen that all was over, the multitude in general, who had stood beholding, smote their breasts and returned. We know not how soon the impression melted away again from many of them; but for the time, at least, it was general, and with many we may believe that it was lasting. O that it might be so with us, in either of the applications of the text which I have been making! that from our sight of Christ crucified, as represented in this week's solemn services, or as daily and every week set forth in the sin committed all around us, or by ourselves, the generality of us might turn away truly grieving! that from that sight, under whatever form exhibited to us, we might derive a hatred of sin with all our hearts and souls, whenever we see it in others, or in ourselves! I do not say for an instant "hatred of those in whom sin is," for as we certainly shall never hate ourselves, so neither should we hate others in whom sin may be manifested; but the sin itself, whether in ourselves or others, we should hate with a perfect hatred;.

for the strength of that hatred of sin is the exact measure of the strength of our love of Christ. We should hate it and make war upon it unceasingly, to destroy it utterly out of all our coasts; for this is the lesson of the destruction of the Canaanites with all that belonged to them, — that we should hold no intercourse with it, make no peace with it, allow it not the least harbor amongst us, that, having overcome that deadly enemy which crucified and crucifies our Lord continually, we may turn to him with joy, and share with him in the glory of his resurrection.

I was very tired towards night, when Clara came and whispered to me. She thought, if I left the room a little while, the baby would be quiet with her, and she had made a little fire in the air-tight stove in my room, if I would only go up and rest myself. I came up into my room, and found it quiet and warm. Clara had drawn an easy chair up to the fire, and a little table, on which she had placed my favorite books. It was very still and peaceful here, and I had a little time for thought. And I gave thanks. And I laid off, for a little while, the responsibility that hangs above me so constantly with regard to my children. Surely they were not worse than other people's children. Because I loved them better, I am anxiously conscious of all their faults, and feel myself to blame for them, but how much there is in them to give me hope! How thoughtful and unexpected was this little act of Clara's! She is the gay one of the family. From one week's end to the other, she keeps us laughing with her fun, and seems filled only with the joy of life. But lately I have seen some very pleasing traits in the midst of her apparent thoughtlessness. There is a generosity in all the little things she does, and a sensibility to the little troubles of others. Indeed, let me in future look to these encouraging traits in my children. Of late, perhaps, I have been weighed down too much by the care of them, not joining in their joy, or growing young in their youth. Let me in future leave the care of them in the hands of God, and trust that he has given them to me for a blessing. And for my boys! If Christ shall ask of them to drink of his cup, and be baptized with his baptism, may I hear them answer, and may I too, be willing to hear them answer, " We are able!"

ST. JOHN'S DAY.*

"Peter, seeing him, saith to Jesus, Lord, and what shall this man do? Jesus saith unto him, If I will that he tarry till I come, what is that to thee? follow thou me."

Lord, and what shall this man do?
  Ask'st thou, Christian, for thy friend?
If his love for Christ be true,
  Christ hath told thee of his end.
This is he whom God approves,
This is he whom Jesus loves.

Ask not of him more than this;
  Leave it in his Saviour's breast,
Whether, early called to bliss,
  He in youth shall find his rest,
Or arméd in his station wait
Till his Lord be at the gate.

Whether in his lonely course
  (Lonely, not forlorn) he stay,
Or with love's supporting force
  Cheat the toil and cheer the way,—
Leave it all in His high hand,
Who doth hearts as streams command.

Gales from heaven, if so he will,
  Sweeter melodies can wake
On the lonely mountain rill
  Than the meeting waters make;
Who hath the Father and the Son
May be left, but not alone.

---

* Keble.

Sick or healthful, slave or free,
  Wealthy or despised and poor, —
What is that to him or thee,
  So his love to Christ endure?
When the shore is won at last,
Who will count the billows past?

Only, since our souls will shrink
  At the touch of natural grief,
When our earthly loved ones sink,
  Send us, Lord, thy sure relief;
Patient hearts, their pain to see,
And thy grace, to follow thee.

THE SIXTH STORMY SUNDAY.

THE BIBLE.

"Stars are poor books, and oftentimes do miss;
This book of stars lights to eternal bliss."

HERBERT.

21

THE SIXTH STORMY SUNDAY.

THE BIBLE.

HERE are six stormy Sundays that we have had in succession, and to-day I was particularly disappointed that I could not go to church, for our friend Mr. R. was to preach for us, and was spending the Sunday with us. My friend Anna, who is staying with me for a few days, and who had depended, too, upon hearing Mr. R. preach, was much disappointed. Last night we looked out upon a bright starlight, and were hoping for a pleasant Sunday at last. But in the night the storm rose; we heard the wind blowing the snow against the panes of glass of the window, as though it would dash them through. This morning we found the house more blocked up than it has been all winter. Mr. R. and George looked out in dismay, and George early began his efforts in bringing round the sleigh and the horse, through the heavy drifts, from the stable to the house door. This was accomplished at last, and in due season before the hour for the church services, that they might have plenty of time to fight their way through the snow to church. At first Anna and I insisted that we would go, too; but we were plainly shown that we should be in the way, and nothing but a burden, and that George and the horse would have as much as they could do to get "the minister" to church in season. So we bade them good by for the day, for they would not return till night. We watched them for some time, for the sleigh was overturned three times, and I thought they would have to give up their efforts to pierce through the drifts. At last they disappeared from sight, and we turned away from the window, Anna very despondingly. "I do not understand," she exclaimed, "how you have been able to survive five quiet, solitary, stormy Sundays! I must confess I should find it very hard. I am afraid at the last I should be sighing for my knitting!"

Then Anna went on to say she should find it very hard to read what were called "good" books all day long. She liked the services at church, she liked summer Sundays, when the quiet and beauty of nature suggested a quiet and beautiful peace within. But this succession of stormy Sundays, — was not it very dreary?

I told her I had found it difficult to occupy the time heartily and happily. But I thought some

of her complaints should be charged to a retired
life, to having my house so far away from other
people, rather than to the fact of its being Sunday. If I had five stormy weeks that kept me
away from the rest of the world, I should find
my week-day occupations, however varied they
might be, grow monotonous and dreary without
the zest of interruption. But I should not like
to say that my resources were not equal to five
separate, uninterrupted Sundays, — my resources
of a library and my own thoughts, — that I should
be reduced to knitting or sewing, which I am not
fond of doing week days, and, on the other hand,
am glad to be relieved from.

Anna confessed that the novelty of sewing on
Sunday might give it a charm that it did not have
to her on other days. "Perhaps," said she, "it
is the sighing after a forbidden fruit, sour though
the fruit may be." Then she asked how much I
read of the Old Testament on such days, and we
fell to talking of how much or how little it is read
now-a-days. Anna said she had found very little
interest in the Old Testament; that it seemed to
her to present a picture of a God such as she
could not comprehend, — cruel and unjust; that
the lives that were held up to be the lives of good
men were far from being immaculate and pure;
that she could not look upon it as a book to be
read every day as a lesson for her own daily life,

because, at best, it was a history of people who lived long ago, and under less light than we are living in now.

I agreed with her somewhat in this last, but I asked her if she had come at this impression through her own reading of the Old Testament. She said that she had not; that indeed she had read the Old Testament very little. She remembered hearing it read aloud in her childhood, and liking the history of Joseph; the greater part of what she had read then, had left little impression upon her. But lately she had read a great many of the books that discussed the inspiration of the Bible, and she more and more wondered that it should be bound up with the life of Christ, and she found it impossible to waken any interest in it.

" There are the Psalms," I said; " certainly they contain very beautiful poetry."

" Yes," she said. " But in the midst of the Psalms, in the midst of the most beautiful poetry, are the prayers of David against his enemies, that seem to me savage and cruel."

" The prayers may be savage and cruel," I said, " especially to us, who are taught to forgive our enemies. Yet perhaps many in our times might not spare the lives of their enemies, as David spared the life of his greatest enemy when he was thrown into his hands, as you remember."

"No, I don't remember," Anna said; "and my impression of the Psalms is vague, as I heard them read at a school, where we read on, day after day, in a mechanical way, from the Old Testament. 'Strong bulls of Bashan have beset me round.' I remember that verse struck me once. Of what sort of use could that verse be to me?"

"I remember," I said, "that it is from a Psalm that always impressed me very much, because the first words of it are the words with which Christ cried out in agony upon the cross, 'My God, my God, why hast thou forsaken me?' I have often read the rest of the Psalm, wondering if at that moment there might not have presented itself to Jesus some of the words that follow: 'Our fathers trusted in thee, they trusted, and thou didst deliver them; they cried unto thee, and were delivered, they trusted in thee, and were not confounded. But I am a worm, and no man, a reproach of men, and despised of the people. All they that see me laugh me to scorn; they shoot out the lip, they shake the head, saying, He trusted on the Lord that he would deliver him; let him deliver him, seeing that he delighteth in him. . . . . . They part my garments among them, and cast lots upon my vesture. But be not thou far from me, O Lord! O my strength, haste thee to help me!' It seems so natural that the scene

before him should have called to him words that
seemed to describe it. And this is a way that
the Old Testament is to me connected with the
life of Christ; because, from all his teachings,
we can see that he learnt something himself from
' the Scriptures.' "

"If only," said Anna, " we had not been made
to read the Old Testament in such a mechanical
way."

I thought perhaps I had been very fortunate in
that way. I reminded Anna of the interest we
had felt in ·Mrs. Child's book, of the Religious
Ideas of Different Nations.

" Yes," said Anna, " I was glad to read that;
it told me a great deal I did not know. It is
very curious to read the early history of those
old nations."

" I have felt that interest too," I said. " It
seemed as if one might learn something of the
nature of religion by tracing it up to its earliest
sources, and I had always seized hold of such
histories with a particular eagerness. Often I
had begun to read carefully of the old Hindoo
faith. But in the history of this, and in other
similar histories, I had met with one great difficulty. I was sorry to say they had grown *dull*.
After a while, Vishnu and Siva, Devi and Krish-
na, Brahmin and Buddhist, even mingle themselves in my mind. The account interests me

awhile for a study, in some of its singular coincidences, but it does not keep its hold on me, and I never get beyond a certain point with it. I can study it for a while, but it does not leave any powerful impression upon my mind. Now, the history of the Hebrew religion, as told in the Old Testament, affects me very differently. That is represented as it existed in the lives of men and women. We pass over the long account of the laws and their details, by which they were commanded to live, to read how far they were able to preserve these laws in their hearts and their lives. Very full of faults were these lives, full of the sins of their times and of their own sins, but they wonderfully preserve in them the belief in the one God. This belief, alas! failed often to control their lives, as we allow our Christian faith to fail us in our daily duties, because we make it a thing apart from ourselves, — a form, and not a life. David offers a heart-felt prayer to God, forgets God when the hour of temptation comes, and then again pours out a strain of remorseful penitence for his sin. We look down upon this, as we shall some day look back upon the course of our own lives, as last summer we looked down from the high mountain on the hills and valleys below. We saw the little lake, lying far below us; above it rose the little cloud that had formed itself from its vapors; the cloud lay

far below us too, and at a distance, on the green
fields by the side of the lake, lay the shadow of
its cloud. We see the purity, the sin that followed, and then the shadow of the sin, in its
remorse."

On the whole, Anna and I agreed very nearly
in our opinion of the Old Testament. We thought
it far more imposing, not considered as a verbal
inspiration of God, but as an account of man's
idea of him, the human history of God's revelation to man. And it is to me more valuable, as
presenting the history of the nation from which
Christ came into the world, and thus forming a
necessary introduction to his life. The first
chapters of Matthew and Luke are taken up with
the genealogy of Jesus Christ, as though a long
list of names were necessary to found or exalt
his claims. For us who look upon the bright
light that comes down through the eighteen hundred years from him, this light illumines the history behind, and gives it some of his glory. As
in the pictures of the Nativity, the light from the
child streams upon the wise men just leaving the
background, and upon the shepherds round the
manger.

To me the life of David loses very much of its
interest after he becomes a king, — prosperity is
a heavier temptation than his adversity. And
throughout the Old Testament there must needs

be passages of unequal interest, details of forms of customs that have long ago lost their vitality, lists of the names of inefficient kings that forgot their God. But these indeed form but a small part of the whole history. For our own personal advancement in religion, to help us in our daily trials and temptations, we may not find assistance in the lives of those who saw in God a stern and severe judge. Yet in their aspirations we find a common bond of sympathy. Dante gives them a place in Paradise as "Christians about to be," and perhaps we can trace in them a faith in something purer than they found in their own lives, that gives a fire to their devotion. Certainly some of the prayers and utterances of the Psalms and the Prophecies have something in them which warms us who have strayed away from · Christ.

At any rate, we need not be more prejudiced against it by the superstitious and mechanical way in which it has been sometimes regarded, than we are influenced by the devotional feeling which it has awakened in many others. However it has been regarded by others, we ought, as we ought from all other things, to create our own life, not bound, not prejudiced by others, yet willing to receive what light they will give.

We may speculate as we will upon the authority of the Old Testament, study its character and its teachings according to the bent of our intellectual constitution; speculations on this and other subjects akin to it may serve as food and occupation for the starving and waste hours of our mind. For our guidance in our every-day lives we need the inspiration that was in the life of Christ; through him can we come to the Father, the Father who was imperfectly conceived in the Hebrew faith.

Christ found encouragement in the lives of the men whom his nation revered. The prophets, whose words he heard in the humble synagogue of his home, were familiar to him in his childish days. He lingered in the temple to hear and learn of them, when his life was opening upon him. He used their words when the hour of temptation came, to put back the tempter from his soul. And already he must have become intimate with their spirits, before Moses and Elias appeared to him on the mountain of the transfiguration.

We read, Anna and I, two sermons by F. D. Maurice. He has brought out from the passages of the Old Testament, which he read as fixed "lessons of the day," lessons which he has made appropriate to the present day, and has given a vitality to what might become a dead form.

DAVID THE SHEPHERD AND THE OUTLAW.

"He chose David also his servant, and took him away from the sheepfolds; as he was following the ewes great with young ones, He took him, that he might feed Jacob his people, and Israel his inheritance." — Psalm lxxviii. 70, 71.

Objectors to the history of the Old Testament have dwelt much upon the title, " the man after God's own heart," which is given so continually to David. " Is he not," they have said, " directly charged with adultery and murder, — murder of a very base kind and for the basest purpose? Are there not passages in his life recorded without condemnation, which are indefensible upon any moral principles which we acknowledge? Do not some of his worst acts belong to his later years, when one would have expected to see his passions subdued, his higher qualities matured and perfected? Is this the man whom a righteous God would declare to be the object of his especial complacency? What must we think of the book which teaches us to believe that he was thus regarded? What impressions must it leave upon us of the Divine character, what possible help can it afford us in forming our own? "

Divines have very often met these questions with an answer of this kind. " The epithet which you complain of," they have said, " belongs to David, not personally, but officially.

He was called out by God to restore the kingdom which Saul had destroyed, to subdue the Philistines and the surrounding nations, to raise up a family of kings of the tribe of Judah. These purposes he accomplished. He did the work which he was appointed to do. He fulfilled God's counsel. So far he was a man after God's own heart. His moral delinquencies are recorded, that we may know where the Divine approbation stops short."

I believe that this explanation never satisfied the minds of those who availed themselves of it. I am sure that it never satisfied the mind of any simple or devout reader. The notion of official virtue belongs to a very low code of ethics indeed. In a very artificial state of society we sometimes separate the workman from the work; we speak of that as done faithfully and honestly, while he is unfaithful and dishonest. The possibility of such a separation undoubtedly exists; but we all know that it is one of the greatest and most frightful anomalies that it should exist; we all long for the time when it shall exist no longer. Statesmen possessing no high-flown morality, trained in the school of party politics, have rejected the vulgar distinction between the bad man and the bad king, as inconsistent with experience. Lying, the great sin of the individual, has been proved to be the fatal sin of the monarch, that which makes all aptitude for business, all clearness of perception, all skill in devising theories, even higher qualities than these, practically inefficient, or positively mischievous. How then can a believer in the Bible transfer to it a habit of thinking which we are trying to banish from common life? How can he imagine that the book which he holds to be essentially true, should sanction and consecrate one of our most pernicious falsehoods?

A very little reflection upon the words themselves, still more a slight study of the history of David, should surely have prevented any man from resorting to *this* kind of apology. "God," we hear again and again in Scripture, "trieth the reins." That general principle is applied expressly to the case of David. The Lord said to Samuel, when he was about to anoint the eldest son of Jesse, " Man looketh on the outward appearance ; but the Lord looketh on the heart." What can be so direct a contradiction of this statement, as the notion that David was after God's own heart, because he did certain outward acts which were in conformity with the Divine mind and pleasure? And surely if there is a man in the sacred history or in any history whom it is impossible to think of merely as an official actor, that man is the shepherd-boy who became king of Israel. There is no one who has so marked a personality, no one with whose inward life and struggles we are so well acquainted. Whatever he is, we feel that his whole mind and will are thrown into the words which he speaks and the deeds which he does. And in no life are the king and the man so entirely and inseparably blended. In his highest raptures, in the utterances of his greatest anguish, we are reminded continually that he is to become a king, or that he is one. On the other hand, his sins are not treated as what we call, in our artificial nomenclature, private sins; they are the sins of a king, affecting multitudes besides himself. As such they are denounced, as such they are punished.

I think it must have been the obviousness of this fact in the Scriptural records, which misled the commentators into this dangerous method of justifying them. They saw that David was spoken of as intended by God for a king, while he was a shepherd-boy. They perceived that all his various and romantic adventures were preparing him for a throne; they were struck with the consciousness, in his own mind, of a destiny and a work which were to be accomplished. They could not but be aware, that everything which was greatest, best, purest, in him, had reference to a divine mission which he was to execute for his country. They could not be mistaken that he was educated for a special office. Unhappily they forgot to ask themselves what the education for such an office implied, what we are actually told about it in the Bible. Had they followed the guidance of the history for which they were trying to make ingenious excuses, they might have found how truly the education of the divine king was the education of a man; they might have come to understand what it was in the old days to be a man after God's own heart, what it is in our days; they might have attained through that knowledge to a far deeper sense of the nature and cause of David's sins, to a more earnest repentance for their own. Some of these blessings may, I hope, come to us, my brethren, while we seek to understand the nature of David's discipline. I shall confine myself this afternoon to the years which he passed before the death of Saul, the period which is indicated by the words of the text. The time of his actual government, described in the following sentence, " So he fed them with a faithful and true heart, and ruled them prudently with all his power," I reserve for another occasion.

When I speak of David as having the consciousness of a divine calling or mission in every period of his life, I do not mean that he was haunted in the sheepfolds with dreams of some great honor to come upon him hereafter. Those to whom such dreams come, are commonly impatient of the mean position in which they find themselves. What I apprehend he felt was, that he had a call to the work in which he was then engaged. He must have believed that the God of his fathers, He and no other, had appointed him to take care of the few sheep in the wilderness which Jesse had trusted him with. A strange thought, that the tasks which fell to him because he was the youngest son of the house, could be tasks in which the Most High God, who filled heaven and earth, interested himself. But it was *the* thought which made David's life tolerable to him, the only one which could have enabled him to work without becoming the slave of his work. The shepherd's life brought him into wide, open plains, to hill-sides that were lonely by day as well as night. How awful to feel himself there, him the poor shepherd, an atom amidst the infinity of nature! But an atom which breathed, which thought, which, in the depth of its nothingness, felt that it was higher and more wonderful than the universe, which was able, and sometimes seemed ready, to crush it. Shepherd-boy, what art thou? Child of the covenant, what art thou? Fearful questions, to which the hills and skies could give no answer. But the boy pursued his task. He led the sheep to their pastures, he took them to the streams, he followed them into thickets and ravines where they had lost themselves. These poor, silly creatures were worthy of David's diligence. And then the answer came, " The Lord is *my* shepherd ; I shall not want. He maketh *me* to lie down in green pastures. He leadeth *me* beside the still waters. He leadeth me in the paths of righteousness. Yea, though I walk through the valley of the shadow of death, I will fear no evil ; for Thou art with me. Thy rod and Thy staff, they strengthen me." What a revelation to the soul of a youth! A Guide near him, with him, at every moment, — as actual a guide as he was to the sheep ; a guide who must watch over a multitude of separate souls, as he watched over each separate sheep, who must care to bind them together in one, as he cared to bring the sheep into the same fold!

Let us not suppose for an instant that David, as he practised these duties and meditated upon them, gained some fine metaphors respecting the relations of faithful men to their Creator, which afterwards served to make him the poet of Israel. These thoughts and the shepherd life did bring forth that divine poetry, just because they were so intensely real, and because it was so intensely real. They sprung out of intense anxieties respecting himself. What had such anxieties to do with metaphors? His thoughts associated themselves with the humblest toils. What had they to do with metaphors? His meditations were upon the I AM, upon Him before whom Moses hid his face, who spoke in thunders upon Sinai. How dared he make Him a subject for metaphors? When God taught David to think of Him as a shepherd, He took away that cold cloud-drapery with which we are wont to invest Him; He brought him into contact with His actual presence and government. And do not fancy that, because this apprehension was direct and personal, it was narrow and local. Then, when he could think of God as one nigh and not afar off; then, when he could believe that He cared for him and cared for each of his brethren; then he could look up into the open sky with wonder, but without trembling, and say, "When I behold thy heavens, the work of thy hands, the moon and the stars which thou hast ordained; Lord, what is man that thou art mindful of him, and the son of man that thou visitest him? Thou hast made him a little lower than the angels, thou hast crowned him with glory and honor. Thou madest him to have dominion over the works of thy hands, — all sheep and oxen, yea, and the beasts of the field. O Lord, our Lord, how excellent is thy name in all the earth!" Then first all nature could sympathize with him, could call forth instead of crushing the energies of his own heart. For the heavens, as they shone clear and bright before him after a long night-watching, declared the glory of the God who was his shepherd ; the firmament showed His handiwork. Day unto day, and night unto night, uttered speech and showed knowledge. The sun came out of his bridal chamber, he went forth as a giant rejoicing to run his race, carrying a message to all nations concerning One whose law converted the soul of man, whose statutes made wise the simple.

This was a hidden education, the education of a young man's heart. But it was cultivating the seeds which were to bring forth fruits in manly acts. Here we are told, in David's words, of some of the earliest of those fruits. "Thy servant kept his father's sheep, and there came a lion and a bear and took a lamb out of the flock. And I went out after him and smote him and delivered it out of his mouth. And when he arose against me, I caught him by the beard and slew him." David was learning the secret of invisible strength, what it is, and where and how it works. So there grew in him a scorn of that which lies in bulk and looks terrible to the eye. If the bear and the lion came out against one of his flock, it was his business to encounter them. And seeing that he was a man, made in God's image, made a little lower than the angels, tho child of God's covenant, he could use the dominion that God had given to his race. The strength was not his. In that first battle, as in every one he was to fight hereafter, the Lord of Hosts was with him, the God of Jacob was his helper.

The story tells us that there came to the house of Jesse an old man, whom all knew to be a prophet; that he came upon a strange errand, which he scarcely understood himself,—to anoint one of the sons of that family; that the eldest passed before him, and that the prophet was struck by his look and stature, and would have poured the oil on his head; that he was told that the Lord did not look on the outward appearance, but tried the heart; that the other sons all passed by; that one was missing (he being the youngest, and with the sheep); that when this youth, ruddy and fair to look upon, came in, Samuel was bidden to rise and anoint him.

Here was the sign that all the inward discipline and preparation of David had an object, another object than merely to make him a faithful keeper of sheep, or even a wise and righteous man. But a divine sign is not a mere ceremony. It would be deceitful and insincere if there were not a present blessing denoted by it, the communication of an actual power to fit the man for tasks to which he has not hitherto been appointed. From that day forward, we are told, the Spirit of God came upon David. There was a power within him stirring him to thoughts and acts which connected him directly with Israelites, with human beings. Yet with this new calling, with the consciousness of this new power, he still returned to his old work. It was his till some clear summons drew him from it. It had not lost its sacredness, it could still impart wisdom to one who sought wisdom. There is a time in men's lives, before they enter upon some great work to which they have been consecrated, a time when they are permitted to look back upon the years which they have already past, to see them no longer as fragments, but as linked together, as having a divine purpose running through them which makes even their incoherences and discords intelligible. In such a time of retrospection, when the future is seen mirrored in the past, David may have found his harp much more than the mere solace of lonely hours, the mere response to his inward sorrows and thanksgivings. He may have begun to know that he was speaking for other men as well as for himself; that there were close and intimate fibres uniting men utterly unlike and separated by tracts of time and space; that there is some mysterious source of these sympathies, some living Centre who holds together the different portions of each man's life, and in whom there is a general human life, of which all may partake. The Spirit of God which had taken possession of David may have been teaching him these lessons and inspiring the song which was the utterance of them, before he was prepared to come forth as the actual deliverer. And that Spirit will assuredly have been preparing him for his after conflicts, by making him feel that he had, even then, enemies most fierce to struggle with, subjects most turbulent to subdue. The invisible God does not make known to man that he is his Shepherd, without making known to him also that there are invisible powers more fearful than bears and lions, which would tear his flock asunder, which would bring each separate sheep into the valley of the shadow of death. It may be true that the Psalms of David which speak most of enemies belong to a later period than this, when he was wrestling with flesh and blood; but those Psalms would not have been what they are, they would not have expressed the fears and confidence of suffering people in all times, if the writer of them had not been trained to perceive what are the real and universal foes of God's creatures, before he had to engage with those who were tormenting him and his people.

The passage of the Book of Samuel which describes the battle of David with Goliath, is called

by some of the wise men in our day a fragment
from the heroic legends of the Hebrew people.
I suppose this phraseology conveys some new and
striking impression to the minds of those who
use it, or it could not have become so popular as
it is, here and elsewhere. I confess the old childish notion of a battle between a man with shield
and buckler. and greaves of brass, and a youth
with a ruddy countenance who went forth with
his sling and stone in the name of the Lord God
of Israel, gives me a sense of reality, which I miss
altogether in the modern substitute for it. Why
the story should be looked upon as an interpolat-
ed fragment I cannot conceive. It is entirely
in the spirit of all that goes before and of all that
follows. David no doubt became a hero in the
eyes of the men and the virgins of Israel. But
nothing is said by the historian to make us think
him a hero. He comes down with food and a
message from his father to his brothers; he hears
from them only scornful words about the sheep
he has left in the wilderness; Saul smiles at his
boldness in thinking he can meet the Philistines;
Goliath laughs at him, and curses him by his
gods. Everything is said to make us feel the
feebleness of the Israelitish champion; everything to remind us that the nation of Israel was
the witness for the nothingness of man in himself,
for the might of man when he knows that he is

nothing, and puts his trust in the living God. We may write the Bible again ; but as long as it remains what it is, this must be the sense of it. And this is the sense which human beings want now as in the times of old. We want to be reminded, as much in the age of all mechanical inventions and triumphs as in the age of greatest barbarism, that the shield and the helmet, and the greaves of brass, do not constitute strength ; that the sling and the stone in the hand of one who believes in invisible power, are ever the symbols and pledges of victory. If to disbelieve this is to cast off Hebrew old clothes, it is also to put on the most vulgar, worn-out garments of tyranny and superstition ; it is to fall down and worship brute force, to declare *that* to be the Lord. How soon we may come through our refinements, our civilization, our mock hero-worship, to that last and most shameful prostration of the human spirit, God only knows. But *He* does know. And because He lives and is true, He will make it manifest in his own due time, that the law of his universe is not changed, and that by that law all true strength must be made perfect in weakness.

David, however, did become a hero in the sight of the people; they celebrated in their songs and dances the shepherd who had become the son of the king, and who slew his ten thousands, while Saul slew his thousands. A fearful crisis surely for him who had been learning by such slow, silent discipline, and now by such a signal triumph, whence all glory comes! A dizzy height for a man to stand upon, who had also received the mysterious anointing, and who might well dream that a kingdom was within his reach! He must have learned then, that there were stronger and nearer enemies than Goliath, who might turn his boast into confusion, his life into a lie. He must have struggled hard with those enemies; for we are told that he behaved himself prudently, that he was glad to soothe Saul when he was tormented by his evil spirit, that he fled from him instead of provoking his wrath. But if he had been under no better conduct than his own, his prudence, and the higher wisdom which was the source of it, would both have forsaken him; he would have snatched at a power which he could only turn to the ruin of those over whom he exercised it. He was under a Teacher who did not leave him to himself, who was leading him through the terrible discipline of flattery, as He had through the quieter and safer experiences of his youth, to understand what a king is and what his dangers are; and who had yet higher lessons for him, to be learnt in another way.

David as an outlaw is to many a far less pleasant subject of contemplation than the same David as a shepherd, or as the champion of Israel. Most people feel the beauty of the story of Jonathan's love for him, which binds these two portions of his history together. They can understand that the man who called forth such affections must have had deeper qualities in him than those which command the admiration of a multitude, — if this admiration was not itself paid to those qualities, to the frank, warm, trustful heart which spoke out in his deeds, rather than to the deeds merely in themselves. But the captain " to whom every one resorted that was in distress, and every one who was discontented," the freebooter who made a foray one day upon the Philistines, and another went down to punish Nabal for not giving food to support his followers, affronts all our notions of what is decorous, and makes us think that we are reading the exploits of a border chief, rather than a passage of a divine record. We certainly should not shrink from describing David in the terms in which the Bible itself describes him, nor try to make out a case for him or it by distorting a single fact, even by giving it a different color from that which it would have if we found it elsewhere. If we met with the tale as simply told in a profane author, we should admit that many of the acts attributed to David, however strange and out of place they would be in an ordinary legal condition of society, were perfectly just and honorable when all formal bonds were broken ; some of them (e. g. his conduct to Achish) we should say were natural, but not justifiable, in his circumstances or any other circumstances. We cannot vary our language because the standard of the book we are reading is more divine. The difference is, that while the Bible sets before us broadly and without comment just the temptations which a man in such a position would be likely to fall into, and leaves it to our conscience, enlightened by its own teaching, to say when he did or did not fall into them, it takes still more pains to make us understand what the man himself was, the purpose of his being, the light by which he was guided. David, in the cave of Adullam, amidst his wild, reckless comrades, is essentially the same man as David in the sheepfolds, or David fighting the Philistine. He had not chosen his own circumstances, he had been thrown into them. He did not rebel against Saul. He did not deny his authority, or plot against his life, even when he had cast him off. He had no home, and he was compelled to seek one where he could. I do not know where a better home could have been provided for him than among these men in distress, in debt, in discontent. If it behooved a ruler to know the heart of his subjects, their sorrows, their wrongs, their crimes, to know them and to sympathize with them, this was surely as precious a part of his schooling as the solitude of his boyhood, or as any intercourse he had with easy men who had never faced the misery of the world, and had never had any motive to quarrel with its laws. He was now among the lowest of those whom he would afterwards have to govern, not hearing at a distance of their doings and sufferings, but partaking in them livingly ; realizing the influences which were disposing them to evil. And here he was acquiring more real reverence for law and order, more understanding of their nature, than those can ever arrive at who have never known the need of them from the want of them. He was bringing his wild followers under a loving discipline and government which they had never experienced; he was teaching them to confess a law, which no tyrant had created, no anarchy could set aside. He instructed them by his example to bow before female grace and gentleness, to reverence the person of an enemy, to treat a king as the Lord's anointed. "Come, ye children," he says in a Psalm which a reasonable Jewish tradition connects with this part of his life,—"Come, ye children, and I will teach you the fear of the Lord. What man is he that lusteth to live and would fain see good days? Keep thy tongue from evil, and thy lips that they speak no guile.

Eschew evil and do good; seek peace and pursue it The eyes of the Lord are over the righteous; his ears are open to their cry." This is no dull sermon of a man discoursing to wretched people against sins to which he has no mind. It is the honest, hearty, sympathetic voice of a captain speaking to a band, each one of whom he knows, telling him of a right way which they may follow together, and of a wrong way into which he is as much in danger of straying as themselves. He speaks to them of a God who thinks of them, who is watching over them, who does not despise their poverty, who will avenge their wrongs; but who desires above all that they should be right, who is willing and able to make them right.

And this was the lesson which David was at the same time taking home to his own inmost heart. Through oppression, confusion, lawlessness, he was learning the eternal and essential righteousness of God. He had been taught to despise the brute force of the lion and the bear and the Philistine before; he was now taught to despise all power whatsoever, lodged in men circumcised or uncircumcised, which was maintaining itself against right. He was set in the throne who judged right. "Hear the right; attend unto my cry!" he could say, with confidence that the prayer would at last be answered. He was sure that, though the kings of the earth might gather together, and say, " Let us break these bands of right asunder, and cast away these cords from us," He that sitteth in the heavens would laugh, the Lord would have them in derision. He had set His righteous king upon the holy hill of Zion, and all the nations must do him homage.

The time came when David's faith in the existence of a righteous kingdom, which had its ground in the unseen world, and which might exhibit itself really though not perfectly in this, was to be brought to the severest of all trials. Saul died on the mountains of Gilboa: the Philistines possessed themselves of the cities of Israel. The new mode of government for which the people craved so earnestly had been tried,—they had become like the countries round about,— these countries were now their masters. They had gained such a king as they had imagined,— a leader of their hosts. They had lost law, discipline, and fellowship; now their hosts had perished. Could there come order out of this chaos? Whence was it to come? From a band of freebooters? That was to be seen. If the chief of this band thought of setting up a dominion for himself, of making his followers possessors of the lands from which they had been driven out, of putting down his private enemies, of rising by the arms of soldiers and the choice of a faction to be a tyrant, his life would be merely a vulgar tale, such as age after age, civilized and barbarous, has to record, — a tale that would be merely dull and flat from its frequent repetition, from the utter absence of anything but the lowest purposes and the pettiest plotting in the actor, if we could lose the sad reflection that millions of human beings are interested in events which the on-looker may be disposed to regard with indifference or contempt, and the consolatory recollection, that, by the crimes of foolish, feeble men, God is bringing forth his wisdom and righteousness into clear light. But if David took this disordered, miserable country of his fathers into his hands, not as a prize which he had won, but as a heavy and awful trust that was committed to him, a trust for which he had been prepared in the sheepfolds, which he could only administer while he remembered that the Lord was his Shepherd and that He was the Shepherd of every Israelite and of every man on the earth, — then, however hopeless seemed the materials with which he had to work, and which he had to mould, he might believe confidently that he should be in his own day the restorer of Israel, and the witness and prophet of the complete restoration of it and of mankind.

This, brethren, was the man after God's own heart, the man who thoroughly believed in God, as a living and righteous Being; who in all changes of fortune clung to that conviction; who could act upon it, live upon it; who could give himself up to God to use him as he pleased; who could be little or great, popular or contemptible, just as God saw fit that he should be; who could walk on in darkness secure of nothing but this, that truth must prevail at last, and that he was sent into the world to live and die that it might prevail; who was certain that the triumph of the God of Heaven would be for the blessing of the most miserable outcasts upon earth. Have we asked ourselves how the Scripture can dare to represent a man with David's many failings, with that eager, passionate temper which evidently belonged to him, with all the manifold temptations which accompany a vehement, sympathetic character, with the great sins which we shall be told of hereafter, as one who could share the counsels and do the will of a Holy Being? O, rather let us ask ourselves, whether, with a plausible exterior, a respectable behavior, an unimpeachable decorum in the sight of men, we can ever win this smile, hear this approving sentence. The words, " Well done, good and faithful servant," are not spoken by the Judge of all now, will not be spoken in the last day, to him who has found, in his pilgrimage through this world, no enemies to fight with, no wrongs to be redressed, no right to be maintained. How many

of us feel, in looking back upon acts which the
world has not condemned, which friends have perhaps
applauded, " We had no serious purpose
there ; we merely did what it was seemly and
convenient to do ; we were not yielding to God's
righteous will ; we were not inspired by His
love " ! How many of us feel that our bitterest
repentances are to be for this, — that all things
have gone so smoothly with us, because we did
not care to make the world better or to be better
ourselves ! How many of us feel that those who
have committed grave outward transgressions,
into which we have not fallen because the motives
to them were not present with us, or because
God's grace kept us hedged round by influences
which resisted them, may nevertheless have had
hearts which answered more to God's heart,
which entered far more into the grief and the joy
of his Spirit, than ours ever did ! And that such
lamentations for the past may not be fruitless, let
us ask, for the time to come, that he may not be
of the class which Christ describes by the mouth
of his Apostle, as neither hot nor cold ; that He
will fill us with a burning zeal in his service ;
that He will make us indifferent where or among
whom our lot is cast, among princes or among
outlaws, whether we are respected or scorned ;
so long as we may but testify to all, that He who
took upon him the form of a servant, He who was

despised and rejected of men, the true Man after God's own heart, the Son of David and the Son of God, is the present and eternal Shepherd, to whom the weary and wandering may turn for help and guidance now, since he has passed through the valley of the shadow of death for them; from whom they may expect fuller deliverence hereafter, seeing that He must reign till He has put all enemies under his feet.

DAVID THE KING.

" And David perceived that the Lord had established him king over Israel, and that he had exalted his kingdom for his people Israel's sake." — 2 Samuel v. 12.

This language, some may think, would have been suitable and pious, if an extraordinary, evidently miraculous event had raised David to the throne of Israel. Such an event might have enabled him to perceive that he was divinely elected to reign; he might have continued to reign with the same comfortable assurance. But he appears to have risen quite as slowly — under the same course of accidents — as other leaders of troops in tolerably quiet conditions of society, to say nothing of those which are utterly anarchical. He belonged to an honorable tribe, he had performed great exploits, he had strong popular sympathy with him, increased by the unfair treatment he had undergone from Saul. He had the command of a body of compact, devoted, even desperate followers. Saul and Jonathan were dead. Battles and assassinations, perpetrated by men hoping to gain rewards from him, or under the influence of private enmity, removed his rivals out of his way. What man, who has not taken some very outrageous method of establishing his power, might not say that the Lord had bestowed his dominion upon him, if that phrase became the lips of the shepherd sovereign?

This is a question which I am not able to answer. I do not know what king might not safely adopt these words, and ought not to adopt them. The danger, I fancy, lies in the disbelief of them, or in the idle use of them when no definite meaning is attached to them. So far from admitting that David would have had more right, or would have been more likely, to think and speak as he did, if some angel suddenly appearing had placed the crown upon his head, I apprehend that the strength and liveliness of his conviction arose from the number of conspiring accidents, often seemingly cross accidents, which had led him into so new and dangerous a position. It was the successiveness, the continuity, of the steps in his history, which assured him that God's hand had been directing the whole of it. One startling

24

event would have made no such impression upon him. *That* he might have referred to chance, or to the rare irregular interference of an omnipotent being. Only such a being as the Lord God of Abraham, only one who had guided each patriarch and the whole nation from age to age through strange unknown ways, could have woven the web of his destinies, could have controlled his proceedings and the proceedings of indifferent, of unrighteous men. Had David, instead of maintaining the ground which circumstances pointed out to him as his, seized violently that which was not his, he would not have perceived that the Lord had made him king of Israel; he would have felt that he had made himself so, and would have acted upon that persuasion.

For the two clauses of the sentence are intimately and inseparably connected. David perceived that God had established his kingdom, and he knew that He had exalted it for his people Israel's sake. A government which a man wins for himself he uses for himself. That which he inwardly and practically acknowledges as conferred upon him by a righteous being, cannot be intended for himself. And thus it is, that the early and mysterious teaching of David while he was in the sheepfolds, bore so mightily upon his life after he became a king. The deepest lesson which he had learnt was, that he himself was under government; that in his heart and will was the inmost circle of that authority which the winds and the sea, the moon and the stars, obeyed. We have seen how the sense of this invisible kingdom was awakened in him, how it was quickened by all joyful and bitter experiences, by the care of sheep and the society of outlaws. To understand that the empire over wills and hearts is the highest which man can exercise, because it is the highest which God exercises; to understand that his empire cannot be one of rough compulsion, because the divinest power is not of this kind ; to understand that the necessity for stern, quick, inevitable punishment arises from the unwillingness of men to abide under a yoke of grace and gentleness ; to understand that the law looks terrible and overwhelming to the wrong-doer, just because he has shaken off his relation to the Person from whom law issues, in whom dwells all humanity and sympathy, all forgiveness and reclaiming mercy, — this was the highest privilege of a Jewish king, that upon which the rightful exercise of all his functions depended.

Two memorable passages in the history of David, the establishment of his capital, and the removal of the ark to the hill above it, illustrate the principles upon which his kingdom stood, and show wherein it differed from the great Asiatic empires which were contemporary with it, and which had existed nearly in the same form perhaps centuries before the birth of Abraham. The first sign of the unity of *these* monarchies was the building of some great city, Babylon, or Calah, or Nineveh. The inhabitants of such cities felt that they were a people, because they were compassed with walls. Within those walls there speedily were built temples to some of the powers of nature which they feared. Very soon, as we now have such good means of knowing, the arts of sculpture came forth, doing honor to animal forms, which for their strength or their swiftness were believed to be divine. With a great hunter as a ruler, with one of these cities as the centre of their strength, with divinities thus conceived and visibly represented as their protectors, these Asiatic worlds continually enlarged their limits, absorbed new tribes into themselves, acquired the titles of conquest and glory for one or another of their temporary masters. The commonwealth of Israel began in open plains and pastures. A single man, who had not a foot of earth for his possession, was its founder. A family of colonists, still dwelling on a land which was not theirs, succeeded to him. These became a race of Egyptian captives. They acquired laws, festivals, a polity, first in a wilderness. They struggled hard for generations with the corrupted people of the land into which they came. Only after centuries of conflicts, discomfitures, humiliations, they acquired a king, and a city which he could make the centre of their tribes. But these had been centuries of moral and political progress, of the deepest experiences for individuals and for the whole nation, respecting the grounds of their social existence and the relation in which they stood to the visible and invisible world. All this time they had been learning to worship a Being who was not to be made in the likeness of things in heaven above or in the earth beneath; to apprehend him as a present, unseen Lawgiver, Judge, Deliverer, in whom they might put their trust. They learnt that a nation built upon fear and distrust must be evil while it lasts, and must at length come to ruin. Here are the two kinds of civilization; the civic life, the life of cities, is in one the beginning, is in the other the result, of a long process. But in the first you have a despotism, which becomes more expansive and more oppressive from day to day: expansive everywhere except in the spirits of those it rules; *they* are more contracted from year to year: oppressive of everything but crime and disorder; *they* possess growing activity and freedom. In the other case, you have a struggle, sometimes a weary struggle; but it is the struggle of spirits, it is a struggle for life. And God himself is helping that struggle, is working with and for the spirits whom he has formed, is bringing them out of darkness into an ever clearer and broader light, out of confusion into a real, at last even to something like a visible and outward unity.

But this unity does not stand in the walls of the capital city, even though that city be the holy city and the city of peace. When David had made this conquest from the Jebusites, and had set up his throne in it, he was impatient till he had brought the ark of God there, and placed it, with songs and shoutings and dancings, on the holy hill. That ark had been the witness to the people that they were one people, because they had the one God dwelling in the midst of them while they were shifting their tents continually in the wilderness, perishing from heat and drought, sighing for the slavery, if they might but have the flesh-pots, of Egypt. It was to be the witness of the same truth to those who were dwelling in settled habitations, who were under a native government, whose hunger and thirst were not quenched by manna from heaven or by water from a rock, but by the produce of ordinary fields and fountains. It spoke to them, as it had to the others, of a permanent Being, of a righteous Being, always above his creatures, always desiring fellowship with them, a fellowship which they could only realize when they were seeking to be like him. " Lord, who shall ascend to thy

tabernacle ?   Who shall dwell in thy holy hill ? ”
— so spake David as he brought the ark to its
resting-place. — “ Even he that hath clean hands
and a pure heart, who hath not lifted up his eyes
unto vanity, nor sworn to deceive his neighbor.”

The moral being of the nation, then, as of each
individual of it, stood in the confession of a Person absolutely good, the ground of all goodness
in his creatures, accessible to them while they
sought him with fear and reverence as the King,
Protector, Friend, of each and of all.   There
could be no lesson to a king so deep and solemn
as this, respecting the nature, condition, and bul-
warks of his own authority ; no warning so fearful against forgetting that the bond which united
him to his subjects was also the bond which
united him to God.   He ruled so long as his
throne was based upon righteousness ; the moment he sought for any other foundation, he
would become weak and contemptible.   All David’s discipline had been designed to settle him
in this truth.   He was the man after God’s own
heart, because he so graciously received that
discipline and imbibed that truth.   The signal
sin of his life confirmed it still more mightily for
himself and for all ages to come.

I have shown in what respect David was not
an ordinary Oriental monarch, but the very opposite of one.   The history tells us as plainly,

that there were points in which he resembled the sovereigns of the East of that day, and the Caliphs and Sultans of later times. He had his wives and his concubines. No divine edict told him that such indulgence was unlawful. For thanks be to God, though he makes use of edicts and statutes, it is not by these mainly that he rules the universe. The Bible, as we have seen, is from first to last the history of a practical education, God leading men by slow degrees to enter into his mind and purposes, and to mould their own into conformity with his. If we want exemplifications of all the miseries and curses which spring from the mixture of families and the degradation of women in a court and country where polygamy exists, David's history supplies them. No maxims of morality can be half so effectual as a faithful record of terrible facts like these. But the thorough correction of this monstrous evil, the full assertion of the principle which is opposed to it, could not, so far as we may judge, be brought out in that stage of the history of society. In later times of the Jewish commonwealth, when the royal power had ceased, when the people had been more instructed in the opposition between their own polity and that of the Asiatic despotisms, there was a very evident awakening of the conscience upon this subject, a growing anticipation of the principle which Christendom has adopted and canonized. The like feeling, however resisted by evil passions and a corrupt mythology, it pleased God to awaken in some of the Pagan nations of the West, — in Greece, in Rome, among the Teutonic tribes. The instinctive recognition of the true law of marriage was a preparation — the most wonderful, perhaps, of all — for the revelation of the one Lord and Husband of Humanity. Certainly wherever polygamy exists there is the most fatal resistance to that revelation ; certainly also, wherever the fact of Christ's incarnation is acknowledged, there is a horror of polygamy which can be explained by no arguments, which resists all subtilties of logic, all pretended authority from the example of patriarchs, which prohibits by a fixed law what was esteemed innocent and ·regal· among those who lived before the kingdom of Heaven was proclaimed, even though they might be the prophets of it.

These facts must be borne in mind, if we would understand what constituted that guilt of David which the Prophet Nathan brought home to him by the story of the ewe-lamb. For a king to take the wife of a poor man, — how light a fault may this have appeared to one with the power and privileges which David possessed ! Supposing there was a fixed law against adultery, did this law apply to the ruler of the land ? was

he not in some sense above law? Such are the
arguments and sophistries which would occur to
one who was wrestling with his conscience, either
to give him leave to commit a wrong, or not to
torment him for it when it was done. And then
if the husband of this woman stood in the way of
the full gratification of his purpose, or of the
concealment of it, was there anything strange
that he, who was exposing thousands of his subjects to the chances of battle and death, should
expose this one? Why was his life more precious
than that of any other Israelite? Was it precious
simply because it was convenient to his master
that he should lose it? And so the deeds were
done. Bathsheba was taken; Joab, by David's
order, put Uriah in an exposed place, where he
was sure to be slain. And David, no doubt, performed all his official tasks as before, went daily
to the services of the tabernacle, was probably
most severe in enforcing punishments upon all
wrong-doers. That characteristic feature of a
transgressor, his rapid and bitter condemnation
of other transgressors, is strikingly preserved in
the Scripture portrait. " And David's anger was
greatly kindled against the rich man who had
stolen the poor man's lamb. And he said, ' The
man who hath done this thing shall surely die.' "
This energy of virtue, this mighty effort to get
credit with one's self for a lively sense of right

and hatred of injustice, — who does not recognize it? Who should not tremble while he thinks, The evil spirit who prompts to this consummate deceit and hypocrisy, is near to me; I am tempted continually to fly from the light which would show me the foul spots in my own soul, by projecting them outside of me, and pronouncing sentence upon them in another man. But how satisfactory to think, that, while all this was at work in David's heart, it was not left to the ease and comfort which, no doubt, it was seeking for, and striving by all artifices to secure. What availed it that he could so plausibly justify the acts he had done, and give them gentle names, and could prove that they were not adultery and murder in him, though they might be in any one else? What availed it that he could look back to holy prayers and songs in the night, and evident tokens that God was with him. What availed it to argue that he must be the same man now that he had ever been? There was a voice near him saying, " Thou hast done it, and thou canst not change it. God is no respecter of persons. It signifies nothing to him that thou art called king, or saint, or psalmist. Thy heart is not at one with him, and thou knowest it. Thou art living in a lie, and thou knowest it. Thou art a miserable heartless man at this time, and thou knowest it. And to have been called the man after God's own heart, is nothing at all to thee. It only adds a sting and bitterness to thy present self-condemnation, such as another could not feel." He understood this voice afterwards Then the effect of it was mere anarchy, and restlessness of mind, — a condition in which man hates his fellows and wishes to disbelieve in God, and dares not. "When I held my tongue," he says, "my bones waxed old through my daily complaining. For thy hand was heavy upon me. My moisture was turned into the drought of summer." No language ever described so vividly the sense of a weight at the heart, a weight that cannot be lifted; and it was the weight of God's own presence, of that presence which he had once spoken of as the fulness of joy. With this oppression, like that of the air before a thunder-storm, came the drying up of all the moisture and freshness of life, the parching heat of fever. Did the Prophet Nathan bring all this to his consciousness? No, surely. The Prophet Nathan came at the appointed moment, to tell him in clear words, by a living instance, that which he had been hearing in muttered accents within his heart for months before. He came to tell him that the God of righteousness and mercy, who cared for Uriah, the poor man with the single ewe-lamb, was calling him, the king, to account, for an act of unrighteousness and unmercifulness. Nathan brought him to face steadily the light at which he had been winking, and to own that the light was good, that it was the darkness only which was horrible and hateful; so that he might turn to the light, and crave that it should once more penetrate into the depths of his being and take possession of him.

And this was his confession and prayer. He makes out no case for himself; he pleads no extenuating circumstances. I myself have sinned, and done this evil in thy sight. My joy is in the thought, that Thou wilt be clear when Thou art judged. If I did not believe that Thou art altogether just and righteous and true, I could have no hope. Because Thou art this, I believe that Thou canst and wilt make me a clean heart, and renew a right spirit within me. It is not the misery which Thou wilt lay upon me for my sin, that I dread; the misery is to be false, and to continue in a falsehood. But Thou desirest truth in the inward parts, and Thou canst make me to understand wisdom secretly. I fancied, till Thou didst find me out, that I could make peace with Thee by offering sacrifices. But Thou desirest not sacrifice, else would I give it Thee. Thou thyself must give the sacrifice that we may offer it. This one of a broken and contrite heart which Thou hast given to me, I offer to Thee, and Thou wilt not despise it. When Thou hast restored the king to his right state, and built up again the walls of the city which Thou hast promised to bless, then indeed we may come and offer bullocks upon Thy altar, the expressions of united submission of kings and people to Thee, their just and forgiving King and Lord.

What was the answer to this prayer? First, the death of Bathsheba's child; next, the discovery of hateful crimes in his household; finally, the revolt of the beloved Absalom. These—answers to a prayer for forgiveness? Yes, if forgiveness means what David took it to mean, having truth in the inward parts, knowing wisdom secretly. He had had falsehood in his inward parts; he had cherished the delusion that he was free to do what he liked, that laws and rules were not for him, that he might use a subject at his pleasure. The taking the sins home to himself, instead of imputing them to circumstances or to God, had brought him into fellowship with Truth once more. He had known folly secretly; he had dallied with silly, childish excuses; he had lost all freedom and manliness of spirit. Now he had desired to be Wisdom's pupil again. He had begun, with more prostration of heart than ever before, to learn her lessons. And she would assuredly not leave him till she had written them upon his mind. To have his people's heart stolen from him, to have his child for his enemy, to be deserted by his counsellors and his wives, to lose his kingdom, to be mocked and cursed, — this was rough discipline surely. But he had desired it; he had said deliberately, "Make me a clean heart, and renew a right spirit within me." And that blessing, — if it was granted him in part at once, if he rose up from that very prayer a freed man with a free spirit, — yet was to be realized through his whole life, and to be secured by methods which he certainly would not have devised or chosen for himself.

But, as in all his past history, the discipline was not for him more than for his people, not for his people more than for all ages to come. The kingly lesson and the human lesson are nowhere more intimately united than here. That which enabled David, crushed and broken, to be more than ever the man after God's own heart, to see more than ever into the depths of wisdom and love in that heart, was also that which fitted him to be a ruler, by understanding the only condition on which it is possible for a man to exercise real dominion over others, namely, when he gives up himself, that they may know God, and not him, to be their sovereign.

Those who administered the affairs of the English Church in the early years of the reign of Charles II. chose the passage of the Book of Samuel which describes David's return to his kingdom, for the service on the 29th of May. There was a solemn warning in their selection. History has turned it into bitter irony. The use of this lesson forbids us to forget the certain and terrible truth, that years of hard adversity and suffering do not of themselves fit a man to reign; that they may be worse than wasted upon him; that he may come out of them more reckless and heartless, more ignorant of any government exercised over himself, less conscious of any responsibility for the government which he exercises over others, than he went into them. For our own individual benefit, as well as for the sake of nations, we should lay this doctrine, hard though it be, to heart. Adversity is in itself as little gracious as prosperity. Moral death may be the fruit of one, as much as of the other. It was otherwise with David, not because adversity had any especial influence over him which it has not over us, but because he accepted it as God's punishment and medicine, because he believed that God would do the good for him which adversity could not do.

One of the best proofs, it seems to me, that his schooling was effectual, is this, that all his family griefs, his experience of his own evil, the desertion of his subjects, did not lead him to fancy that he should be following a course acceptable to God, if he retired to the deserts, or ceased to be a shepherd of Israel, instead of doing the work which

was appointed for him. It shows how healthy
and true his repentance and faith were, that he
again set himself to organize the people and to
fight their battles, to feed them and rule them
with all his power, when a religious prudence or
self-interest might have whispered, " Do thy best
to make amends by services to God for the ills
thou hast done ; save thyself, whatever becomes
of thy people Israel." These ungodly suggestions
the like of which came as angels of light to so
many Christian monarchs in the Middle Ages and
sent them to do penance for their evils and to seek
a crown of glory in monasteries, may have presented themselves to the man after God's own
heart. If they did, he proved his title to the
name by rejecting them. He showed that he
could trust God to put him in the position that
was best for him, that he knew God did not send
him into the world to provide either for his body
or his soul, but to glorify His name and to bless
His creatures. He was most devoted to God
when he was most devoted to His work. He
prayed fervently because he lived fervently. He
found out the necessity of seeking God continually, of meditating upon His law, of blessing His
name, because he learnt how weak he was, and
how little he could be a king over men, when the
image of the divine kingdom was not present to
him.

25 *

This is the impression which is left upon our minds by the general context of his history after his restoration. There are passages of that history, such as his giving up the sons of Saul to the Gibeonites, which I do not understand. I can perceive in the story a recognition of the continuance of a nation's life, of its obligations and its sins, from age to age. All national morality, nay, the meaning and possibility of history, depends upon this truth, the sense of which is, I fear, very weak in our day. But I cannot in the least tell why the death of Saul's children should have been the needful expiation of the nation's crimes. I do not, indeed, see any pretext for the supposition, of course a very ready and obvious one, that it was an act of policy on David's part to rid himself of a dangerous family; there would be a blackness in the putting forward of a religious motive for such a crime, which all our knowledge of his previous life forbids us to attribute to him. On the other hand, I conceive that we are not bound to assume that the proceeding was in all particulars a just one, because we are told that a divine intimation was the cause of it. The Scripture is most careful that we should feel the reality of these intimations, that we should refer them to their true source, and yet that we should understand how possible it is for a man to pervert them and found wrong inferences upon them, if his own mind is not in a thoroughly pure and healthy condition.

An instance which illustrates and proves that principle occurs shortly after this one. God is said to tempt David to number the people. The thought that it was a blessing and a cause of thankfulness to be the head of a growing and thriving people, — this was divine. The thought that it was well for a ruler to be acquainted with the condition and resources of his people, — this was divine. With the confidence that it was, must have come an assurance, from the very existence of the Book of Numbers, that it was a right thing in itself, a part of the divine ordinance, that each tribe and its families, and the persons who compose them, should be registered. But the determination, just then, to send forth officers for the sake of ascertaining the armed force of the land, — this was the thought of a self-exalted man, aspiring to be a military chief and conqueror; a thought which was at work also in his people, and which threatened to make their organization and his victories steps to their ruin. And this tendency in king and people was checked by a sweeping pestilence, which brought them back to the feeling that their power did not lie in the number of men capable of bearing arms; that, if this were their reliance, they would soon be swallowed up by empires immeasurably greater than themselves, the habits and false notions of which they were adopting. I do not know anything so instructive to us, if we use them as we ought, as these passages in the Bible, which teach us that all good thoughts, counsels, just works, come from the Spirit of God, and, at the same time, that we are in the most imminent peril, at every moment, of turning the divine suggestions into sin, by allowing our selfish and impure conceits and rash generalizations to mix with them.

We have seen that the life of David is the life neither of a mere official, fulfilling a purpose in which he has no interest, nor of a hero without fear and without reproach; but of a man inspired by a divine purpose, under the guidance of a divine teacher, liable to all ordinary errors, as likely as any of us to fall into great sins. The interest we feel in him is strong and personal. It is not won from us by a single exaggeration of his merits, by the least attempt to surround him with some unnatural halo of glory. We should have wished, perhaps, to see his sun setting with peculiar splendor, to be told of some great acts, or hear some noble words, which would assure us that he died a saint. The Bible does not in the least satisfy this expectation. It represents him in the bodily feebleness, in something like the dotage, of old age. The last sentences which are reported of him concern the after administration of his son's kingdom, and the punishment of some of his mischievous subjects. Of all his words, they are, perhaps, those which we the least care to remember. We must turn elsewhere than to the books of the Old or of the New Testament for death-bed scenes. One beautiful record of the first deacon of the Church, who prayed for his countrymen, " Lord, lay not this sin to their charge," is all that we have of martyrology in the Bible. Its warriors fight the good fight. We know that in some battle or other they finish their course. Where, or how, under what circumstances of humiliation or triumph, we are not told. If it pleased God that their lamp should shine out brightly at the last, that was well, for he was glorified in their strength. If it pleased him that the light should sink and go out in its socket, that was well too, for he was glorified in their weakness. Not by momentary flashes does God bid us judge of our fellow-creatures; for He who reads the heart, and sees the meaning and purpose of it, judges not of them by these. And never be it forgotten, that at the death which has redeemed all other deaths and made them blessed, there was darkness over all the land until the ninth hour, and that a cry came out of the darkness, " My God, my God, why hast thou forsaken me ? "

If you would judge of David, of what he was,

and what he looked for, let this Psalm be your guide. " Give the king thy judgments, O God! and thy righteousness unto the king's son. He shall judge thy people with righteousness, and the poor with judgment. He shall save the children of the needy, and shall break in pieces the oppressor. He shall redeem their souls from deceit and violence, and precious shall their blood be in his sight. There shall be an handful of corn in the earth upon the top of the mountains; the fruit thereof shall shake like Lebanon; and they of the city shall flourish like grass of the earth. His name shall endure for ever, his name shall be continued as long as the sun, and men shall be blessed in him. All nations shall call him blessed. Blessed be the Lord God, the God of Israel, who only doeth wondrous things, and blessed be his glorious name for ever, and let the whole earth be filled with his glory. The prayers of David, the son of Jesse, are ended."

And with that aspiration and hope, brethren, may our prayers be ended. May it be the business of our lives to testify, that there is a righteous kingdom established upon the earth, and that God has set it up, and that his Son, who has made himself one with all poor and suffering men, is at the head of it; and that it shall prevail over all oppression and violence; and that all nations shall be blessed by it. Let us grapple this faith to our inmost souls now, when men think, and openly proclaim, that law and order are based not on the will and mind of a gracious God, who cares for his creatures, but are to be the tools and servants of a grasping Mammon; now, when we have proofs openly before our eyes how that low, grovelling, godless conviction leads at last to the trampling down of all law, to the setting up of the most hateful lawless tyranny. Let us not merely detest such outrages upon God's order, but scorn them as essentially weak, as predestined to destruction, however for a time he may permit them for the chastisement of the sins and idolatries of other nations, nay, even if he should see fit to use them for the chastisement of our own. " Rest in the Lord, and wait patiently for him: fret not thyself because of him who prospereth in his way, because of the man who bringeth wicked devices to pass. Cease from anger, . and forsake wrath; fret not thyself in any wise to do evil. For evil-doers shall be cut off; but those that wait upon the Lord, they shall inherit the earth. For yet a little while, and the wicked shall not be: yea, thou shalt diligently consider his place, and it shall not be. But the meek shall inherit the earth; and shall delight themselves in the abundance of peace."

Anna read me a translation of a German hymn that pleased her, and afterwards we read together some favorite extracts of mine.

A HYMN.*

FROM THE GERMAN.

On God, and not on my poor strength,
  Will I my hopes repose,
And trust the Power who made me first,
  And all my weakness knows.
      He who the world
      Guides on its way,
      Will help me bear
      My burdened day.

From all eternity He saw
  How sore my needs would be,
His power could fix my term of life
  My joys and burdens see.
      What says my Lord?
      Is there a grief
      Where love and faith
      Bring no relief?

God knows whate'er my heart desires
  Before it is expressed,
And grants the boon, unuttered still,
  If wisdom sees it best.

---

* Gellert.

Most fatherly
He heeds his Son;
Then, not my will,
But thine, be done!

Is not unbroken happiness
Often more hard to bear,
Than what we call life's sorest ills,
Privation, grief, and care?
Our greatest needs
All end with death;
Earth's honors fly
With our last breath.

The gifts which make us truly blest
To all alike are given,
While outward goods, health, fortune, wealth,
Make not the soul a heaven.
He who God's word
Keeps still in view,
With conscience pure,
Gilds trouble too.

What is life's brightest, glorious hour?
Fading, when brightest burning!
What are its sorest, bitterest griefs?
How soon to blessings turning!
Hope in the Lord,
His aid is nigh;
Rejoice, ye saints,
He hears your cry.

26

EXTRACTS FROM SERMONS OF F. W. ROBERTSON.

What is your religion? Excitability, romance, impression, fear? Remember, excitement has its uses, impression has its value. John, in all circumstances of his appearance and style of teaching, impressed by excitement. Excitement, warmed feelings, make the first actings of religious life and the breaking of inveterate habits easier. But excitement and impression are not religion. Neither can you trust to the alarm produced by the thought of eternal retribution. Ye that have been impressed, beware how you let those impressions die away. Die they will, and must; we cannot live in excitement for ever; but beware of their leaving behind them nothing except a languid, jaded heart. If God ever gave you the excitements of religion, breaking in upon the monotony, as John's teaching broke in upon that of Jerusalem, take care. There is no restoring of elasticity to the spring that has been over bent. Let impression pass on at once to acting.

It is a perilous thing to separate feeling from acting; to have learnt to feel rightly, without acting rightly. It is a danger to which, in a refined and polished age, we are peculiarly exposed. The romance, the poem, and the sermon teach us how to feel. Our feelings are delicately correct. But the danger is this; — feeling is given to lead to action; if feeling be suffered to awake without passing into duty, the character becomes untrue. When the emergency for real action comes, the feeling is, as usual, produced; but accustomed as it is to rise in fictitious circumstances without action, neither will it lead on to action in the real ones. " We pity wretchedness and shun the wretched." We utter sentiments just, honorable, refined, lofty, — but somehow, when a truth presents itself in the shape of a duty, we are unable to perform it. And so, such characters become by degrees like the artificial pleasure-grounds of bad taste, in which the waterfall does not fall, and the grotto offers only the refreshment of an imaginary shade, and the green hill does not strike the skies, and the tree does not grow; their lives are a sugared crust of sweetness trembling over black depths of hollowness; more truly still, " whited sepulchres," — fair without to look upon, " within full of all uncleanness."

It is perilous, again, to separate thinking rightly from acting. He is already half false who speculates on truth, and does not do it. Truth is given, not to be contemplated, but to be done. Life is an action, not a thought. And the penalty paid by him who speculates on truth is that by degrees the very truth he holds becomes to him a falsehood.

There is no truthfulness, therefore, except in the witness borne to God by doing his will, — to live the truths we hold, or else they will be no truths at all.

Sweet are the tears that from a Howard's eye
Drop on the cheek of one he lifts from earth ;
And he who works me good with unmoved face,
Does it but half ; he chills me, while he aids,
My benefactor, not my brother man.
But even this, this cold benevolence,
Seems worth, seems manhood, when there rise before me
The sluggard pity's vision-weaving tribe,
Who sigh for wretchedness yet shun the wretched,
Nursing in some delicious solitude
Their slothful loves and dainty sympathies.

S. T. Coleridge.

There is a strange inconsistency in the human mind, which leads men to scrutinize with severity the secrets of their fellow-creatures' souls, which it is impossible they should ever clearly discover ; while they neglect to examine and probe into the springs of their own conduct, which if they do not, they certainly ought to know. The first they are forbidden, and the second they are commanded to do. — *St. Francis de Sales.*

In one of the lower heavens Dante asks of some spirits whom he meets, if they are happy here, or do they desire a higher place, to see more or to make more friends. " Among these shades there was first a little smiling; then one replied so joyous that she seemed to burn with the intensest fire of love, Brother, our will rests on the virtue of love, that makes us wish for only what we have, and is satisfied with nothing else."

" All things," says Hooker, " (God only excepted,) besides the nature which they have in themselves, receive externally some perfection from other things." Hence the appearance of separation or isolation in anything, and of self-dependence, is an appearance of imperfection ; and all appearances of connection and brotherhood are pleasant and right, both as significative of perfection in the things united, and as typical of that unity which we ·attribute to God, — that unity which consists not in his own singleness or separation, but in the necessity of his inherence in . all things that be, without which no creature of any kind could hold existence for a moment. Which necessity of divine essence I think it better to speak of as comprehensiveness, than as unity, because unity is often understood in the sense of oneness and singleness, instead of universality, whereas the only unity which by any means can become grateful or an object of hope to men, and whose types therefore in material things can be beautiful, is that on which turned the last words and prayer of Christ before his crossing of the Kidron brook. " Neither pray I for these alone, but for them also which shall believe on me through their word. That they all may be one, as thou, Father, art in me, and I in thee."

And so there is not any matter, nor any spirit, nor any creature, but it is capable of a unity of some kind with other creatures, and in that unity is its perfection and theirs, and a pleasure also, for the beholding of all other creatures that can behold. So the unity of spirits is partly in their sympathy, and partly in their giving and taking, and always in their love ; and these are their delight and their strength, for their strength is in their co-working and their fellowship, and their delight is in the giving and receiving of alternate and perpetual currents of good, their inseparable dependency on each other's being, and their essential and perfect depending on their Creator's ; and so the unity of earthly creatures is their power and their peace, not like the dead and cold peace of undisturbed stones and solitary mountains, but the living peace of trust, and the living power of support, of hands that hold each other and are still ; and so the unity of matter is, in its noblest form, the organization of it which builds it up into temples for the spirit, and in its lower form, the sweet and strange affinity which gives to it the glory of its orderly elements, and the fair variety of change and assimilation that turns the dust into the crystal, and separates the waters that be above the firmament from the waters that be beneath; and in its lowest form, it is the working and walking and clinging together, that gives their power to the winds, and its syllables and soundings to the air, and their weight to the waves, and their burning to the sunbeams, and their stability to the mountains, and to every creature whatsoever operation is for its glory and for others' good.

There is the unity of different and separate things, subjected to one and the same influence, which may be called subjectional unity, and this is the unity of clouds, as they are driven by the parallel winds, or as they are ordered by the electric currents, and this the unity of the sea and waves, and this of the bending and undulation of the forest masses, and in creatures capable of will it is the unity of will or of inspiration. And there is unity of origin, which we may call original unity, which is of things arising from one spring and source, and speaking always of this their brotherhood, and this in matter is the unity of the branches of the trees, and of the petals and starry rays of flowers, and of the beams of light, and in spiritual creatures it is their filial relation to Him from whom they have their being. And there is unity of sequence, which is that of things that form links in chains, and steps in ascent, and stages in journeys, and this, in matter, is the unity of communicable forces in their continuance from one thing to another, and it is the passing upwards and downwards of beneficent effects among all things. And it is the melody of sounds, and the beauty of continuous lines, and the orderly succession of motions and times. And in spiritual creatures it is their own constant building up by true knowledge and continuous reasoning to higher perfection, and the singleness and straightforwardness of their tendencies to more complete communion with God. And there is the unity of membership, which we may call essential unity, which is the unity of things separately imperfect into a perfect whole, and this is the great unity of which other unities are but parts and means ; it is in matter the harmony of sounds and consistency of bodies, and among spiritual creatures, their love and happiness and very life in God. — *Ruskin.*

THE OLD TESTAMENT. *

The Psalms (or, according to the Hebrew title, the Book of Hymns) are a collection of songs, some shorter, some longer, written by very different authors, and at very different times, all arranged to be sung or recited with a musical cadence. The titles of the several Psalms can scarcely have anything to do with their authors, but must have been added by others, since there is sometimes an error observable in them. One Psalm, the ninetieth, is ascribed to Moses, but certainly erroneously. Seventy-two Psalms are attributed to David, among which are some that were written much later. David was a poet and a musician, and after he became king, he set apart, as we read in 1 Chronicles, chap. xxv., two hundred and eighty-eight persons for singers in the house of the Lord. They were placed under three leaders, Asaph, Jeduthun, and Heman. The king, Jehoshaphat, was also a lover of temple music (2 Chronicles xx. 18 – 21). In his time a part of the singers were called, from their master, the sons, that is, the scholars, of Korah, to whom eleven Psalms are ascribed, while to Asaph twelve Psalms are attributed. The

---

* From *Die religiose Glaubenslehre*, by Dr. K. G. Bretschneider.

word Selah, which occurs fifty-one times, is not a Hebrew word, but a musical sign for the use of the singers, written with letters (S L H), by which, it is supposed, a mark of repetition is denoted. The expression " a song of degrees," is a Hebrew one, meaning either a song sung on the way up to the temple, or a hymn in a certain rhythm. The Psalms, considered as poems, have mostly a high poetic worth, and are especially valued because they all have a religious character, and all have reference to God both in nature and human life. As they are mostly effusions of earnest religious feelings, they are also fitted to awaken these feelings in others. They have, therefore, always been considered as consecrated songs in the Christian world, and are still so held, and deserve to be. For proof of this, read Psalms i., ii., viii., xxii., xxiii., xxix., xlii., xliii., xlv., l., li., lxv., lxxxiv., xc., xci., civ., cxviii., cxxi., cxxvi., cxxviii., cxxxix., cxlvi., and others. But not everything expressed in the Psalms is suitable to the spirit of Christianity. Since they come down from a time of an incomplete revelation, it should not surprise us that they express at times views, feelings, wishes, and prayers in which the Christian cannot share, where, for example, hatred towards the heathen and enemies is required, such as Psalms ii. 9, v. 10, vi. 10, ix. 15, xxxv. 1 – 8, xlvii. 3, 4, lix. 14 – 16, cxxxvii. 7 – 9, cxlix. 7 – 9, etc.

The Proverbs follow the Psalms, a collection of wise sayings in short sentences which were collected and put together by one of the Jewish Rabbins. The compiler of their writings says himself, chap. i. 1, that this is a collection of the sayings of Solomon ; but as he repeats this superscription, x. 1, xxv. 1, it is evident that he has presented three collections of wise sayings, which were ascribed to Solomon. He adds, in chap. xxx. and xxxi., the sayings of other wise men. History testifies authentically that Solomon was renowned for his wise sayings. It may be doubtful whether he had anything to do with writing down these proverbs himself, but it is not to be doubted that others, from the admiration bestowed upon Solomon's wisdom, certainly began early to collect the sayings attributed to him. Thus can be explained the three collections of proverbs of Solomon, which we here find united. Whether they all came from the mouth of Solomon, and exactly as we read them, cannot be ascertained. It does not affect their value, that Solomon in his later years gave himself up to the worship of idols, for with regard to their worth *for us*, we must decide from the contents of the Proverbs, especially in their religious connection. Their contents are in part moral teachings, in part prudent admonitions. Although they contain much that is noble, instructive, and true, they must still be read and used by the Christian with wisdom, that is, with constant reference to the more complete moral teachings of Christ.   For they come to us from a time when the idea of the divine law was but imperfectly developed, and the knowledge of mankind and the world was limited.   See chap. i. 26, ii. 21, 22, x. 27, xxxi. 6, 7.

In the order pursued in the Hebrew Bible, the Book of Job follows.   It is still uncertain in what century this was written, or who was its author. Job is here described as an Arab Emir.   Since the Arabs place the name of Job among their holy men, there must be some true history in the book ; for instance, Job, although he was pious and guiltless, was attacked by a series of painful misfortunes.   The account of these given in the first chapter was probably handed down by oral tradition.   But this historical point is a mere secondary consideration, for the book is throughout an instructive poem upon the question whether it fares well in the world with the good and the guiltless, or worse than with the bad ? This question is treated in the conversations with Job and his friends, which form the principal part of the book.   The three friends proceed wholly upon the idea, frequent among the Jews and constantly expressed in the Old Testament, that misfortunes must necessarily be divine punishments, and they consider, therefore, that Job deceives himself, or dissembles, when he holds himself as guiltless, or that, at least, he must have secret sins that God is visiting upon him. Job, on the other hand, asserts firmly his complete innocence, and the purity of his life. The contest is brought to a close in an answer from God, which declares that man is much too weak to apprehend the wisdom and justice of God's providence, but that, if he cannot comprehend this wisdom, he must *believe* it, since it is so manifestly proved in the world of nature and man; that Job has failed in this, since he has charged God with injustice, and has not submitted to his trials with resignation; and that the three friends (chap. xlii. 7) have not spoken rightly towards God, and have made themselves displeasing to him. Hence it appears, that the author of this book himself shows that the words he has placed in the mouth of the three friends are erroneous, and therefore the Christian reader must be careful not to seek for universal truths in the words of the three friends, nor consider them as divine teachings.

The Song of Songs, which is ascribed to Solomon, follows the Book of Job. It is a little collection of songs of high poetic beauty, but which, as is betrayed by the idioms of a later time occurring in it, cannot have been by Solomon. The compiler of the Old Testament placed these songs in the third portion of the national writings, and accepted them, though their contents lacked the religious element, either because, as remains of so highly honored a king as Solomon, they ought not to perish, or because they represented, in a pictorial sense, the love of Jehovah for the Jewish people ; a representation which in the example of the prophets was already prevalent. Since the connection between God and Israel reached its issue in Christianity, this connection itself, in so far as it relates to the history of revelation, is ended in the Old Testament. Therefore this Song, since it wants the religious element, is not available for Christian edification. The symbolic conception, by which Christian readers would explain these love-songs as between Christ and the Church, his bride, is far too artificial and unnatural to be of any advantage to piety.

Ecclesiastes, or the Preacher, is not written by Solomon, for its language is of a later idiom, which is first found in the time of the captivity, and its contents betray an acquaintance with the Greek philosophy, which the Jews first learnt to know after the captivity, and which holds that the wisest manner of living lies in a gay enjoyment of the moment, and of the present, without questioning the future or bemoaning the past. The main points are : — All things are vain and transitory, even the joys and the goods of life, as well as care for the future, and all wisdom and splendor. It is the same with the good as with the bad, with the just as the unjust, with men as with beasts, all will in the same way be swallowed up by the grave. "Behold," says the preacher, "that which I have seen: it is good' and comely for one to eat and to drink, and to enjoy the good of all his labor that he taketh under the sun all the days of his life, which God giveth him; for it is his portion. Every man also to whom God hath given riches and wealth, and hath given him power to eat thereof, and to take his portion, and to rejoice in his labor; this is the gift of God. For he shall not much remember the days of his life; because God answereth him in the joy of his heart." (Chap. v. 18 – 20.) The whole book shows a heart utterly wrong towards God and froward to his rule, unacquainted with the wisdom and justice of destiny, and its complaints of the vanity of earthly life rise from the want of the great idea of religion, from its ignorance of immortality. This the writer shows plainly (chap. iii. 20 – 22), and the expression (chap. xii. 7), that the spirit shall return, in death, to the God who gave it, suggests no knowledge of immortality, but rather supposes the return of that breath of life with which God has animated the body into the essence of God. This book, written at the close of the Old Testament revelation, is, therefore, a sign of the great need of a revelation of the idea of immortality, or the need there was in the human heart for Christianity. For this idea not only solves the riddle of human life, but displays to us rich treasures, which elevate the spirit as well as make it happy. The Christian, therefore, when he reads Ecclesiastes, must always remember how much happier he is as a Christian than this wise man of olden time, for Christianity has solved for him the riddle that so easily led into sadness and error the spirit of wise men, before the days of Christ. We can see that the philosophy presented in Ecclesiastes was found among the Jews of Alexandria after the captivity, from the book of the Wisdom of Solomon, supposed even by them to be apocryphal, where (chap. ii. 1–9) the same opinions with regard to earthly life are expressed, but are there combated. It appears plainly that the book of the Wisdom of Solomon was written to oppose that of Ecclesiastes, which the Jews themselves hesitated to read in their synagogues......

The highest and the only religious point of view in which the Old Testament can and should be considered, is this; that it contains the history of the divine revelation of religious ideas; that it shows when and through whom there entered into the consciousness of mankind the first ideas of religion, with regard to God, his relation to the world, his laws, and a reverence for him; and through what means they were upheld and cultivated, and how in the course of time they were developed, as far down as the Christian era. The principal thing that concerns us in the Old Testament, therefore, is what belongs to the history of the rise and development of religious ideas; but much else which appears in the Old Testament is of secondary importance, however weighty it might appear to the Jewish nation. All that is most important to the Christian, which has served as foundation and introduction to Christianity, we find in the Mosaic writings, and in the Prophets, to which the Psalms, the Book of Job, and the Proverbs may be added. It is also the inner history of the gradual illumination of the spirit of man by God, which the Christian must heed, as appertaining to revelation.

But the external history of men and nations, of the people of Israel themselves, is to be considered as a part of the general history of the world and of nations, and has no closer connection with religion or with revelation. It is an historic relation which stands on the same line as other historical narratives of the olden times, and is to be estimated by the same measures. To this belongs the history of remote antiquity, and the first spread of mankind in Genesis, the history of the departure of the Israelites from Egypt, their conquest of Palestine, (the Book of Joshua,) and the further outer development of the Israelitish government (the Book of Judges, the Books of Samuel, of the Kings, of the Chronicles, Ezra, Nehemiah, and Esther). Although the history related in the Old Testament possesses a peculiar character, because all the events that occur to the nation, and all the political regulations and measures, are supposed to proceed from Jehovah, and to follow his command, yet this part, as has already been expressed, is only a form of conception arising from the nature of a theocratic state government, which can offer no religious dogmas for Christians.

From what has been said of the necessary connection of religious ideas with the existing knowledge of the world, and the gradual progress of the development of ideas, the religious element in the Old Testament must be recognized as incomplete and limited, from the very meagre state of knowledge existing in the world. We, as Christians, since we have the full light of revelation, are not obliged to take into our minds these limitations and deficiencies, but must consider them as unavoidable, compelled by the state of human culture at that early time, while we are better informed by the Christian revelation. All the religious elements of the Old Testament must be compared with the Christian measure,—its conceptions of God, of creation, of the government of the world, the law of God and the kingdom of God, and our durance after death. And it must be always remembered, that the Old Testament contains only the foundation of true religion; its outer walls and its inner temple were finished by Christ. It was a mistake when men looked upon the entirely external history of the world, of Israel and other nations, related in the Old Testament, as a revelation, and would fain make the incomplete forms in which the elements of religion present themselves articles of faith for the Christian world.

On the other hand, it were wholly a false procedure, for the opponent of revelation to take occasion, from these narratives of external history, and from the yet deficient form of the religious element, to inveigh against the Old Testament, and make little account of it as a record of revelation. This external history appears nowhere in the Old Testament as a revelation, but throughout as a human historical narrative; and the still incomplete form of the religious element was, as we have seen, a necessity, which was unavoidable in those remote ages, and which even bears witness to the great age and truth of this earliest illumination of the spirit of man.

THE WAY, THE TRUTH, AND THE LIFE.

We complain, often, that there are so many ways that we cannot find which is the right one. Every hour brings up new duties which cannot all be performed, but from which we must choose one, and we do not know how to choose the right one. Take the best maps that we will, they do not show which is the true road; and often we have to wander back to find our starting-point, or sit down bewildered and lost in the close wood that shuts in all pathway. We study old writers, we plunge into philosophy and into speculation, and try to learn the way to God. We hear the whirlwind and the noise of the earthquake, but we hear not his voice. The ways all seem uncertain, the ways to Him,.the way through life, the way, even, through the little duties of the day.

We want the truth to guide us. But the truth is hard to find. One teacher and another claim to show it us, but in all they show there is something wanting. It is very fascinating to study the theory of life, to speculate on its beginning, or course, or end. Some minds naturally occupy themselves with such subjects, and cannot rest from them. They are every moment asking new questions, and then discouraged when there comes no answer. And we all want to know what is the truth. We want to see clearly what is before us.

But the faithless heart does not find the truth either in books or in friends, and the heart itself is deceitful; and at the same time that the way appears uncertain, the truth seems dimmed and insecure, and we do not know where to find either.

Amidst all these doubts the life fails. How can we learn to live if we do not know the way to live, and have not the truth to guide us? We ask in despair, What is life? We begin to fear it is only a dream: Some of us live wholly in the other world. A mistaken conscientiousness, a fancy that this is a religious life, leads many to putting their thoughts so wholly in the future world, that they neglect to live in this. It is true the body holds them down and demands of them little daily duties. But they go through these with a sadness and a martyr-spirit, as if they felt they were made for heaven, but some mistake had set them here for a time. We cannot say they live. For all the work they do here is that of a machine which does not live. There are such days of existence to all of us, when some weight on our spirits has put us out of tune with life here. Our duties no longer seem ours, they are distasteful to us, we fancy ourselves made for a higher sphere, and wish to take our hands from the plough that is waiting in the unfurrowed earth. There is no heartiness in our greetings, for these are not the friends we would like to meet; there is no earnestness in our labor, because we believe it beneath us; there is no warmth in our prayers, because we have grown faithless towards God, who would not give us a better world to live in, or better tools to use in this world.

Some are living in another extreme, for this world only. And this too is not living. The time is given up to gain and business and pleasure, which inthrall both body and soul, but give neither a chance to live. It is again a mechanical round, not a life. It needs the inspiration of something higher; it needs the wakening of some great purpose and aim; it needs to be roused by the thought of immortality, of the presence of God, of the life of Christ.

For there is a way and a truth and a life for those who will seek for them. We can come back from our speculations and our dreamings to study the life of Christ. We can learn what is the way, because he knew how to tread it. It leads us among the suffering; it leads us away from selfishness; it leads us towards God. God is no longer a vague and abstract being, not only the upholder of the universe, but he is our Father, to whom we may come with our daily cares. The way to him is not far; it is not long. We have not to seek his temple in distant mountains, nor to wait for heaven, but we may listen to his voice within us. By following in this way, we learn the truth. The words of Jesus are simple. "Believe ye that the Father is in me, and I in him." "Abide in me, and I in you. As the branch cannot bear fruit of itself, except it abide in the vine; no more can ye, except ye abide in me." If we believe in the words of Jesus, their truth shines before us.

It is he that teaches us to live. His life was an example of true living. It was full of courage and of faith. We are always faltering, always complaining, sometimes making much of this life, as though it were all, sometimes despising it, as though it were a poor gift for God to make. Jesus said, "He that loseth his life shall save it"; and yet he did not think lightly of life, for he said, "Greater love has no man than this, that he lay down his life for his friend." We must begin with faith in him. A little faith, faith like a grain of mustard-seed, is all he asks. With this faith we must look upon his life, we must see its self-sacrifice and be inspired by its teachings. Other teachings come to us like dry proverbs, or are the studied efforts of a silent, retired life, or want the sanction of a holy life. Or else they are uttered in doubt and uncertainty, they are feeling for truth, but are not the truth itself. They impress us just because they strike some sad, sympathetic chord in our own hearts, but they do not give us strength. They all end with the same unsatisfied questionings with which we began them.

But the words of Christ are in harmony with his life. They are a part of that life. There was the same inspiration in his words that there was in his deeds. He said, " My Father worketh with me." They were always called out by the need of the moment, so they could not be dry, dull teachings. And they were uttered in perfect faith, there was no doubt or uncertainty in them. They contained no promises but *rest* and *peace.* " Take up the cross, and follow me." " Leave all, and follow me." The object in life for which he lived was " to do the will of the Father."

There is much to be learned of the outer history of the Gospels, when and how they were written. There is much to be read of the various opinions concerning their writers, of the effect that is produced in different minds by the differences found in the various Gospels, — these differences in some minds producing a conviction of the accuracy of the record, in others startling them away from this conviction. But it is pleasant to turn away from these conflicting opinions, to read the life of Christ by the lamp of our own faith, — to turn away from discord and find

harmony.   For we do find a harmony, the words
and the deeds both represent the high aim of his
life.   The more we study them, the more complete, the more precious do they become.   They
have something for every sufferer, they bring consolation to every doubter.   "Lord, to whom shall
we go?   Thou hast the words of eternal life!"

28

THE SEVENTH STORMY SUNDAY.

PAIN.

Since I am coming to that holy room
  Where with the choir of saints for evermore
I shall be made thy music; as I come,
  I tune the instrument here at the door,
  And what I must be then, think here before.

DONNE.

THE SEVENTH STORMY SUNDAY.

PAIN.

To-day there has been storm without and storm within. Without, a wild struggling of the elements; within, the struggle of the soul and body. A whole day of pain! Sometimes giving strength with the wonderful excitement it brought to the nerves, sometimes weighing down body and soul into the most depressing weakness. What is the office of patience under incessant pain? I *must* submit. It is no time for me to summon the grace of patience; I *must* bear the burden. I must bear it alone. It is easy for me now, since there is no one for me to express my complaints to, no one to hear my cry of agony if I utter it, — no one but God, and already he knows my suffering.

Must I submit in silence? And can I bring myself to say that this is good for me? I remember I used to test my sufferance of pain by asking myself whether there were any other per-

son in the world to whom I would consent to give
it rather than bear it myself. And my consent-
ing to bear the pain myself I considered a test of
my endurance. Indeed, it is far easier to bear
such pain than to look upon it in another; for, as
some one has said, the pain from which we see
another suffering appears to us infinite, because
we cannot measure it, while we know the breadth
and length of our own suffering.

This pain I have been willing to bear myself,
and alone; but, alas! not without complaint. After reading the strengthening words of others,
after recalling the courageous resolutions of quieter hours, after words of prayer for strength, I
have been driven back to the complaining excla-
mation, "O, release me from this pain!"

In pain one is swallowed up in the present, in
the same way as in extreme joy. In moments of
great happiness we are willing to forget all other
happiness; the moments that lie behind are quite
lost in the present, and we scarcely allow ourselves time to look forward. The beautiful scene
falls upon our soothed eyes, the gentle sounds
lull our delighted senses, a happy companionship
fills all the wants of sympathy, and the present
moment is sufficient and full of life. Sometimes
we say that this only is true life, that it is the
happiness that God has given to his children, and
that we were ungrateful if we brought into its

enjoyment any memory of the past or any shadow of the future. And they are moments that are necessary for the life of the soul and the body. Both of them are often cast down by privation, by weakness; and this earthly happiness is needful for the refreshing of the body and the soul. I can call it earthly happiness without meaning to put upon it a low term. It is the happiness that the flower draws out from the earth, and which from its own life and joyfulness it changes into color and perfume. It is the happiness that the bee drinks from the flower, on which the bird feeds in its fruit. It is the happiness that the summer brings. In one summer day what richness of life is poured forth, seen and unseen! Whirring insects, flocks of birds, waving grass, dashing streams, by the side of quiet lakes still full·of life, broad green swards on which rest peaceful flocks, and great seas in majestic motion. And all such life seems full of joy, so that it can hardly rest in its expression of joy. It is the happiness of our earth which lends some of its vapor to receive the tints of the sunset sky. We were ungrateful if we too could not enter into the joyfulness that the summer day brings forth.

And a day of pain stands in severe contrast. It is a heavier contrast than the words summer and winter bring to us. Winter, it is true, checks all these sources of life, puts to sleep the insects, exiles the gay birds, stays the streams with its icy hand, and chills the lake, and cuts down the grass in the broad fields. But over all seeming decay and destruction it spreads the snowy covering; if it robs the trees, it leaves a graceful outline of trunk and branches against the sky, and hangs around the stayed stream a silver tracery as varied as summer foliage. But the pain that comes to us in the place of happiness has no such snowy mantle of peace to distract us from its presence. We must look it in the face; it is there, we cannot turn away from it. And so we find ourselves far more taken up in the " present " of pain, than we were even in that of joy. For it is of very little help to recall that such a pain may be of short duration. It is but little consolation to say, " This pain is so violent, that in a few hours I may be relieved." I say this is of little help, and of little consolation, because under the influence of present suffering, in the weakened state of the body, it is so hard to reach the higher faith that can submit, that can look forward to a release. Such a faith the early Christians reached when they could speak of their affliction as "light, but for a moment," in comparison with the " eternal weight of glory," looking as they did towards the " things not seen." It has made me smile to read such a suggestion as that I met with the other day, that the belief in the approaching end of the world, held by the disciples, is "a diminution of their credit for disinterestedness and self-sacrifice."   As if this "belief" were an easy thing to enter upon, — as though it required no disinterestedness and self-sacrifice!

It is difficult to endure merely a violent toothache for an hour, even if one could hope for an entire release from it at the end of that hour. It must require some self-sacrifice to enter upon a voluntary physical suffering, even if repose and reward lay visibly within reach.   Far more difficult must such sacrifice be, accompanied with contumely from others, self-distrust, and that human weakness that surely only a high faith can subdue.   In our calm, painless moments we can easily say we should be able to bear what "the saints" endured, if we had their faith!   An hour's physical suffering, half a night's suspicion of our best friend, a few moments' distrust of ourselves and of our cause, might show us how hard a thing it is to reach such a faith.

It cannot be reached by the momentary effort at resignation that we strive after in the midst of suffering.   It cannot be reached by the mere painting of imagination, which may try to picture the crown of reward and a future repose. Imagination may sometimes be of assistance in relieving the thoughts in what would be dreary hours of endurance.   But more often it lends a deeper agony to the throb of the excited nerves; it can seldom carry us away even from mere physical suffering. If the " things unseen " became so present to the Apostles that they could forget their " light momentary affliction," it was no sudden flash that opened to them a future joy, or a new elevation, that lifted them from their present suffering; it was their religious faith which they had worked out for themselves, the same faith that acknowledged the presence of God in their hours of satisfaction, and recognized him now in their hour of affliction.

For these hours of extreme joy and pain do not make up our life. We seldom pass through days of desert emptiness, nor can linger long in a paradise of delight. Joys and pains alternate with each other. The sum of our life is a series of " little things," a succession of little duties, the necessity of constant little decisions. Over these hangs sometimes the arch of sunlight, sometimes they are canopied with clouds. One day suffices to present all these changes. We cannot pass our life in a constant joyousness, for suffering in the shapes of pain and sorrow looks us in the face. And we cannot turn away from the refining power of its discipline. But the buoyancy of gratitude that has given the zest to our days of joyousness can help us to bear the heavy weight upon our spirits, when body and soul are both suffering, when no outward happiness avails to turn our eyes from our inward struggle.

There is then one help that stands by us in all the changes of our life; it is the true religious faith, the faith that sees God in all things. This praises him in the hours of exaltation and of joy, and submits in the hours of privation. It makes a seemingly monotonous passage of time glorious with the presence of Him to whom one day is as a thousand years, and a thousand years as one day. It brings a consistency to a life that at times seems too much agitated with its changes from joy to pain. There is one God that rules over both. It gave to Peter the power to say: "Beloved, think it not strange, concerning the fiery trial which is to try you, as though some strange thing happened unto you; but rejoice, inasmuch as ye are partakers of Christ's sufferings; that, when his glory shall be revealed, ye may be glad with exceeding joy." And James could say: "Be patient, therefore, brethren, unto the coming of the Lord. Behold, the husbandman waiteth for the precious fruit of the earth, and hath long patience for it, until he receive the early and latter rain. Be ye also patient; stablish your hearts; for the coming of the Lord draweth nigh. Behold, we count them happy which endure!"

And Paul said: "Where the spirit of the

Lord is, there is liberty; but we all, with open face beholding as in a glass the glory of the Lord, are changed into the same image from glory to glory, even as by the Spirit of the Lord. Therefore, seeing we have this ministry, as we have received mercy, we faint not.

"For we preach not ourselves, but Christ Jesus the Lord; and ourselves your servants for Jesus' sake. For God, who commanded the light to shine out of darkness, hath shined in our hearts, to give the light of the knowledge of the glory of God in the face of Jesus Christ.

"But we have this treasure in earthen vessels, that the excellency of the power may be of God, and not of us.

"We are troubled on every side, yet not distressed; we are perplexed, but not in despair; persecuted, but not forsaken; cast down, but not destroyed; always bearing about in the body the dying of the Lord Jesus, that the life also of Jesus might be made manifest in our body.

"For which cause we faint not; but though our outward man perish, yet the inward man is renewed day by day."

A PRAYER.

FROM THOMAS À KEMPIS.

O Lord, thou knowest what is best for us; let this or that be done, as thou pleasest. Give what thou wilt, and how much thou wilt, and when thou wilt. Deal with me as thou thinkest good, and as best pleaseth thee, and is most for thy honor. Set me where thou wilt, and deal with me in all things just as thou wilt. I am in thy hand; turn me round and turn me back again, which way soever thou pleasest.

Behold, I am thy servant, prepared for all things; for I desire not to live unto myself, but unto thee; and O that I could do it worthily and perfectly!

Grant to me thy grace, that it may be with me, and labor with me, and persevere with me even to the end. Grant that I may always desire and will that which is to thee most acceptable and most dear. Let my will be thine, and let my will ever follow thine, and agree perfectly with it. Grant to me above all things that can be desired, to rest in thee, and in thee to have my heart at peace. Thou art the true peace of the heart, thou its only rest; out of thee all things are hard and unquiet. In this very peace, that is, in thee, the one chiefest, eternal Good, I will sleep and rest. Amen.

OF PAIN AND TROUBLE.

BY LEIGH HUNT.

The pain that affects ourselves only, and not the comfort or interests of the many, let us learn to keep in subjection, in order that it may not subject us. Let us lord it, as much as we can, over physical evil, that we may bend circumstances to our will. Let us be respectful wrestlers also with intellectual suffering, that we may win it to do our bidding. As men, let us be manly; as women, womanly; thorough helpers; forgiving friends; not querulous with evil, both for the sake of others and ourselves; but nevertheless doing all we can to master it for the same reason; counting pain at what it is worth only; forcing what would be more evil, to become a part of good; and opposing, to what we cannot subdue in its effects on others, a resolution that will at least hinder ourselves from being conquered. Let impatience be quickly over. If we cannot master it by ourselves, let us take it with us to God, and under the sense of his all-embracement it will not abide.

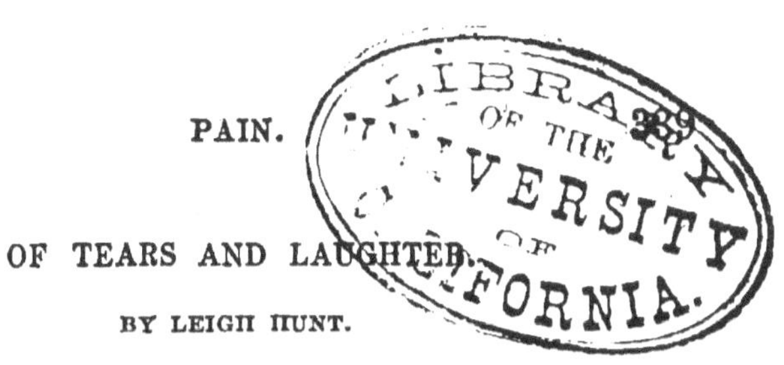

OF TEARS AND LAUGHTER.

BY LEIGH HUNT.

We must not call earth a vale of tears. It is neither pious to do so, nor in any respect proper. We might as well, nay, with far greater propriety, call it a field of laughter. For as there is more good than evil in the world, more action than passion, more health than disease, more life than death (life being a thing of years, but death of moments), so there is more comfort than discomfort, more pleasure than pain, and therefore more laughter than tears. But as it would be a disrespect to sorrow to call earth a field of laughter, so it is a sullenness to joy, and an ingratitude to the goodness of God, to call it a vale of tears.

God made both tears and laughter, and both for kind purposes. For as laughter enables mirth and surprise to breathe freely, so tears enable sorrow to vent itself patiently. Tears hinder sorrow from becoming despair and madness; and laughter is one of the very privileges of reason, being confined to the human species.

It becomes us, therefore, to receive both the gifts thankfully, and to hold ourselves, on fitting occasions, superior to neither. To be incapable of tears would be to lose some of the sweetest emotions of humanity; and the proud or sullen fool who should never laugh, would but reduce himself below it.

FROM "THE SAYINGS OF RABIA."

BY R. M. MILNES.

Round holy Rabia's suffering bed
   The wise men gathered, gazing gravely.
"Daughter of God!" the youngest said,
   "Endure thy Father's chastening bravely;
They who have steeped their souls in prayer
Can every anguish calmly bear."

She answered not, and turned aside,
   Though not reproachfully nor sadly.
"Daughter of God!" the eldest cried,
   "Sustain thy Father's chastening gladly;
They who have learnt to pray aright,
From pain's dark well draw up delight."

Then she spoke out: "Your words are fair;
   But oh! the truth lies deeper still;
I know not, when absorbed in prayer,
   Pleasure or pain, or good or ill;
They who God's face can understand
Feel not the motions of his hand."

"We have this treasure in earthen vessels." — 2 Corinthians iv. 7.

I am going to try to set in order some thoughts on the religious value of sickness. I suppose there is apt to be some vagueness of notion about it. This is a pity. For sickness certainly affords at times decided advantages in our religious growth. It is, I think, as often — because not rightly used — a decided drawback to that growth. It is a pity, then, not to watch it closely enough to know when it promises one of these results and when the other. I should say that, in general, people look with a sense of mystery upon it; almost as they did in old pagan times, as if it had certain magic power upon the soul. Have you never observed, that when people are subdued, and do not wish to talk of worldly things, they fall to talking of the illness in the community around them, with an air of seeming sanctity? And I am afraid it is still true, that a great many people, who are very practical in lesser affairs, are so unpractical about their soul's training as to put it off till sickness shall give occasion for it; — as if sickness made a sort of long Sabbath, which nature had provided for such an emergency.

Of course, in fact, sickness is one of God's angels. Its real heavenly lesson may be learned, always, by those who have ears and can hear.

29 *

It will not be learned, however, in any such superstitious estimate as I have hinted at ; and it will be but a broken stay, if we have not well trained ourselves to make use of it when it come. That training, like most training, requires times of health, and therefore I call your attention to it here and now, while we are together well.

Of the real solemnity which sickness has, apart from this half-superstitious notion, I will only say one thing, by way of introduction. It is quite enough to give the fitting gravity to our meditations. It is this, — that almost all the seriousness with which we are used to invest the idea of *death* itself belongs, not to the event called death, but to the sick-bed which precedes death. The real seriousness of death is simply that it is an instantaneous passage from life to life, from man to God. All the notions beside this, which we hang about it, of pain, or of struggle, as our pictures of ghastly faces, of hollow cheeks, and of skeleton forms, are notions or pictures which belong to sickness, not death ; and we do but borrow them from sickness to dress up with them our idea of what follows. " The pain of death is but in contemplation " before death comes ; and it is the witness of long struggling sick-beds, which makes it as dreadful as it is supposed to be to the great company of men.

It is not, then, too much to say, that the thought

which we give to the angel of Sickness, and the
eager forecast with which we look forward to his
ministrations, should be and might be even more
serious, more solemn, and more patient than those
which look to the angel of Death, when he acts
suddenly, without the intervention of sickness.
Because of sickness we know and see so much,
while of death itself we see in fact so very little.
A passage from world to world! All that we
can say of it is, that, in itself, it must be momentary. Most likely the soul starts surprised when
it is over, — surprised ever to find that it is begun. While of sickness, each instance teaches us
more; and leaves us, if we will, better able to
meet another.

This relation of sickness to the instant of passage which we call death, shall be, in the first
place, the guide of our meditations.

I. In a celebrated sermon on sickness which
Mr. Buckminster preached after his recovery from
one of those severe attacks which at last closed
his earthly career, he enumerates seven benefits
of sickness : —

1. It calls attention directly to God.

2. It reminds us of the uncertainty of human
pursuits, and

3. Of their vanity.

Again, it shows our dependence on each other;
it softens our own hearts towards others' suf-

ferings; it teaches us also the· value of our health.

Lastly, and chief of all, it shows us " how idle, how fatal the notion, that hours of weakness or of suffering will .be hours favorable to quiet reflection and pious thoughts, how vain his scheme of life who has relied upon them entirely."

These lessons are addressed not only to the sufferer, but to those around him as well, — his friends, his physician, his nurses, his neighbors. Now, will you observe that each of these invaluable and eternal lessons is complete and effective, without any allusion to death as the probable consequence of illness? It is not dangerous illness only which teaches them. Long, wearing confinement of whatever kind instils them. They are not borrowed from the treasure of death's admonitions; but have a value and origin all their own. So true is it that sickness, of itself, has many a lesson, which death itself cannot teach to us.

Practically, you may make the same observation thus,—in seeing, that, of all the persons who would meet the instant of death bravely, not one in a hundred probably would bear as bravely the sentence of a year's languishing. For instance, most of *us*, I think, would receive firmly, without much outcry or expression of grief, the announcement that in the next instant to this he must die. An instant's resignation to God's will is not so difficult but we might yield it. But to resign one's self every instant for months or years is another thing; and the training which has fitted one to meet death does not, of course, prepare us to meet this harder trial.

And thus we are led to our first practical lesson for use in sickness; namely, that we avoid, in counselling our sick friends, or in arranging our own thoughts on the sick-bed, the habit of looking mostly at death, as if that were the one business for which God had placed us there. We have two different things to learn, — how to meet death, and how to bear sickness. Of these the latter is vastly the harder. And yet it is at each, the instant, the certain duty, and that which is at once essential. The Christian sufferer then leaves till to-morrow to-morrow's care ; and turns to-day's prayer, to-day's resolution, not to to-morrow's possible result, but to to-day's essential duty. How best shall I discharge the duty of this sick-bed ? How best ease the trouble and anxiety of these friends ? How best keep my mind at peace, and this angry temper soothed ? How best, O God ! keep my spirit of devotion ordered, and my soul near to thee ? Harder questions these to meet than that vague one, " Am I ready to die ? " to which mistaken physicians to the soul beg him to turn his attention, — harder, and yet vastly more essential to be answered.

For God so orders life that my right discharge of to-day's duty always implies a preparation for to-morrow's. Have I learned to-day's lesson thoroughly, to-morrow's follows very simply, be it a lesson in arithmetic or a lesson in life. And therefore, though bold readiness to die by no means implies fitness to bear long sickness, the counter proposition is true. Steady duty in long sickness does imply, does bring about of itself, a perfect fitness to die. Is your body purified by this patient subjugation to which you have brought your appetites? Is your mind disciplined, are your anger and quick temper tamed, by patient submission here in your sick-room? Is your attention turned off earthly pursuits as you have lain here, with so little to remind you in your chamber's monotony of the world's changes? Why, then body, mind, passions, and eager appetites are all trained, and in readiness for you to pass on. And when the Angel Death whispers to say, "Are you ready?" you look round to array yourself, and find you are arrayed; to throw off your encumbrances, and behold they are gone; to take your staff, and see the discipline of sickness has fitted it to your hand. You smile, surprised, and say, "Lead on!" He smiles, with the smile which has seen that glad amazement of

humility so often before; and we who wait beside know only that the change is a blessed one;
and we are left for a few years to wonder how it
came. This only we know, that because, each
day, you were prepared for a day of sickness,
when the last moment came, you were prepared
for death.

And this reflection then shall guide us, when,
as comforters or counsellors or friends, we go to
stand by other beds of sickness. Not that any
one of us will be afraid to think or speak of
Death! God forbid! For God sends him, as
one of our dearest friends. Not because we fear
death, but because we fear to fail in to-day's
duty, will we turn distinctly to the duty next
our hand in the sick-room. What can we say,
what do, that this sufferer may meet to-day more
patiently, more bravely? For *that* is his duty.
So to help him in *that*, is ours. Most like we
do not help him by discussing death with him.
Most like he knows more of that than we. Let
us help him to patience under pain; let us cheer
him in discomfort or disappointment; let us
bring him to God, and God to him, by joining in
his prayer, or by helping him with ours; and
then, if we have been really living, we have done
our blessed duty for that day, and helped him in
his as well. If we have wisely remembered his
weakness, if we have cut short our words and

our presence, so as not to weary him, (the most essential duty of such a friend,) then we have a right to trust that we have brought some help there, such as we may hope to receive in our turn !

II. I pass now to the systematic treatment necessary that we may bear sickness well and secure its lessons. We remember, of course, what I quoted just now from Buckminster, " that the hours of torturing pain and languishing confinement are not the hours most favorable to quiet reflection and pious thoughts." While we remember this, however, we must acknowledge that God never brings upon us a trial which we have not strength to bear, and that every trial has somewhere its compensations and helps, teaching us or suggesting to us how to bear it. So, I should say that the one special service which sickness renders in regard of religion is that it gradually and certainly weans us from external occupations. It compels us to find occupation within ourselves. If you cannot walk in your garden, it is harder for you, while imprisoned on your bed, to occupy your heart and thought there, although it is not impossible. If you cannot go to your counting-room, it is not of course that your mind will be engrossed there, and when you do go there, that is of course. We must in sickness find occupation in ourselves. Well, this may be a gain or not, as we choose to make it. For there is no certainty that this occupation will be religious occupation, or that it shall tend to make us religious. But this is certain, — that the abstinence from your accustomed interests suggests to you this question : " What other interests can I brood over in these silent hours ? " If, as you lie, windows curtained, temples throbbing, mind quivering, — if the interest, which last week was so fascinating, of a mercantile adventure or a deliciously balanced romance or poem, become disgusting to you, so that your tired fancy pushes it out of the way, — this question must come instead : " What interest is less transitory than these ? " " These were everything ; now they are nothing. What interest, what thought, would abide with me and remain, though my mind do quiver, though my temples do throb, in this darkened chamber ? " Sickness helps you so far as to suggest that question. God grant you find what sickness does not of itself give, the right answer ! God grant you, that in well life you prepare for that question ! God grant that so your subdued spirit whisper, " These three abide and shall eternal be, — faith, hope, and love ! " That so, as you lie there, not asleep, yet not speaking or spoken to, the hours may fly by, rather than crawl along, as your grateful heart feeds itself with these eternal interests. As your faith in a present God, who shares with you that darkened room, becomes more faithful, as your hope for **a** higher life becomes more tangible and clear, and as your love of these dear friends — of that Saviour who is best friend of all, and of the God who is just now next your heart of any — grows fresher and more childlike till it is your all; so is it that sickness may bless you in withdrawing you from care, by bringing you so near to God, and him to you!

A blessing, I have hinted, for which some preparation of well days is needed. Make that preparation like a man studying facts, and not from fancy or notion. Pain does weaken you. A fever does cut down your strength. Sickness does tame your proud spirit. Do not, when you are well, imagine that when you are ill you are going to stand out against any such changer, of your own strength. Do not talk of training yourself to insensibility to pain. Do not rely on any chivalrous, pride-born resolution. The loss of a few ounces of blood will cut down all such resolutions, as surely as a wound in its roots makes a tree's leaves wither. You need better rest than that. That is a mere struggle of your will, and a struggle ending in failure. You want to have sickness even work good for you. That is the aim. To most men it seems an evil. You want to make it work good. There is only one way in which it can be made to work good. But this way you may rely upon.

For this practical fact, announced by the highest faith, proves true on the closest detailed observation, namely, that all things work together for good to them that love God. Your panacea to be gained in health, is this abiding love of the Father in whose image you are made. Love him, as you love your nearest friend. Love him, as he loves you; that he may not call you a servant longer, but call you a friend; letting you see what he does, letting you enter into his system. Then, though you suffer, you suffer willingly. You grow faint, knowing that he holds your swooning head. You wait through sleepless nights, confident still in him that sleepless nights are fraught somehow with blessings to the world; your sleepless night is, though you are such a little child, as truly as the sleepless night of Paul shipwrecked, — nay, as the sleepless night on which the dew fell in Gethsemane. If only you love God, you feel how gently he deals with you; that it is those whom he loves whom he chooses for his chastisements. So fades away the mean suspicion of false theologies, that your strength fails because you have incurred his wrath; and that the chamber of sickness is to be doubly saddened, as being the torture-room where a Father is dealing his vengeance upon his child!

Is it another's sick-room which you enter, or is it your own where you lie bound, take thus the Holy Spirit, the One Comforter, to be with you. First, remember that you have there a graver lesson even than the lesson of death to trace along. Secondly, then the sick-room does offer for the true lesson its share of advantages, in its seclusion, if you will use them. But chiefly and behind all, remember that this is God's angel of mercy, and not of anger, whom you would question. With that memory may the Comforter inspire us! With the memory indeed of one who was made perfect through his own suffering, — was acquainted with grief, and so indeed our Saviour; who brought blessing to so many sick; who so often entered the sick-room and knew its life so well, — knew so well, too, the tears, the hopes, of so many sorrowful hearts. So shall come the life which abides, even when the nerves quiver; so come the faith which is cool, even though the blood boils. So shall each day of sickness be sufficient for each day's duties. No day shall look nervously forward to anticipate the lesson of the last day. If such sickness ends with recovery, you find that such imprisonment has trained you for your freedom. Or, does it end with death? Well, when your last day comes, behold! its duty will have been already accomplished, in hours which did not think that they were attempting it. And, at the threshold of eternity, you find that you are ready, — that there is no parting lesson to be learned.

"I will lead them through paths they have not known."

How few who from their youthful day
　Look on to what their life shall be,
Painting the visions of the way
　In colors soft and bright and free !
How few who to such scenes have brought
The dreams and hopes of early thought!
For God through ways they have not known
　　　　　Will lead his own.

The eager hearts, the souls of fire,
　That pant to toil for God and man,
And mark with eyes of keen desire
　The upland way of toil and pain, —
Almost with scorn they think of rest,
Of holy calm, of tranquil breast.
But God through ways they have not known
　　　　　Will lead his own.

A lowlier task on them is laid,
　With love to make their labor light;
And there their glory must be shed
　On quiet home, and lost to sight;

30 *

Changed are their visions bright and fair,
But calm and still they labor there;
For God through ways they have not known
     Will lead his own.

The gentle breast that thinks with pain
 It scarce can lowliest tasks fulfil,
And, would it dare its life to scan,
 Would ask but pathway low and still, —
Often such lowly heart is brought
To act with power beyond its thought;
For God in ways they have not known
     Will lead his own.

And they, the bright, who long to prove
 In joyous way, in cloudless lot,
How fresh from each their grateful love
 Can spring without a stain or blot, —
Such youthful heart is often given
The path of grief to tread to heaven;
•For God in ways they have not known
     Will lead his own.

What matter what the path may be?
 The end is clear and bright to view;
We know that we a strength shall see,
 Whate'er the day may bring to do.
We see the end, the house of God,
But not the path to that abode;
For God in ways they have not known
     Will lead his own.

In Cicero and Plato, and other such writers, I meet with many things acutely said, and things that excite a certain warmth of emotion, but in none of them do I find these words: " Come unto me, all ye that labor, and are heavy laden, and I will give you rest." — *St. Augustine.*

Worldly hopes are not living, but lying hopes; they die often before us, and we live to bury them, and see our own folly and infelicity in trusting to them; but at the utmost, they die with us when we die, and can accompany us no farther. But the lively hope, which is the Christian's portion, answers expectation to the full, and much beyond it, and deceives no way but in that happy way of far exceeding it.

A living hope, living in death itself! The world dares say no more for its device, than *Dum spiro, spero;* but the children of God can add, by virtue of this living hope, *Dum ex spiro spero.* — *Archbishop Leighton, from " Aids to Reflection."*

A part of the day I was able to spend in reading another sermon of Tholuck's, in the German, — a sermon preached at the beginning of a new year.

SERMON.

BY A. THOLUCK.

We stand at the beginning of a new division of life. Would that we did not need such epochs! Happy is the youth, happy the man, to whom such periods are not necessary to recall him to himself, who, while the stream of his life rushes by, stands upon the shore, and, with thoughtful meditation, keeps his glance fixed upon the flowing wave. But it is not so with us; the waves come, the waves go, and often we know not of them. Therefore must every one make fresh starting-points in his life, even in his inner life. In what spot of your heart do you trace the beginning of this new period of your existence? Do you glow with holy zeal, like the combatant, who sees before him the course he is to run through, — like the warrior at the moment the battle is to begin? I can easily see this is the case with many of you. At least it is the case with reference to the planting of that fruit which the world will some time demand of you. And even this is to be praised, for in many cases the fruit which the world demands is no other than that which God will some time ask of you. But, beloved, there are also fruits which the world does not ask of you, and concerning which you will be questioned only at the day of judgment. The Apostle says: "It is a very small thing that I should be judged of you or of man's judgment, yea, I judge not mine own self; he that judgeth me is the Lord." Many of the fruits that the world demands of you will pass away when the world passes away. Are you determined to bring forth fruit that shall remain,— remain through all eternity ? Do you enter upon this new portion of your life with an earnest determination to cultivate the fruits of the spirit and of righteousness that are of worth in the sight of God ?

Let us animate ourselves to this resolution with the words of the Lord (John xv. 1–16) : —

" I am the true vine, and my Father is the husbandman. Every branch in me that beareth not fruit, he taketh away; and every branch that beareth fruit, he purgeth it that it may bring forth more fruit. Now ye are clean through the word which I have spoken to you.

" Abide in me, and I in you. As the branch cannot bear fruit of itself, except it abide in the vine, no more can ye, except ye abide in me. I am the vine, ye are the branches : he that abideth in me, and I in him, the same bringeth forth much fruit; for without me ye can do nothing. If a man abide not in me, he is cast forth as a branch and is withered; and men gather them, and cast them into the fire, and they are burned.

"If ye abide in me and my words abide in you, ye shall ask what ye-will, and it shall be done unto you. Herein is my Father glorified, that ye bear much fruit; so shall ye be my disciples.

"As the Father hath loved me, so have I loved you; continue ye in my love. If ye keep my commandments, ye shall abide in my love; even as I have kept my Father's commandments, and abide in his love.

"These things have I spoken unto you, that my joy might remain in you, and that your joy might be full.

"This is my commandment, that ye love one another, as I have loved you. Greater love hath no man than this, that a man lay down his life for his friends. Ye are my friends, if ye do whatsoever I command you.

"Henceforth I call you not servants; for the servant knoweth not what his Lord doeth; but I have called you friends; for all things that I have heard of my Father I have made known unto you. Ye have not chosen me, but I have chosen you, and ordained you, that ye should go and bring forth fruit, and that your fruit should remain; that whatsoever ye shall ask of the Father in my name, he may give it you."

Let us occupy ourselves to-day with these words of the Lord, — "that we are ordained to bring forth fruit, that shall remain." And we will first consider what such an admonition requires of us, and, secondly, what help we have in obeying its request.

Life is a field fit for sowing, the little human heart is a large seed-chamber, and eternity the day of harvest. Look, my friends, into the confused bustle of life, how men plough and sow and labor, how the fruit grows and increases beneath their hands! O tell me, how much of the fruit that all men produce is that fruit that will abide, — abide when the world passes away?

Dear brothers, tell me how much fruit will remain of *your* seed, which you have strewn, when the world passes away? And yet, you have only fulfilled the destiny of your life, according to the measure in which you have sowed *such* seed. So grandly, so sublimely, has our Lord traced out for us the destiny of life when he says, "I have ordained you, that ye should bring forth fruit." Again, "Herein is my Father glorified, that ye bear much fruit." Sluggish, earthly spirits, do you understand this? For this lofty aim has your Heavenly Father created you, since Christ has chosen and ordained you in his kingdom, for the high end, that you bear fruit that shall remain. If this bearing of fruit that shall abide, is indeed the whole aim of life and of Christianity, O tell me, do you not hold it as a necessary requirement in the life of every Christian, that he should preserve one quiet hour of every evening when he may ask himself what fruit he has brought forth for eternity that day? And if each day does not own such a quiet hour, ought not at least each great division of life to present one?

And what is this bearing of fruit? The Scriptures speak of a double fruit of the Christian;—of a fruit within, which is called the fruit of the spirit and of righteousness; of an outer fruit, of souls won to the kingdom of God; as when the Apostle says, that he would have gone to the Romans, "that he might have some fruit in them also, even as among other Gentiles." What this fruit-bearing is, the Lord himself shows in the passage we are considering, when he describes it in the words, "If ye keep my commandments"; and again he explains what it is, when he says, "Continue ye in my love"; and, "This is my commandment, that ye love one another, as I have loved you." I have wished to present to you the greatness of the Lord's requirements, and when I offer you this explanation, you think, perhaps, that his demands are limited. For to continue in his love, and to love one another,—if it depends upon this only, you say,—who can fail? O holy, sublime word, love! How men drag thee to the dust, how they imprison thy infinity in narrow limits! *Only, merely*, to love Jesus and our brethren! As easily can you say, *only* to be for ever damned or for ever blessed. That this is not a little thing, that everything is expressed by it, you ought to perceive, since it is written, " Love is the fulfilment of the law," and since the Lord here portrays the keeping of his commandments as the manifestation of love. Those fruits of the spirit, as Paul recounts them, love, joy, peace, long-suffering, gentleness, goodness, faith, meekness, temperance, — are they not, all, the fruits of the heart that dwells in the love of Jesus? And, again, the fruits that were gathered for the kingdom of God from a world that had been lost without Christ, what else has gathered them, but the love that, after the example of Jesus, seeks for that which is lost? Would you behold a tree in the garden of God, rich with all the fruits of righteousness, which shine golden in the rays of the sun of mercy, look upon Paul. Would you have an idea of the fruits with which his inner man is adorned before God, learn from the mouth of a man who speaks only the truth: " I therefore so run, not as uncertainly; so fight I, not as one that beateth the air; but I keep under my body, and bring it into subjection, lest that by any means, when I have preached to others, I myself should be a castaway." Would you behold

31

the fruit which he gathered in the world for the granaries of his Master, learn it, when he says, " From Jerusalem, and round about Illyricum, I have fully preached the gospel of Christ," and when he is able to speak of " those things that are without, that which cometh upon me daily, the care of all the churches. Who is weak, and I am not weak? who is offended, and I burn not?" And what is the water of life, that streams through this fruit-laden tree, from the root to the branches? " For though I preach the gospel," he cries, " I have nothing to glory of; for necessity is laid upon me; yea, woe is unto me if I preach not the gospel"; for the " love of Christ," as he elsewhere says, " constraineth me." To bring forth fruits from within and without, which shall remain, and to love Jesus and our brethren, is, truly, one and the same thing.

But a question presses upon us here, a weighty question. Is the fruit which we have here mentioned indeed the only fruit that shall abide when the world passes away, of what use then, you ask, are the occupations of our daily life? Shall we not let them stand aside for those who serve the gods of this world, and, that we may save our own souls, flee ourselves to the solitude of monastic cells? Here we touch upon a point, that shows why all you hear in this holy place leaves you frequently so cold. Here is preached

to you a love towards Jesus and the immortal
souls of your brethren, and when you go out from
here, there waits for each one the toil and sweat
of a calling, which, as it appears, brings forth
only fruits which will pass away. You see no
living connection between the demands of the
church and the daily duty of your life. High as
the church-tower rises above the tumult of life,
above your houses and homes, as high stands the
church with its preaching above your daily occupations. You look up to it, but it remains to you
a strange land; high as the heavens, it enters
not your homes, your cottages, your workshops,
or parlors. Brothers! the profession and the
calling should not stand *near* the kingdom of God,
but *in* it. If it only brings forth fruits that will
pass away, when the world passes away, it is *your*
fault. Let us begin with the lowest pursuits of
life! Tell me, is it not necessary to preserve the
temple of God, in which dwells the spirit that
is to bring forth fruit that shall abide? And
those members of the body which are most in dis-
honor, are they not as necessary for the support
of life as the most honorable? No calling which
is necessary for the support of social life is in itself ignoble. Is only love towards God and your
brethren the source whence flows that fidelity
with which you perform the lowest concerns of
life, then do you bring forth fruit which shall re-

main. There remains the *inner* fruit, for your
fidelity has preserved in your own heart the purity of your love, and you will take this enhanced
and purified love away into eternity; there remains the outer fruit, for you have so labored,
that your earthly condition shows in what way
souls can be drawn towards heaven. Is this true
of the lower pursuits of life, how much more of
those that demand knowledge! Has love to Jesus
and your brethren driven you to seek truth with
fidelity and divine earnestness in any sphere of
knowledge, then the fruit of such fidelity abides
in your own soul. It remains also in the world.
For wherever beams of truth press into the common life of men, then it must serve to glorify him
who is King in the land of truth. Since all truth
has come forth from God, so must all truth, of
whatever nature it may be, lead back to him. If
your pursuits in life are apart from your life in
the kingdom of God, so that they only bring forth
fruit that passes away, then it is *your own* fault,
because all that you do and that you pursue, you
do not through love of the Son of God and your
brethren.

Arise, then; you know now what it is to bear
fruit, and you have heard the saying of the Lord
that you are ordained to bring forth just such fruit.
Then, brethren, begin with this new term of your
life upon a new season, when you will ask your-

self daily, with an earnestness quite different from any you have shown before, whether the fruit which shall abide increases in you. Beautiful Christian words dwell upon your lips; well, these are the *leaves* of the tree of life. Holy feelings throb at times through your heart; these are its *blossoms*. But there will come a day when the Lord of the vineyard will ask not for the leaves, nor for the flowers, but for the *fruit*. Therefore, are you in earnest with regard to your salvation, let there not be wanting, in a single day of your life, one quiet hour of the morning or evening in which you may ask yourself concerning the growth of this fruit. Manifold are the relations of your life. You are a workman or scholar, father or child, son or daughter, master or servant; all these relations are branches of the tree of life. Do the fruits of righteousness hang on all these branches? Is it seen of all men, in all these relations, that you are a disciple of Christ? Friends, who can in the quiet hour question himself earnestly concerning the fruits of his faith, without casting down his eyes in shame, and needing some great, strong consolation to save him from throwing away all hope?

But is the demand great that springs from these words of the Lord, yet is that which supports us in fulfilling it also great. For has the disciple of the Lord, as we read in this passage,

once become "a branch of the vine" of Jesus,
then also is the Father the husbandman.   When
you were without Christ in the world, O how
often must it have happened to you, that, in that
hour when on your right stood earnest duty, on
the left alluring pleasure, you clutched your own
breast, to find there the strength for victory,—
and in vain!   The disciples of Christ seek not
after such strength in vain.   Is the saying of
Christ true, "Without me you can do nothing?"
So also are the words of Paul true, "I can do all
things through Christ which strengtheneth me."
There is a mysterious connection between the
glorified Redeemer and you, which you cannot
have learnt from experience, but may believe
through faith in the word of God!   There is a
mysterious connection with the glorified Redeemer, through which, as the juice of the grape swells
through the vine, strength rises for the Christian
for every good work,—for everything for which
the demand comes to us from without.   For to
do everything is not allotted to all,— only to do
that work for which each finds a demand in the
relations of his life, only what can be looked upon
as the duty enjoined by the Father.   But all this
you are able to do, are you only planted in Jesus,
and become one with him, and have drawn near
to him.   With all these strong expressions do
the Scriptures portray the connection between the

spiritual branch and the spiritual vine. And how is such a close connection formed? The band which thus draws together the branch which is upon earth, and the vine which is in heaven, is called *faith*. This is the first consolation which our text offers us.

But there is a second, that we have a heavenly husbandman who cares for the branches. When you were without Christ in the world, you were a wild tree in the field, whose leaves were torn by every storm, whom no kind hand watered when it was dry, whose branches no gentle hand bound up when they were broken. Since you have believed in Christ, you have been transplanted to a favoring soil, you have found a gardener who, when the storms rise, protects you, who, when it is dry, gives you water, who binds up the broken branches. Since you are a branch of the vine of Christ, the Heavenly Father who planted this vine is also your husbandman, who purgeth his branches that they may bring forth more fruit. To *purge* the vine, that is to prune the shoots that deprive the branches of the vine of their strength. My beloved, since we have become branches of the vine of Christ, whatever withdraws strength from the vine, these are the offshoots, they are those ungodly inclinations that have no connection with the kingdom of God, and by them that strength is destroyed which should bring forth goodly fruit. The more any one is satisfied to stand in so loose a connection with Christ, by which, it is true, he brings forth leaves and flowers, but no fruit, so many more offshoots remain in him. There prevails in our time a Christianity in which there is frequent talk of Christly doctrine and Christian feelings, without earnest self-examination, without purging of the offshoots which spring from the nature of man. There prevails a Christianity which preaches finely how noble Christ is, but says not how pitiful is man, so that it never reaches a repentance daily renewed, nor a faith each day fought for anew. Such a Christianity will not stand at the day of judgment. The Lord declares in the parable we have quoted, that the branches which bring forth no fruit shall be hewn down, and shall be burned. Observe, he says this of the branches, even of those who already stand in a certain relationship with him, who can say in a certain sense they are Christians, who can point to the leaves and blossoms which the spirit of Christ has produced, but no fruits. O, is it not pitiful that it is possible to be a branch of the vine, and that the branch may be hewn down? Ah, how deceived will they find themselves, who allow themselves to be satisfied with their leaves and blossoms, when an earnest voice shall ask them, Have I not ordained you to bring forth fruit, — fruit which shall abide?

Yet, beloved, the beginning of even such a connection with Christ brings its blessings with it. You who have made this beginning, if you do not yourselves bring the knife to such offshoots, lo! you stand beneath a heavenly husbandman, who from heaven reaches down a hand towards them. In the life of every Christian there are hours when the pruning-knife cuts, where the heart clings to Christ, deep into those bonds of a love that is not consecrated to God,—into every inclination of the soul that is not newly born. O, he who has not sought for a fervor higher than himself lives to see with astonishment how in the course of his life God's pruning-knife touches him just in that spot where he is most sensitive, where his connection with the world is the strongest! There is—yes, brethren, there is truly in the life of every Christian a mercy of discipline from God. Yes, the words are true which the Scriptures tell us: " Whom the Lord loveth, he chasteneth ; if ye endure chastening, God dealeth with you as with sons."

If everything came to you
Exactly as you willed,
And God took nothing from you,
No burden gave to bear,
How would it at your dying,
O children, be with you ?
Your hearts would sink in anguish,
So dear the world to you !

If one after another
Your dearest ties are loosed,
Then joyous can you wander
Towards heaven through the grave.
Your trembling then is over,
While hope inspires your souls ;
This truth, so often spoken,
Is ne'er too often told !

Now, dear friends, lie still when you observe that God's pruning-knife is cutting away your off-shoots, even though the heart bleed. "That they may bear more fruit," — for this reason he purgeth his branches, and without the fruits of goodness you cannot enter into his kingdom. My brethren, he would prepare you all fully for this, by your sorrowful as well as by your happy hours.

THE EIGHTH SUNDAY.

SUNSHINE.

" Thy sun shall no more go down ; neither shall thy moon withdraw itself ; for the Lord shall be thine overlasting light, and the days of thy mourning shall be ended." — ISAIAH lx. 20.